GROUNDED

G.P. CHING

Grounded, The Grounded Trilogy Book One
Copyright © G.P. Ching 2014
Published by Carpe Luna, Ltd., PO Box 5932, Bloomington, IL
61704
www.carpeluna.com

Second Edition: November 2014

ISBN: 978-1-940675-12-1

Cover art by Christa Holland
www.paperandsage.com

v2.5

Books by G.P. Ching

The Soulkeepers Series
The Soulkeepers, Book 1
Weaving Destiny, Book 2
Return to Eden, Book 3
Soul Catcher, Book 4
Lost Eden, Book 5
The Last Soulkeeper, Book 6

The Grounded Trilogy
Grounded, Book 1
Charged, Book 2
Wired, Book 3

Contents

Prologue

September 2062

The night Frank found her it was raining, a wrath-of-God type of downpour Crater City hadn't seen in a decade. The power was out, but that was nothing new. The grid was unpredictable in any weather.

Later, he'd call it divine providence. If not for the rain, he wouldn't have grabbed his jacket to take out the trash. And it was the jacket that would save his life.

In the alley behind the fire station at the corner of Fifth and Lincoln, Frank escaped the endless drone of his fellow firefighters by volunteering to dispose of a smelly nest of takeout containers. Without power, the men didn't have the city's monitoring equipment to keep them busy. They became downright nostalgic by candlelight. Hell, if you let him, Jonas would drone on about his three freckle-faced girls until sunrise.

Frank could not deal. He didn't have a family. Not anymore.

He might not have noticed her at all in the blackout, but when he tried to lift the dumpster lid, a shock ran up his arm. The jolt made him drop the stack of waxed cardboard he was carrying, and he bent over to clean up the mess.

"What the—?" Frank crouched for a better look.

A newborn baby girl, in a worn pink T-shirt and wrapped in a plastic grocery bag, blinked at him from under the lip of the dumpster. Frank would have liked to think there was some compassion in the effort—that whoever left her meant for the thin sheath of plastic to keep her warm and dry, but under the abandonment law, it was legal to leave a newborn inside a public building. The fact that she wasn't safely indoors was a testament to what type of scum had abandoned her.

"Hi, sweetheart. Oh, you're cold. Don't worry, old Frank will take care of you." He lifted her into the cradle of his arms and shuffled under the awning of the alley door. By the light of the moon, he wiped the raindrops off her face with one burly thumb. Cuddling her tiny body against his chest, he enjoyed the innocent shine of her eyes and her slight weight in his embrace.

Frank's atrophied spirit stirred from a long, deep sleep. He smiled. And smiles were hard to come by since the day a semitruck T-boned a Range Rover and turned Frank's family into just Frank. One tiny hand wrapped around his pinky finger, and that was that. She might as well have handcuffed his soul.

Shuffle-scrape. Shuffle-scrape. He searched the alley for the source of the sound. A sewer rat? Since the war, they grew as large as dogs. Better to be safe; consider the babe. He groped for the doorknob behind his hip.

A deep voice rasped from the darkness, "Don't! You've got to get her out of here." From the shadows, a man stepped into the swash of moonlight; at least, Frank thought he was a man. The guy was a piece of raw meat with more bruise than face and open sores up both arms. Soaked to the bone, he wore bloody white hospital scrubs that clung like a second skin. The water sheeted off him, his breath a foggy reminder of the cold night air.

"Who are you?" Frank asked, tightening his hold on the little girl.

"Never mind that. They know we're here. It's just a matter of time. You've got to run. You've got to hide her."

"Hey, buddy, it's legal to abandon a baby here. Why don't we all go inside and warm up? There are places you can stay, get a hot meal."

"*Listen to me,*" the man implored. "Everything you need is with her."

Frank ran his hand around the newborn. Sure enough, under her back the corner of a thick envelope scraped his palm.

"I'll take care of her," Frank said in his most reassuring tone. "We've got resources inside."

"*No!*" The man's voice broke and his eyes widened. Large, wounded eyes. Desperate eyes. "You can't tell anyone."

No stranger to desperation, Frank took pause. He'd been there once. The way the guy let the rain pound on him, with no attempt to move for the shelter of the awning, was a blatant cry for help.

"What's your name?" Frank asked.

The man eyed the street with twitchy apprehension.

"Come on inside," he continued. "Let's talk."

"They're coming," the stranger said, shaking his head. "We're out of time."

Damn, the guy's pale skin seemed to light up the alley. Or was he actually glowing? At first, Frank thought it was a trick of the moonlight, but the sky beyond the awning was no different than before. He closed his eyes, opened them again.

The sizzle of electricity echoed off the brick wall of the fire station. Was the grid coming back up? No, the source of the sound was the stranger! With each crackle, neon blue veins wormed beneath the man's translucent skin. Frank's mouth gaped. That was not normal. It sure as hell wasn't natural. He curled the baby closer and pressed into the door.

"You've got to get grounded, and fast." The man's stare bore into Frank. "You're a fireman. You know what happens when electricity and water mix. I can't hold back much longer."

Heat bloomed from the stranger's body, blue-white energy that extended a foot around his profile. The rain evaporated on contact, filling the alley with steam.

How hot must his body be to do that? Eyes narrowed against the glare, Frank pressed into the wall, forced back by the iridescent heat.

"Promise me you'll take care of her," the man begged.

One look at the baby girl in his arms and there was only one answer Frank could give. "I promise."

The stranger nodded. "Go. It's time."

If Frank had any ideas about handling the situation in an official capacity, those thoughts burnt up in the blue inferno that chased him from the alley. Hunched protectively over the babe, the blast singed his back just short of pain and infused the air with the acrid scent of scorched, flame-retardant fabric. Thank the Lord he'd put on his coat to take out the trash. Throat tight, he hurled himself behind the concrete wall of the covered parking garage bordering the fire station. Was the babe hurt? He peeled her away from his chest as he ran, relieved when she made a small mewing noise, like a good solid cry was coming on.

His faithful antique pickup waited in its usual spot overlooking Fifth Street. He fished the key from his pocket to let himself in and cranked the heater as the babe cried in earnest. "Cold we can deal with, baby girl. If you're hungry, you're out of luck for now."

Through the windshield, Frank's view was unobstructed as the stranger exited the alley, tendrils of steam heralding his blue glow. "Radioactive son-of-a bitch," he murmured, his head buzzing with theories about the stranger's condition. Toxic drugs, industrial exposure, alien DNA. Each as unlikely as the next.

The stranger stopped beneath the dead traffic light and faced a street abandoned due to the storm and the time of night. Abandoned, until a fleet of black Humvees roared up Fifth and unloaded a barrage of gunfire in the stranger's direction.

"Holy God in heaven!" Frank threw the truck into reverse, peeling out of the parking space. His transmission groaned as he forced the vehicle into drive and raced for the exit. In the rearview mirror, he expected to see the stranger's bloodied body in the street but slammed on the brakes at what he saw instead.

The man wasn't dead. He was a living lightbulb.

Holding the baby, Frank craned his neck over his shoulder for a better view. Lightning flew from the man's hand, igniting the first Humvee and catapulting another weighty vehicle into the air. A moment of flight and the fiery descent turned the jeep into a missile. The vehicle ripped through the advancing fleet, an oily, twisted mass of metal. Another lightning bolt flew, and then another. Like children's toys, the military vehicles popped skyward and folded accordion style, rolled and rumpled in the stranger's ire.

The glowing man stepped around the wreckage and advanced toward the next wave of Humvees.

Frank floored the accelerator, patting the now wailing baby as he exited on to Fourth Street at the back of the garage. He raced away from the flames and the rancor of burning rubber. Sirens blared from every direction but he did not stop. With nothing to lose, and no one who mattered to miss him, Frank ran.

It would be a long time before he stopped running.

Chapter 1
Lydia

Seventeen years later...

Bishop Kauffman often preaches we are to be *in* the world but not *of* the world. I've never understood why he bothers. The only world I've ever known is Hemlock Hollow, and you can't be more set apart than us.

I press my cheek into Hildegard's tawny belly, and she stomps her hooves in disapproval. She's uncomfortable with my pace, but I don't slow my milking. I can't. I have my responsibilities, but there are also my priorities.

"Sorry, girl," I whisper. "We need to hurry."

I kick a clump of hay toward her head. The cow stretches her neck for a nibble, temporarily distracted from my tugging. The sky lightens beyond her hindquarters, distinct rays visible on the horizon. As planned, my bucket is full before the sun is up.

To Hildegard's relief, I set her to pasture and then return to the barn to get my bucket of milk. Mary Samuels arrives just as I'm leaving for home, rubbing her eyes and yawning. Behind her, the cow she leads looks as tired as she does.

"Already finished? Oh, to be a morning person like you, Lydia," she says. She straightens her apron with one dark brown hand, darker than usual due to her work in the sun this time of year. I curse the vulnerability of my fair complexion. Any other time, I'd enjoy a long talk with Mary, my dearest girlfriend, weighing the benefits of our various gifts, dark skin versus a morning disposition, but not now. Not this morning.

"Good to see you, Mary." Arm bent to keep the bucket a safe distance from my side, I hurry past her toward the house. Inside, I dump the fresh milk into the stainless steel receptacle we keep in our one and only modern convenience, a methane-powered refrigerator. Quickly, I wash my pail out for tomorrow and check on breakfast. The risen dough is ready for the bread pan. I've already gathered the eggs. My father will be in the field for at least another hour, plenty of time.

Without delay, I hasten toward the hay barn. Jeremiah sidles up to me, also finished with his chores. He wears the same black trousers and vest as all the other boys, but Jeremiah stands out to me. His eyes are the color of cornflowers and he's always smiling, even when none of his teeth show.

"Good morning, Lydia." He straightens his straw hat. His steps quicken until his feet slap the gravel ahead of mine.

"Good morning, Jeremiah." I match him step for step.

Lengthening his stride, he speeds up until he's ahead

again. "Are you going to do the wise thing this morning and start breakfast early?"

"No, I don't think so. I think I'll be going to the haymow." I elbow past him.

"Yeah?" He smiles, breaking into a jog. "That's where I'm going, too."

Race on.

I launch into a full-out run, balling my long skirt in my hand. More of my tights show than is proper but I trust Jeremiah won't tell. Anyway, the shape of my calf might distract him. I can't allow him to beat me to the hay. Of all the mornings I've raced Jeremiah, he's only won twice, and I've never lived down either of those times. If he wins, he'll tell me with a quirky half-smile that maybe I've finally learned I'm a girl. He'll offer twenty times a day to help me carry the eggs or knead the bread, because the race has proven he is more capable. Not again. Not if I can help it.

My legs pump underneath me. I pant from the exertion, the air heavy with late summer heat and the smell of fresh hay. The pounding of Jeremiah's feet beside mine pushes me harder, faster than I've ever run before. Lucky for me, I'm fast for a girl.

We burst through the red and white doors of the hay barn at the same time and sprint past the mound of fresh hay to the worn oak ladder. I reach it first. With a smug grin, I skip rungs as I scramble up, Jeremiah nipping at my heels. His laughter behind me reminds me what I'll face if he wins. I tumble over the top rung and onto the loft, eyeing the huge pile of fresh hay beyond the unobstructed edge. The mound calls to me, but my head swims with vertigo at the space between the precipice and its welcoming fluff.

"You should still let me go first," he calls from the ladder as he pitches over the edge and onto the loft.

"Why? I beat you fair as feathers this time."

"To test the fall. A boy should jump first, just in case."

"Not a chance. You'll have to play the chivalrous male for someone else. I'm going." I shuffle to the far wall and bolt for the edge before he can stop me.

"You're going too fast," he protests. "Slow down!"

I don't listen. I leap for the hay, stretching my body flat in the air. Wind rushes over my *kapp*. My stomach drops. The thrill and exhilaration catch in my throat. For a moment, I fear Jeremiah is right; I've jumped too far, too fast. Unable to gain control, I collide with the top of the hay and bounce across the pile, toward the edge. I dig my fingers into the bales and jut my leg out to the side to slow myself down. My momentum stops just in time, one arm and leg dangling.

Slowly, I roll onto my back. Jeremiah stands at the edge of the loft, eyes wide and arms crossed over his chest.

A self-satisfied grin creeps across my face. "I'm fine." I laugh. No matter how many times I make the leap, the fall sets my heart fluttering in my chest. I don't care if I do bounce off someday. I wouldn't give up this feeling, the free-falling excitement, for anything.

His lips part, and his tight, worried expression softens a little. "Thank the good Lord," Jeremiah mumbles.

"Well? Won'tchya jump, Jeremiah Yoder? Are you

afraid?" I taunt him by lacing my fingers behind my head. Just resting in the hay. Not a care in the world.

His face relaxes into a lopsided grin. He answers by removing his hat and throwing himself over. He lands with a rustle a few feet away from me, and then rolls flush against my side. Propped up on his elbow, his cheeks pink from the exertion of the run, I am reminded of when we were children and would spend our days playing by the river. Not much has changed in seventeen years. We're simply taller and craftier than our younger selves.

Still, Jeremiah embodies everything sweet and good in this world. Of that I am sure.

"You could've let a man be a man, Lydia. What if we were courting? What about *demut*?"

Demut means "submissiveness" in the old language, Pennsylvania German. We still go to German School on Saturdays, although the realities of Hemlock Hollow dictate speaking like an *Englisher*. When Jeremiah says *demut*, he's referring to a wife's role with her husband. It's a way for him to tug at my heartstrings.

"I was protecting you from *hochmut*, Jeremiah." *Hochmut* means arrogance, about the worst trait an Amish can have. "And besides, by the time you choose to court me, you will have years of experience with my disposition and trust that I can leap just as far and as fast as you." As long as he's known me, I've been this way, a girl who likes to plow just as well as quilt and who has to win the race, every time. A risk-taker. Maybe being raised without a mother has cost me my femininity. I don't miss it.

He laughs in the deep baritone that reminds me of his

father. Jeremiah is seventeen like me, but I can tell he will be a great man. He's already an accomplished carpenter.

"I brought something for you," he says.

"You did?"

From his hat he pulls a shiny piece of folded paper. My heart skips a beat.

"Eli brought it back with him."

Unfolding the slippery page, I examine a picture of a woman on a runway. If her skirt were any shorter it would be a belt, and the way her blouse sags off her shoulder makes me blush. In our *Ordnung*, our church law, we are taught to value simplicity. We strive to be plain. The woman's dress is sinful and contrary to everything I believe. Still, as a seamstress, I am fascinated. I trace my finger along the perfect stitching, the sheath of lace that falls just below the hem. Orange. Bold and unapologetic. What would it be like to wear orange?

"Do you think they all dress like this?" I ask. "Her shoes look painful."

"I don't know. But we could find out. When will you ask your dad about *rumspringa*?"

"Not this again. I've told you, there's no way he'll allow it."

"Come on, Lydia. Almost everyone in Hemlock Hollow lives outside the community as an *Englisher* before they commit to the *Ordnung*. They say it's better in the long run, in case you *have* to go someday. What they teach us in school is barely enough to get by in their world. Even the bishop encourages the tradition."

"I hardly think living as an *Englisher* is necessary to a

happy Amish life. Besides, everything I need is here."

Jeremiah rolls his eyes. "Everything you need is here because other folks bring it back for you from the English world. I don't recall you spinning and weaving the cloth for that dress."

I shake my head. "You know my father. He lives the most modest life, and he hates the English world. There is no way he'll agree."

"Did you ask? Did you speak to him about it?"

"Not exactly. I know how he feels by hearing him talk about the others. Remember when Jacob left?"

"Yes."

"My father said, 'Such a waste of a good upbringing. It's like dipping a lily-white lamb in a tar bath.'"

"He did not!"

"He did. Every chance he gets, he reminds me of how he lost my mother and brother in an automobile accident in the English world. 'The world outside ain't safe, Lydia,' he says. 'It's the devil's playground.'"

Jeremiah lets out a deep sigh that blows strands of hay over my shoulder. "I'm not goin' without you."

"Don't be silly. If you want the experience, go. I'll still be here when you get back."

His fingers hook into mine, and I stare up into his unbelievably bright eyes and clean-shaven face. What will he look like with the traditional beard of married Amish? Will his chin be as blond as his curls?

"There are more important things than *rumspringa*, Lydia. But I hoped we could experience the English world together. An adventure to talk about later when we're…"

"When we're what?" I flutter my lashes at him innocently, knowing full well what he means. We've been two peas in a pod since we could walk, and it's long been accepted that we would court. I can't help myself. I want him to say it. I want to hear the words.

Jeremiah lifts a corner of his mouth and then opens it to respond.

"Lydia? Lydia Troyer!" Katie Kauffman, the bishop's wife, calls from outside the barn.

Jeremiah rolls onto his back and flattens himself against the hay. Strictly speaking, we aren't supposed to be alone together unchaperoned.

I swing my head over the side. "Yeah?"

"What are you doing in there, child? I thought you were milking?"

"I finished. Having a rest."

"You must come. I'm sorry. It's your father."

I toss my legs over and jump to the barn floor, a good six-foot drop. "What about my dad?"

"He collapsed. Isaac Bender found him in the field. Rode all the way to the English neighbor on his fastest horse to call a doctor. They took him back to the house—"

I do not wait for the details. Without concern for social formalities, I dash for home, only yelling my thank you to the bishop's wife as an afterthought. As much as I complain about my father, he's all I have. I love him deeply and he's my only kin. Unlike most Amish, I have no brothers or sisters. When my mother was killed, she took with her any hope of more siblings. My father never remarried, and my grandparents, aunts, and uncles are dead. I have cousins, the Benders and the Kauffmans, but our house is rarely full.

I scale the wooden steps of our porch in one leap and grapple with the uncooperative doorknob. It turns much too slowly. Inside, a circle of Amish friends pray around my father. He's propped up with pillows on our sofa, eyes closed. The Benders, the Samuels, the Kauffmans—familiar faces pale against the dark wool of their clothing—whisper solemn appeals for health and healing. Thankful for the prayers and for the company, I place my hand over my heart.

Amish prayers are strong. God is listening.

The door slams behind me, and my father's eyes open at the sound. One of his hands twitches when he sees me; his mouth tugs unevenly to the left. I run to his side, pressing the twitching hand between mine.

"What happened?"

He mumbles an unintelligible response. Something is very wrong. Only half of his body moves and my usually quick-witted father barely acknowledges me. His eyes drift away from my face every few seconds.

The thunder of a car engine turns my head toward the front of the house; the English doctor has arrived. His name is Doc Nelson—he's treated members of Hemlock Hollow before in extreme circumstances. Isaac Bender opens the door before the doctor has a chance to knock and I move out of the elderly man's way without being asked.

After a thorough examination, Doc Nelson addresses

the bishop. "I believe Frank has had a stroke. I need to take him with me to the hospital to confirm and to give him proper treatment."

My eyes meet Bishop Kauffman's, leader of our *Ordnung* and my oldest male relative, my father's cousin. For anyone to leave our community is against English law. In fact, most *Englishers* don't know we *can* leave. But with permission from a bishop, we still do. English law isn't our law. Amish understand that breaking the English law is a necessary part of living in a sinful world.

Even without speaking, the exchange between the Bishop and myself is clear to me. My father wouldn't want to be treated with English medicine, but he might die without it. The bishop must decide. He knows my father as well as I do, but the way he searches my face tells me he's waiting to see if I will voice my father's wishes. More importantly, I think he wonders if it's God's will that I become an orphan.

I've always had faith. Moments ago, I'd told Jeremiah that I would live and die in Hemlock Hollow. But now that it's my father who needs the English medicine, I'm not so willing to dismiss the value of the English world. The difference between Dad and me is this: he trusts that prayers will heal him, while I understand that God sent the doctor.

I remain silent and lower my eyes. It's what Amish women do when they submit to male authority. But by not speaking, I'm sending the bishop a message, my desire for my father to be treated by the English.

"Take him, Doctor Nelson," Bishop Kauffman says.

"Please."

I raise my eyes and breathe a sigh of relief.

With surprising speed, the men load my father into the doctor's black automobile. How is the world still turning? I can't lose him. *I can't.* Practiced prayers rattle through my brain as the only family I've ever known races away from me. All I can think is my father would find the car he's riding in as sinful as the hospital that, God willing, will save his life.

Chapter 2

"**Y**ou shouldn't be alone," Mary says to me. My dearest friend pulls me into a hug and rubs my back.

Martha, Mary's mother, nods. "You're welcome to stay."

After my father was taken to the English hospital, Mary insisted I come home with her. Her mother took me under her wing, fed me until I thought I might burst, and kept me busy the rest of the day at her shop, where I am an apprentice seamstress. I finished six dresses and two pairs of pants she'd started earlier. She worked me harder than usual to be kind, so I didn't have time to think about what happened. I am grateful for their charity but loathe to overstay my welcome.

"I want to sleep in my own bed and pray from my own Bible," I say.

"Well, you know best what you've gotta do. Door's always open," Mary's father says. "Benjamin and Samuel will help with your farm while your father is away."

Mary's two brothers nod in my direction.

"Thank you. I could never manage on my own."

With warm hugs all around, I leave, knowing a strong dose of reality is in store for me without their distraction. Freed by the quiet of the walk home, my mind swims in a sea of insecurities, trying to make sense of my father's infirmity. He's always been my rock, my anchor. What will happen if they can't save him? Can I survive tossed about on the waves of my own independence?

I have a place, a secret place I go to think. My sacred space.

To get there, I cross through a field of summer wheat, caressing the soft bristles with my fingertips as the grassy stalks tug against my skirt. My hickory tree is at the edge of the wood. Struck by lightning, half the tree is dead and rotting, but the other half defies the odds, covered in lush green leaves. I run to its trunk and throw my arms around its bark as if the green branches could hug me, pat my back, and say everything will be okay.

The rotting side has a hollow heart that keeps my secrets. I plunge my hand into the hole, retrieving the treebox Jeremiah carved for me. It's made from hickory wood and the lid is carved in the likeness of my tree. Inside, there is a hodgepodge of mysteries. A flexible transparent rectangle Eli says is a phone. A piece of rubbery fabric Anna told me adjusts to size when made into a garment. There's a disintegrating paper cup with a picture of a kidney bean on it and the words Ready Bell Express. I add the photo Jeremiah gave me this morning, taking one more look at the woman in orange with her tall shoes. I sift through the box until my brain buzzes with thoughts of the outside world.

"Why do you keep that thing if you don't ever plan to go on *rumspringa*?"

I flip the box closed and turn to face Jeremiah, whose

teasing tone does not match the grim tilt of his lips. He's as worried about my father as I am. I shrug. "I'm curious, I guess." It's a simple answer, although my feelings are far from simple.

"Come on, Lydia. Tell me the truth."

I stare at the box in my hands for a moment before answering. "Remember a few years ago, Benders had that dog with something wrong in its head?"

"Yeah, the biter."

I nod. "The Benders had to keep it chained so it wouldn't kill their sheep. That old dog would tug against that chain until his neck was bloody." I rub my neck. "Fur worn away by rubbing leather."

He nods.

"One day, the rain made the yard soft, and when the dog tugged against the chain, he pulled the spike from the ground, yanked it free from the mud."

"I hadn't heard. Did it kill a sheep?"

"You would have thought after all the tugging. But no. Instead he lay down at the edge of the yard with his head between his paws. The Benders found him like that, crying and shaking."

"What has that to do with *rumspringa*?" he asks through a smile.

I sigh. "Maybe I'm a bit like that dog. I want to know about the outside world, but I can't bring myself to leave home to do it. The English world is a novelty and a temptation. It calls to me, promising excitement and adventure." I shake my head. "But I'm thankful for the life I have. My father always says the dream of a thing is often better than the reality. The English world could never live up to my expectations."

He hangs his head. "Or maybe you're afraid it will."

I purse my lips. "Anyway, Dad will be back soon, I'm sure, and everything will return to normal."

"I'm sure it will, Lydia," Jeremiah says.

I hide the box again inside the hollow of my tree and then pull myself up into the lowest green branch. Jeremiah follows my lead and positions himself next to me. We sit in the shared silence of old friends. No words are necessary.

The red-molasses sun drips behind the twelve-foot wall that surrounds Hemlock Hollow. From here, the nuclear reactor in the Outlands is clearly visible. The towering concrete hunkers in the distance, both our blessing and our curse. There are guard towers on the wall, where my father says there used to be soldiers years ago, but the radiation made them sick and eventually the Green Republic couldn't get anyone to work there. By that time, the government thought all my ancestors were dead or dying. Some did, but the ones who lived learned to adapt. And because the Green Republic is afraid to come here, they haven't a clue about us. The reactor preserves our way of life.

"He's made of tough stuff, Lydia," Jeremiah says. "This is why we have the lessons. This is why we prepare. Your dad will blend in, get healed, and come home. Don't you worry." His hand comes to rest on the branch next to mine. Our little fingers touch. My cheeks warm and I have to look away.

"It's you who should be worried about what your mother will do if she catches you here after dark," I say to him.

He grins and jumps down from the branch. Tipping his hat, he says, "Good night, Lydia."

He disappears into the wheat. A few minutes later, I follow, arriving home by the light of the moon. I let myself into my house, hyperaware of the whine of the door hinges and the creak of the floorboards underfoot.

I fall into bed exhausted, but there's no rest for me. Nightmares fill my head. Nightmares of dark wolves chasing me.

* * * * *

It's two days more before I hear anything. Two days I spend in prayer and fasting, even though Martha Samuels and others try their best to feed and comfort me. I don't want to be a burden. I do my chores and help with my father's. I stay in my own house.

When the knock comes, I approach the door, the weakest I've been since the time I fell into the river at nine years old. My limbs are just as shaky, and my heart pounds as it did when I had to tread water for hours to stay alive. I've never been sick, not even a cold, but maybe this is my first flu. I'm overdue.

On the other side of the door waits a slight man with minimal gray hair and a kind smile. He holds his hat at his waist.

"Bradford. Do you bring news of my father?"

"I do." His mouth pulls into a tight line. For a moment, I'm afraid to hear what he has to say.

Bradford Adams and his wife, Hillary, have been friends of Hemlock Hollow for some thirty years. The Adamses live a mile west of the wall, and it was their phone Isaac used to call the doctor. Bradford and Hillary are the only *Englishers* besides Doc Nelson I know and trust.

I remember my manners. A bicycle leans against the porch and there is no car in front of the house. "You rode your bike all this way." I motion for him to come in and sit down.

Bradford nods. "Out of respect for your traditions." The man limps into the house and takes a seat on the sofa.

By way of the kitchen, I return with some lemonade, pouring him a tall glass before plopping down ungracefully in the chair across from the sofa. "Please, tell me what you've learned."

"Doc Nelson called today. First, let me relieve your fears. Your father is alive. The doctor says he's progressing normally."

"Praise the Lord." I take a deep breath and let it out slowly. "When can he come home?"

"That's the trouble. See, your father had what they call a stroke. He can't speak or walk. The doctors on the outside can fix it. They have ways."

"I can take care of him while he recovers."

"Once they fix him you won't have to, honey. The only thing is, the treatment will take several weeks."

I shake my head. "No. Dad can't stay for that long. He

wouldn't want to."

"It's too late to bring him back. As far as the *Englishers* are concerned, he's a plumber from Willow's Province. You have to understand, in the outside world, no one leaves the hospital before they're treated. If he leaves early, they might trace him back here. You and I both know that would be disastrous." He takes a sip of his lemonade. "They're moving him to a rehabilitation center in Crater City."

"Crater City? But that's so far away!"

"He's in good hands, but he will not be back for quite some time."

I press the heels of my palms over my eyes. I can't do this. I can't pretend anymore. As strong as I want to be, tears seep down my cheeks. I come apart tear by tear.

An arthritic hand pats my shoulder. "Don't cry, darling. If you want me to, I can take you in my car to visit."

It's a sweet offer, but it's unrealistic to expect Bradford to support multiple weekly visits to my father, especially considering I'd have to masquerade as an *Englisher*. The risk is too great. Even if I accepted, the time commitment would be burdensome on both of us. Crater City is more than three hundred miles away.

"I'm sorry. I need some time to think." I attempt to stand to show him out, but the walls start to wobble. My bottom hits the chair hard enough to slide the legs backward on the wood floor. I close my eyes. When I open them again, there is a glass of lemonade in front of my lips.

"For your father's sake, please take care of yourself," Bradford says.

"I'm so sorry. Don't trouble yourself with me. I'm just tired." I sip the lemonade and force a smile. "Thank you for coming. I'm going to rest now."

He watches me take a gulp of lemonade and shifts his weight from one foot to the other. The corners of his mouth sag.

"Really, I'm fine. I need rest, that's all." I give my most convincing smile.

"Okay. I'm going to go. Come see me if you need my help."

As soon as he leaves, I set the lemonade down and bury my face in my hands, giving in to the wave of grief that plows into me. The door opens again. I rub my eyes in a weak attempt to cover my tears. "Did you forget something?"

"It's me."

I lower my fingers.

Jeremiah frowns at me, a large basket hanging from his arm.

"I don't want you to see me like this."

He remains silent but sets the basket down. The next thing I know, he's swept me up into his arms. Carrying me to my bedroom, he props me up on every pillow he can find. Then leaves the room and returns with the basket. "Dinner, compliments of *Maam* Yoder."

"Jeremiah, you didn't—"

"She insisted." Out of the basket, he pulls a soup urn and a spoon and sits down beside me on the bed. He ladles the hot soup and brings it to my lips. The savory liquid courses down my throat, so delicious I moan.

"You're hungry," Jeremiah says.

"Chicken dumpling. Your mother's was always the best in Hemlock Hollow."

Jeremiah feeds me again. While I chew, his attention sweeps away from me toward the wall. "I've always loved that quilt."

How embarrassing. The blue and gray log cabin style on my wall was my first. "Don't tease me."

"I'm not. I love it."

"The corner is messed up."

He spoon-feeds me another bite of soup, locking eyes with me. "I love it."

"Thank you," I say around the bite.

He rests the bowl on his leg. "Bradford told me about your father's condition."

I nod.

"This is our chance. *Rumspringa*."

I swallow the bite of chicken in my mouth. "Not this again. Don't you understand? My father wouldn't want me to go."

"That was before, but now your father isn't here."

"Just because he's sick doesn't give me the right to disobey."

"You don't understand what I'm saying. He isn't here, Lydia. He's out there. If we go on *rumspringa,* you can live where he is, in Crater City. You can see him every day. Maybe this is God's way of telling you it's the right time."

I try to derail his logic but come up short. Clutching

the base of my neck, I attempt to calm my racing heart but the untrustworthy organ pounds against my palm, speeding at the thought of leaving home. Even after a few deep breaths my shoulders are still hunched in tight knots.

"I've known you since you could walk," Jeremiah says. "I think, maybe, it's not just about your father's wishes or about the dream being better than reality. I think, maybe, you might be afraid. A little bit?"

For a moment, I'm speechless as I ponder the accusation. Me? Afraid? "I trust my father and if he says the world outside is dangerous, I believe him. I want to visit him but I *am* afraid. I think we both should be."

"It's normal to be afraid. Everyone is. But we aren't the first Amish to do this. There's an English house that helps people like us with the transition. They provide papers, names. They'll help us find jobs at places that will be discreet about us. We'll get to see all of those things we've talked about. Remember how Eli told us about the television? Don't you wonder what that will be like? Or how it would be to flip a switch to light up any room, instead of hanging the gas lamp from the hook above the table? I know it's scary, but it might also be wonderful."

I squeeze my eyes shut and try to ignore the pounding in my ribcage. I picture what it would be like to live in a house with Jeremiah. Without the expectations of Hemlock Hollow hanging over our heads, we might finish what we started in the barn. His lips look soft, wanting. We've been inseparable for as long as I can remember, but we've never even kissed. In the English world there would be no limits, no chaperones.

My cheeks burn. Emotions swirl within me that I can't even name. I press my hand into my chest as if I can hold my heart at bay. Pressure on a wound stops the bleeding, after all. But a flood of memories comes back to me. Ever since I was a baby, my father has lectured me on the evils of the English lifestyle. This is one edge I'm not sure I can throw myself over, even if Jeremiah is holding my hand.

"Open," he says.

I obey, drinking in the spoonful of broth he brings to my lips.

"Good girl." Jeremiah drops the spoon into the bowl and sets the lot down on the bedside table. Then he leans over me. With a hand propped on the bed on either side of my chest, he accepts my eye contact as he would an outstretched hand. I relax into the down pillow. The sight of him hovering over me fills me with intense joy and a sense of security. If we had time alone, if we shared an uninterrupted kiss, would I feel for Jeremiah what a wife feels for her husband?

"Please, Lydia. Just this once, do as I say. Come with me. I want you to be the one I experience the world with. We're seventeen years old. A few months—just until your father has recovered—and then we'll come home."

The way he says home, his breath brushing my face, sends a shiver across my skin and makes my heart skip against my breastbone. He says home like the word is intimate: *our home.*

"Besides," he continues in a whisper, suddenly intent on my mouth. "Until old Frank is home, I have no one to

28

ask to court you. And I will court you, Lydia, whether the English way, the Amish way, or both."

A curl of his blond hair falls across his forehead. I sweep it aside and caress his cheek with my knuckles.

Some decisions are carefully constructed towers of logic framed in lists of pros and cons, shingled in trusted advice. As I throw my arms around Jeremiah, pressing the apron of my dress against his vest, the choice I make is based on none of those things. It springs straight from my heart to my lips.

"Yes, Jeremiah. I'll come with you. I'll go on *rumspringa.*"

The smile he gives me is as much a reward as the embrace that leaves me longing for more and anxious to begin.

Chapter 3

Bishop Kauffman agrees to my *rumspringa* request with little concern. In fact, the way he claps me on the shoulder suggests he expected the turn of events. Literally, *rumspringa* means "running around," the only time in Amish life when the *Ordnung* overlooks transgressions. The Amish only baptize adults, so as a teenager I'm not bound to church law, but at seventeen, I'm considered old enough to make my own decisions. That means between now and the time I choose to be baptized, I am free of all expectations except those of my conscience.

But my conscience has a loud voice. My father has made sure of that.

"Lydia," Bishop Kauffman says, placing a calloused hand on mine, "where you are going, they don't have rules like we do. The reason we've come to this, living behind this wall, is because they chose a life without limits, without conscience, and we chose to preserve ours. I want you to go and experience that life so that you know what it is you're giving up, the good and the bad. But remember your roots. Remember who you are. You may walk through the valley of darkness, but remember you come from the light."

I smile and nod. "I won't let their world change me."

As the words leave my mouth, I truly believe them.

His eyebrows dart toward the ceiling. "Oh, child, that's not what I'm saying at all. You *should* let it change you. When you leave here, there is no halfway. You will live, dress, and speak the English way. There's something wrong if living that life doesn't change you."

"Oh," I say. I knit my eyebrows.

He gives my shoulder a gentle shake. "It should make you more committed to our way of life."

I bob my chin. "Okay." My stomach twists with my impending reality. I will have to live English. All of my lessons, my schooling, it was all for this moment—so I could walk among them if I had to.

"Then, go. We'll take care of your father's farm while you're gone. I will miss you."

Tossing my arms around his neck, I squeeze hard enough for the hug to last until I return.

* * * * *

Balanced between reluctance and excitement, I pack my father's small brown suitcase. I start with a *kapp* to cover my head and the box of pins I use every morning to bun my hair under it. Will they make me cut my hair? Winding a loose tress around my finger, I watch the honey brown tighten like a noose against my pale skin. I bite my lip. I don't want to change my hair.

Head shaking, I resolve not to worry about a problem that hasn't even happened. *Keep busy*, I tell myself. The modest gray dress I pack is without zippers or decoration, and the tights I've sewn myself. Leather shoes made by an Amish neighbor go in next. It all fits easily. I won't be able to wear this clothing once I'm on the outside, but I want a change of clothes for the trip home. Plus, it feels good to bring something of my life with me into the void.

I clean my house spotless and turn off the gas that powers the lamps and refrigerator at the tank. Both run on methane collected from heating pig dung—an Amish invention. The Yoders will use our pigs' chips while I'm away. As for the water, I turn that off too and empty the pipes, in case I'm not back before the first freeze.

Everything is prepared, but I startle anyway when Jeremiah knocks. I scurry to the door, a mess of jittery limbs.

His smile melts when he sees me. "Are you all right?" He takes my waist as if he expects I might fall over at any moment. "You look pale."

"Just nervous," I answer.

"Do you need to sit down? Some water?"

"No, I'm fine." I turn to grab my suitcase. "Besides, I shut the water off."

"Just as well. I have a surprise for you in the buggy."

Through the door, I notice the Amish buggy in front of the house. *Huh?* "I thought we would be going in a car. Won't someone see us in that?"

"Baby steps, Lydia. Baby steps." He lifts the suitcase from my hand and leads me out the door. "The safe house is in Willow's Province, just outside the gate. The only neighbors are Doc Nelson and Bradford and Hillary Adams. No one will see."

It sounds risky, but I trust in his plan. Besides, the familiarity sets me at ease.

Jeremiah's horse, Abe, swats flies with his tail, the jingle of metal against leather mixing with the songs of sparrows in the summer wheat. It's all the encouragement I need. I climb into the cab and wait as he loads my suitcase. He takes the bench next to me and scoops up the reins. With a cluck of his tongue, Jeremiah spurs Abe into the road, where he quickens to a rhythmic trot.

"So, what is this surprise?"

Jeremiah raises an eyebrow. "Patience is a virtue."

"And so is initiative. Should I look for it myself?"

"No need. It's there." He motions behind me with his head.

I pull the covered pail that rests next to Jeremiah's suitcase toward the bench. When I lift the lid, the most glorious scent fills the cab. Two soft drinks are wedged next to a large, colorful paper bag with the Ready Bell Express logo.

"You brought fast food from the English world?"

He flashes me a conspiratorial grin. "Jacob met me last night to make arrangements and brought it. I thought you might like lunch. Reheated it this morning myself. Cheeseburgers, French fries, nuggets, and something called a pie that looks nothing like one. And soda, still cold from the fridge."

"You are my favorite person in the world right now." I kiss his cheek, then pull the drink from the pail. The ice-cold cola bubbles up the straw, courses down my throat. After the last swallow, I burp appreciatively.

I've only had soda pop once before, when Mary returned from *rumspringa* with a case of it. It was just a small taste because we all had to share. I slurp on the straw again, anxious to have my fill. Wedging the cup between my feet, I unwrap a cheeseburger, offering the first bite to Jeremiah, since he's holding the reins and can't feed himself properly. He wraps his lips around half the burger, only thwarted by the ridge of paper I'm holding.

"I see that large mouth of yours is *gut* for something, Jeremiah." I use the German pronunciation for emphasis, like a mother scolding her child. "Did ya leave any for me?"

"Not *gut*, Lydia. Good. From here on out, you have to speak like an *Englisher*. We can't slip into German, ever."

"Gooood," I drawl.

Waving a finger, he says, "When in the English world, act English. Always. Have you been looking through your book?"

He's talking about the book each of us is given with pictures of new technologies so that we don't embarrass ourselves the first time we see a dish sanitizer or an irradiator. Of course I've reviewed mine. As if the eight years of English culture we had to take in school weren't enough.

"How's this for acting English?" I shove the entire other half of the burger into my mouth until my cheeks bulge.

Laughing, he shakes his head. "There's more in there, you know. Please don't choke on my account."

I shift the half-chewed mass to my cheek. "It tastes

funny. Mushy and bland. Is this beef?"

"I think so." Jeremiah glances toward the bag.

"So, how far is it?" I swallow and reach for another burger.

"Just a few miles past Bradford Adams's place. Jacob is coming home to be baptized. He's going to drive the buggy back for me."

"I guess the tar didn't stick," I say, looking out over the fields of crops that line both sides of the road. I can almost hear my father talking about Jacob. *Like a lily-white lamb dipped in a tar bath.* Is that what Dad will think of me when all this is over?

"I guess not." Jeremiah's quiet chuckle brings me back into the moment.

Abe's rhythmic *clip-clop* provides background music. This is how it is with Jeremiah. I'm not compelled to speak to fill the quiet. The miles skip by. Fields give way to hickory and birch trees and then the road melds into two dirt ruts. This isn't the fastest way to the wall, but it's the only way to the gate.

Hemlock Hollow borders the Outlands, territory ravaged by radiation during the war. Most *Englishers* won't live anywhere near the Outlands because of the radiation levels. There are rumors that certain animals have mutated. Dangerously large rats and bears with two heads are said to make their homes near the remains of the reactor. Once the wall went up, a bunch of men from Hemlock Hollow knocked a hole in the concrete, at the part deepest within the Outlands, and built a wooden gate. I don't know why the English didn't think we'd do that.

Amish are talented builders and our faith makes us brave. If I were to guess, I'd say it was because they underestimated us and assumed we'd go quickly into death.

I think the rumors about the continued impact of the radiation are made up. While it's true, I've been told, that many people died that first year after the war from the sickness, people in Hemlock Hollow live long and happy lives now. For as long as I've been alive, no one has ever seen anything like a bear with two heads. Our homes are built as far away from the Outlands as possible, within the bounds of our walled existence. I don't really understand what radiation is or why the English are so afraid of it. All I know is, it doesn't seem to bother us any. Not anymore.

We reach the wall, and Jeremiah jumps out of the cab and swings the gate open. I take up the reins, guiding Abe through. He closes and locks it behind us. The forest is dark here, thick with trees that twist and tangle together. I scan both sides of the path for two-headed bears, then giggle at the ridiculous thought. Jeremiah climbs back in, and Abe breaks into a trot again.

"Why do you think Bradford and Hillary Adams choose to live so close to the Outlands?" I ask.

"My father says the houses are cheaper in Willow's Province. Plus, it's the place you live when you want the government out of your business. The Province is rural and keeps poor records. I'm guessing they aren't big fans of the Green Republic and decided to take their chances with the radiation."

"That makes sense. I think the radiation is hogwash

anyway. Some invisible force that makes you sick? I don't believe it."

Jeremiah shrugs and laughs through his nose.

The forest opens up and Abe's feet *clip-clop* on paved road again. We pass the Adamses' small stone cottage. By the time Jeremiah guides Abe up a long driveway toward a sweet-looking yellow house with a white wraparound porch, I regret eating the second burger.

"Please tell me this is it. I think my stomach is rejecting the fast food." I blow my cheeks out as a wave of nausea washes over me.

"This is it, Lydia. Fifty-four Lakehurst Drive. Your temporary English home."

He pulls the buggy up next to a corroded blue hatchback and reins in Abe. Hopping out first, Jeremiah offers his hand to help me down.

"Thanks," I say.

On the surface, the house looks similar to the ones in Hemlock Hollow, but there are subtle differences. A glass cage over the door houses an electric lightbulb. There's no knocker. Instead, the button on the frame is an electric doorbell. I've never used one, and I decide in advance that I won't push it. I'll knock on the wood with my knuckles. A string of party lights in the shape of chili peppers wrap around the porch railing. It's late afternoon, so they aren't lit, but I can picture what they must look like glowing in the darkness.

An Amish home would never have such decoration, not because of the electricity required to run them, but because it would be considered a form of vanity. It would be viewed as an attempt to make a house look better than its neighbor. An Amish community is grounded in sameness and humility. It's virtuous to hold others above self.

Still, they *are* beautiful; my eye is drawn again and again to the cherry red plastic hanging like ripe fruit from an electric vine. They seem harmless in this setting, where they can be enjoyed without judgment.

"Are you ready to go in?" Jeremiah nudges my elbow, his hands filled with our luggage.

"I'm sorry. Let me help you carry that." I reach for my suitcase, but Jeremiah shakes his head.

"No, I've got it. Can you knock on the door?"

I climb the two steps to the porch and pound my knuckles twice against the wood. The door whips open before I can make contact the third time. A boy in a T-shirt and cap holds his hands out toward me.

"They're here! Everyone, come see. The newbies are here," the boy yells.

I don't recognize the face in front of me, but I do recognize the voice.

"Caleb? Is that you?" I ask.

"In the flesh." He removes his cap to reveal a headful of spiky brown hair.

"We never heard what happened to you," I say.

"Well, I decided not to go back. I'm not surprised Hemlock Hollow didn't advertise my refusal of baptism. I'm the custodian here now."

"Oh." I balk at the permanence he puts behind the words and glance toward Jeremiah, who's joined me on the porch.

"Come on in, you two."

I follow Caleb through a sparsely decorated living room. A plain boy stands next to the sofa, hat in hands.

"Jacob!" I throw my arms around his neck for a quick hug then retreat a proper distance. Jeremiah ducks between us to shake Jacob's hand. "You look…exactly the same!"

The boy shakes his dark mop of hair and smiles. "Well, I didn't yesterday, but I'm ready to go home."

"Living English hasn't changed you, then?" I ask.

There is an awkward pause while Jacob studies the floor; the smile fades from his face. "Yes, Lydia. Living English has changed me. The people here don't value each other the way we do back home. People are tools here."

"Hey, that's your opinion, man," Caleb interjects.

"Yes," Jacob states. "That is my opinion." The smile returns to its proper place on his face. "Lydia, Jeremiah, *gut* to see ya again. I'll take Abe back for ya. Hope to see you both again soon." Without even a glance at Caleb, Jacob bounds to the front door.

I wave goodbye as he glances back and nods in my direction. What was that all about? He's lived here for months and not even a handshake for his host? I want to ask but it's none of my business. Still, tension hangs thick in the air as the door closes and Caleb doesn't acknowledge Jacob's leaving. Moments later, Abe's rhythmic *clip-clop* grows soft with distance.

After an awkward moment of silence, Caleb claps his hands together as if he means the sound to clear the heavy mood. "Let me give you guys the tour."

I exchange glances with Jeremiah. He shrugs.

Caleb holds his hands out toward a faded blue sofa with worn edges, a matching chair, coffee table, and end tables. "This is the family room."

"It's plain," Jeremiah says. He means it as a compliment.

"Glad you like it, because it's where we spend most of our time when we're home." Caleb turns around and points into an arched doorway. "That is the kitchen."

I step forward and peek in. The refrigerator is gigantic and strangely quiet compared to our gas-powered one. I recognize the irradiator and the dish sanitizer, but something is missing. "Where's the stove?"

"We don't use them anymore," Caleb says. "The new irradiator cooks the food while it sanitizes it."

"Oh." I run my fingers over the smooth silver top of the device, wondering if it will be difficult to use.

"Don't worry. I'll show you how it works later. Gotta warn you, the food tastes like crap."

I glance at Jeremiah, but he's opening and shutting the irradiator experimentally. Caleb does not expound on the quality of the food.

We follow Caleb back through the family room to a hall near the rear of the house. He points into a small rectangular room with a well-used twin bed and dresser. "It's not paradise, but it will have to do," he says to me.

"It's perfect." The quality of the furniture isn't important to me. I didn't come here to sleep, and I hope to spend as little time as possible in here anyway.

Jeremiah sets my suitcase down on the bed. I walk to the only window and look out. Fields of corn go on and on, as far as I can see. I guess the English world isn't so different after all. If I wasn't so excited to be here, I'd be disappointed. "Looks like Hemlock Hollow," I say.

Caleb laughs. "You might not want to judge by that view." He motions toward Jeremiah.

"You're right next door. Let's get you settled in."

The boys slip from the room, giving me a moment alone.

It doesn't take long to unpack everything I own, and I begin to wonder where we're going to get our *Englisher* costumes. I return to the living room to ask. Caleb isn't there, but a girl in a tight T-shirt and jeans is reading a magazine on the sofa. She glances up at me.

"Lydia, I'm so excited to have you here." Her bright blond curls bounce over her shoulder with the movement of her head.

"I'm sorry, do I know you?"

"Don't you recognize me?"

I concentrate on the makeup-covered face in front of me. The girl's skin is flawless. Silver eyeshadow feathers across her lids and over her eyebrows toward her ears. It looks like she's wearing silver, wing-shaped glasses that have melted to her skin. The color contrasts sharply with her robin's egg blue eyelashes—long, thick lashes. A wide black line surrounds each eye and her lips are puffy and blood red. But under it all, I recognize the bow-shaped mouth and narrow nose. "My word, Hannah, is that you?"

The girl nods, bounding from the sofa and spreading

her arms.

I accept her embrace. "You are so beautiful. Look at your hair, your makeup. It's like something from a painting... or a dream."

"You'll look like this too. It's expected here."

"Oh, I couldn't."

Hannah opens her mouth but is interrupted when Jeremiah and Caleb enter the room.

"Great, everyone's here. We can do the welcoming ceremony," Caleb says.

"What's the welcoming ceremony?" I ask.

Caleb and Hannah move to the windows and shut the blinds, plunging the room into darkness.

"Hannah, can I have a drum roll, please?" Caleb asks.

Hannah drums her fingers on the coffee table and trills her tongue off the roof of her mouth. Ritualistically, Caleb approaches the wall, chin held high with the exaggerated step-together-step of a formal occasion. His eyes fix on a switch. A *light* switch. Suddenly, I understand what all the fuss is about. This will be the first time Jeremiah or I have ever seen an electric light work.

Plain folk aren't against electricity per se. Our community is against dependence on an ungodly world. That's why it's okay for us to use gas to power our homes. Gas isn't connected physically to the grid, and frankly, we could live without it in a pinch. Still, whether it's the novelty or taboo that draws me in, I'm excited for this experience.

I smile, oddly breathless with anticipation as Caleb's finger hooks beneath the off-white plastic switch. Hannah quits her drumming with a fake cymbal crash. *Click*. The lightbulb in the lamp next to me glows for a moment. The bulb flares quieter than my gas version. But then bluish-white lightning arcs from where the lamp plugs into the wall, dancing for a moment in the storm of its own making.

ZAP! The bolt strikes me in the chest. Sparks fill my vision. A boom rattles my eardrums. Head snapping forward, my feet lift off the carpet and I fly backward until my shoulder blades slam into the far wall. *Crack!* My skull follows my momentum. Pain radiates from my heart to my fingertips as I am suspended for a moment, arms outstretched.

Jeremiah yells my name.

The white light retracts and my body crumples to the floor. I fall as if the hand of God has dropped me from heaven.

Chapter 4

When I wake, Jeremiah and Caleb are hovering over me. Something cold and wet blots my forehead and dribbles down my temple—Jeremiah with a moist handkerchief.

"Did I pass out?" I ask.

"Oh, thank the good Lord," Jeremiah says on a sigh. He slides an arm under my shoulders and hugs me to his chest. "You were electrocuted."

"Electrocuted?"

"I've never seen anything like it before," Caleb says. "You weren't even touching the outlet. How could that have happened?"

"Well, don't ask us. You're supposed to be the expert," Jeremiah says accusingly.

"Jeremiah, it wasn't Caleb's fault," I say. "If he says he's never seen this happen, I believe him. I'm okay." I sit up and rub my chest, still sore from where the electricity struck me. My hand touches skin. "Oh my. It burned through." I grip the singed edges to close the hole in my dress as heat rises in my cheeks.

"Don't worry. We kept you covered." Jeremiah helps me up.

Once I get my feet under me, I peek under my palm.

The hole is the size of a silver dollar and directly over my heart, with crispy brown edges that stand out against my pale skin. Amazingly, my flesh is unscathed. "If you all would please excuse me, I'd like to change," I say.

"You should change into the English clothes I bought for you," Hannah says. "Maybe static electricity was the cause. Wool is the worst material for that. I think it would be safer if you dressed English."

I run my hand down my apron to the thin wool of my skirt. "Yes, I'd like that."

With thoughts of the rubbery fabric from my tree box in my head, I follow Hannah across the hall to a closet brimming with clothes that are as foreign to me as the ceiling fan above our heads. Hannah pulls out a pair of denim pants and three different shirts.

"These look small but the material stretches to fit, even the jeans. They just have one size here that fits everyone. Layer them, like this." She demonstrates.

"Okay." I'm skeptical. The T-shirt looks especially tiny as if it were made for a doll. Will it fit over my head? I carry the items back to my room and shut the door behind me.

Undressing is a process. I shed the skin of where I come from piece by piece, carefully folding my apron and dress, even though they're both ruined. By the time I reach my tights I wish I'd never come. Although the colors, fabrics, and decoration of the clothing on the bed fascinate me, I'm at war with myself over wearing it. I am naked in more ways than one.

Reluctantly, I slide into the pants, which Hannah

called jeans, marveling at how the denim is as soft as a baby's blanket. The midnight blue slithers over my hips, stretching, expanding as I dress. Once I have them on, I tug the zipper, unzip them and zip them again. I smile at the novelty of the interwoven metal teeth. The jeans don't feel that different from tights. I squat and stand, getting used to the feel. Next is an elastic lace undergarment with thin straps. It's snug, lifting my breasts and hugging my waist. In this, I can't even look down my body without blushing. Quickly, I cover myself with a formfitting T-shirt, paper-thin and cornflower blue. This layer has cap sleeves and covers more skin. I can tolerate a look in the mirror now. The color makes my eyes look greener than they actually are.

Everything on my body is snug, stretchy, and leaves me feeling on display. Thank goodness for the last layer, a silvery jacket. Silky and light, I weigh it in my hand. A tag on the collar says it maintains body temperature in all but the most extreme weather. I slide my arms into the sleeves. With a hood and a zipper, it drapes over the T-shirt, giving me some sense of modesty. This zipper is harder to work because I have to start it myself. When I finally succeed in hooking the sides together, I zip it as high as it will go, just under my chin. I frown. I do not look like an *Englisher*. I tug the zipper halfway down, until it looks more like what Hannah might wear and shrug at my reflection. This is how *Englishers* look and how I must look to fit in. It's not too bad.

One more thing. My *kapp* doesn't match the ensemble. Fingers trembling, I pull the meshy white bonnet from my head. Emboldened by my new English clothes, I unpin my hair and let it fall in honey-brown waves around my shoulders. I part it on the side, something no plain woman ever does, and brush it until it shines.

What will Jeremiah think? He's never seen my hair down.

Excited to show him, I slip from the room and quietly return to the living area. Jeremiah is watching something through the blinds of the front window, his fingers spreading the slats. I notice he's also dressed in jeans. Despite my best efforts, my gaze lingers on how they fit his lower body. He's wearing a stretchy black shirt that shows off every muscle, and there's something in his hair that tames his golden curls, making them appear slightly damp. I want to talk about our new clothes, but it isn't a good time. His face is positively somber.

"What's going on?" I ask.

Jeremiah turns, opens his mouth to answer but comes up short of breath when he sees me. "Lydia," he whispers.

Noticing Jeremiah has forgotten how to speak, Caleb pipes up from his place at the far window. "We have visitors. Government vehicles across the field. The green color means they're from Crater City, the capitol. This never happens. I've lived here for three years and we've never even seen the authorities—not even an officer. We're the only house out this way."

"Why are they here?" I ask.

"That's what I'd like to know," Caleb answers. He exchanges glances with Hannah. "They don't have their sirens on. That's a good sign. But we're doomed if they figure out who you are."

"I'll take care of their clothes and things," Hannah says, bolting for my room.

"Looks like you two are getting the crash course in acting English," Caleb says. "No matter what, they can't find out you're from the preservation."

That's what the *Englishers* call Hemlock Hollow, the Amish preservation. In school we learn there used to be some people called Indians who lived on what the English called reservations. After the war, when the reservation system ended badly and the Amish were allowed to keep their independence from the government by being walled in on land nobody wanted, our home was nicknamed a cultural *preservation*. I guess changing the name sounded better to people. No matter how you twist the words, *Englishers* think of our preservation as a kind of zoo and us as animals. Most *Englishers* assume we've either died from the radiation or we live like wild animals, and that's fine with us.

A sharp knock turns Caleb's head. He opens the door without hesitation. On the porch, a man in a dull green military uniform waits, rigid and serious. His black armband sports the emblem of the Green Republic, the same emblem on the vehicles in the driveway.

"Can I help you?" Caleb asks.

"I'm Officer Reynolds," the man says. "Are you Caleb Hunter?"

"Yes, that's me."

"We've been informed that a surge took place at this address consistent with energy scamping. Have you kids been scamping electricity? Before you answer, I'm required to inform you that early admission is a misdemeanor. If you lie and we find out, it's a felony."

"No one here is scamping electricity."

"How do you explain the surge?"

"Lydia was electrocuted." Caleb points toward me.

I cross my arms over my chest to feel more covered in my English clothes. My brain repeats the word *scamping* over and over, trying to figure out what it means. I decide it must be like stealing, but I don't understand how anyone could "steal" the white-blue light that poured into me.

Officer Reynolds pushes into the room, scanning me from head to toe. "She doesn't look electrocuted."

"It was weird. I've never seen anything like it. She was standing next to the lamp and the electricity jumped from the outlet into her chest."

Officer Reynolds takes another good look at me, and then frowns at Caleb. "I'm going to need to search the house. Do you agree to this search?"

"Yes, of course," Caleb says.

With a gesture of his hand, Reynolds urges a team of six officers into action. We watch out the front door as they circle the house at a jog, arms full of buzzing equipment. "Caleb Hunter, you and your property are under investigation for scamping. As such, specialized equipment will be used to detect any device that could drain, store, or emit electricity. As part of this investigation, we've cut power to your home. This power will be restored once the grounds and interior are found

49

free of scamp contraband."

An officer returns to the base of the porch steps. "Sir, the exterior is clean."

"Excellent. Please proceed to the kitchen, Stanley."

Tick-tick-tick. The machine strung over Stanley's shoulder clicks evenly as the man squeezes past Caleb and Jeremiah to enter the house and turns left for the kitchen. I retreat farther into the living room, Hannah's hands on my shoulders. The officer scans the irradiator, the dishwasher, the refrigerator, each appliance and each outlet. The gauge on his detector flutters slightly.

"Everything's normal in here," he calls.

Another man enters the house and then another. Officer Reynolds sends them to the bedrooms with their clicking machines. Out the open door, I see the other three men head for the cornfield with equipment humming. For several minutes we huddle in the middle of the room, listening to the officer's heavy footsteps and the buzz of their equipment. Finally, all three men return to Reynolds, fiddling with the knobs on their devices.

"Can't find nothing," one of them says.

The other three emerge from the cornfield, shaking their heads. "Clean."

Reynolds shrugs. "Sorry to bother you folks."

He turns on his heel to leave. It's all been a misunderstanding. Everything is resolved. But when the one called Stanley walks past me to get to the door, the machine on his hip goes haywire. The alert is loud and all four men turn toward me.

Reynolds grabs the wand from his colleague's hand,

running it up and around my body. The beeping alarm hastens near my head and hands, the gauges on the box a flurry of spiking needles.

"What the f—" Reynolds murmurs, then composes himself. "Identify yourself," he barks in my face.

"I'm Lydia."

"Last name."

"Lane," Caleb blurts. "Lydia Lane." Opening the drawer in the end table that supports the offending lamp, he removes a black leather square. He walks toward me, flipping the wallet open so that I can see the inside. My picture is next to the words *Lydia Lane*. This must be my English identity. He presses it into my hand, speaking volumes with the way his eyes tighten at the corners and his hand squeezes mine.

I wonder where the picture came from, especially considering I'm not wearing my *kapp* in it.

Reynolds removes a silver cuff from his belt and takes a step in my direction. "Lydia Lane, you are suspected of scamping. As such, you are required by law to accompany me to the nearest detention center—"

"What do you mean, she has to accompany you?" Jeremiah interrupts. Too fast, he moves for the officer, his chest out, his arms raised.

Reynolds reaches for the box on his hip, which I'm sure is some kind of weapon.

I shake my head. My heart skips in my chest. *No! Don't make it worse.* Thankfully, Caleb grabs Jeremiah's shoulder and holds him back. "Calm down, man. Everything's going to be okay," he says.

I'm relieved when Jeremiah seems to listen.

"You're carrying a charge," Reynolds accuses me.

"She was electrocuted," Caleb says. "The lamp—"

"I heard you the first time. Unfortunately, that story doesn't jive with the volts she's registering." Reynolds smiles but it doesn't reach his eyes.

"I didn't do anything wrong," I say.

"Okay, listen. That's your story. I hear you. But the sooner we can get you back to headquarters, the sooner we can prove that's true," Reynolds replies.

"I'll go with you," Jeremiah says to me, but Reynolds holds up his hand.

"Sorry, she needs to come alone. It's policy. Like I said, if everyone cooperates, she'll be back in a few hours. But she's carrying a charge, which means she has to be scanned for storage devices before you all can be cleared."

The edges of my mouth turn downward. The last thing I want is to get Caleb and Hannah in trouble with the authorities my first day here, and for something that is potentially my fault. Hannah said wool caused static electricity. If I hadn't been wearing the wool or standing so close to the lamp, maybe none of this would've happened.

"It's okay. I'll go," I say quietly.

"But—" Jeremiah starts.

"Don't worry," I tell him. "I don't have any storage devices inside me. They'll scan me and I'll be back. It's a minor inconvenience."

"Smart girl," Reynolds says. He snaps a silver cuff around my wrist.

52

"What's this?" I ask.

"This is a containment cuff. Be aware that if at any time you try to escape, this cuff will be activated remotely and emit a debilitating pulse. A GPS inside the device will notify us of your location. Understood?"

I gasp, feeling threatened but nodding my head dutifully.

"Where will you be taking her?" Jeremiah asks.

"Crater City Government Energy Facility," he says. "Come along. The quicker we get this over with, the better it will be for everyone involved."

I can't argue with his logic. I allow the officer to lead me to the squad car by the elbow. Before lowering into the backseat, I glimpse Jeremiah, Hannah, and Caleb huddled together on the porch, staring at me. Jeremiah's face is contorted with worry, but Hannah's and Caleb's expressions are much worse. Their entire bodies are in on the frown, as if someone just died. As if this is the worst thing that could ever happen.

Chapter 5

All my life, I've wondered what it would be like to ride in a car. I've seen them when Bradford Adams or Doc Nelson visited Hemlock Hollow, but I've never been inside one. Would it be exciting, like galloping on a horse or falling from the haymow?

In Officer Reynolds's vehicle, behind the protective plastic that separates the front from the back, I don't feel excited. I feel claustrophobic, like the doors are collapsing in on me.

The other Green Officers drive away while Reynolds punches letters and numbers into a screen on the dashboard. Is he entering information about me or where we are going? The engine rumbles to life, much quieter than the Adamses' car, but then this one looks newer. Instead of a wheel, Reynolds uses a stick with a knob to guide the vehicle as we back from the driveway and gain speed. It's not unlike our buggy but faster, much faster. The rush of scenery beyond the window makes my head swim and my stomach turn over. I press my fingers over my lips.

"I'll never understand how you people live offline. But then, you're probably used to this in Willow's Province," Reynolds says, bouncing in his seat and making adjustments to keep us on the uneven pavement. The road here is riddled with potholes. Debris pings against the car and windows. An especially large bump knocks me against the car door.

I lean across the seat and vomit my fast food onto the floor mat.

"Hey! Aww, hell!" Officer Reynolds glances over his shoulder. He presses a button, and the plastic divider stows itself in the seat back. With his free hand, he digs into a compartment in the dash and hands me a towel.

"Thank you," I say. The material is strange with fibers that grip my skin. I rub it between my fingers before wiping my mouth with it. "My head is spinning."

"Why didn't you tell me you get carsick?" Looking annoyed, Reynolds presses a button to his left.

My window lowers half an inch, and a breeze chills the sweat on my forehead. The rush of air sweeps away the smell of sick, and I mop up the mess as best I can. "I'm sorry," I say. "It must be from the electrocution."

He squints at me skeptically. "A few more miles to the grid. Just leave those on the floor for now."

I lean against the seat and close my eyes. Eventually, the jostling becomes more sporadic and the scattering gravel gives way to a smooth hum. The car jerks one last time and then I don't hear the wheels anymore. I open my eyes. Out the window, cars of all shapes and sizes whiz by us, hovering over narrow strips of steel rather than full stretches of pavement. To be sure, there is a road far below us, the kind I am familiar with, but up here in "the grid" as he calls it, layers of traffic speed high above the earth.

Even I know cars can't actually fly. It's an illusion only diminished by the occasional glimpse of the silver mesh that I assume supports whatever technology holds us to the grid. The roads merge and separate at such high speeds, I have to wipe my sweaty palms on my jeans. Above and below us, hundreds of vehicles are nothing but colorful blurs and flashes of light.

"This was not in the book," I mumble to myself.

"What's that?" Reynolds asks.

"I'm feeling better," I say to him.

"Good." Reynolds types something else into the keypad on the dash and grabs a fresh rag before turning his seat all the way around. I have no idea how the car drives itself, but I don't dare ask. He leans over the divider to collect the rag I've left on the floor, wrapping it inside his own.

"Normally I wouldn't risk lowering the divider, but something tells me you're not the violent sort." He laughs a little, eyes darting over my slight frame. A strange defensiveness tugs at me, but I dismiss it.

"I'm not violent. I've done nothing wrong," I say.

"If you're telling the truth, we'll know soon enough." He disposes of the dirty towels in a receptacle in the passenger side door. "Problem is, little girls like you tend to get taken advantage of. A boy will come along and pressure them into doing something they know is wrong. Who can blame them for giving in? Maybe they're hungry. Maybe they want to help their family." He gives me a knowing look.

I stare back, blankly.

"Hmm," he grunts. We ride in silence until the car slows, merging with a full-sized stretch of pavement as we enter a city of silver towers. Officer Reynolds takes the control stick again and stops the car in front of the largest building I've ever seen. Glass, steel, and concrete climb toward the sky and disappear into the clouds. My door won't open from the inside, so I wait as Reynolds exits the vehicle and walks around to open it for me.

"What is this place?" I ask, staring straight up at the endless column of mirrored windows. The entire street is lined with these tall steel monoliths.

"The Crater City Government Energy Facility, CGEF."

"This place controls all of the energy for the entire city?" I ask.

He looks at me strangely. "City? As the capital of The Green Republic, this is the headquarters for our nation. The entire country's power supply is controlled by the people in this building. I'm surprised you haven't had the tour. Usually, they parade all the kids from the area through by the third grade."

I rummage through my brain for a suitable response. "I was homeschooled," I say. It isn't a complete lie. Amish stop going to school after eighth grade so they can learn a trade for Hemlock Hollow. For the last three years, I've trained as a seamstress with Martha Samuels. It is a type of homeschooling.

Officer Reynolds shoots me a sideways glance. "Homeschooled?" He shakes his head and takes a deep breath. "I guess Willow's Province does things their own way." He points toward two glass panels and moves behind me as I walk toward them. I try not to startle as the doors open for me and a vast atrium of polished white floors and silver furniture greets me with a blast of cool air. A woman with hair so blond it has a lavender tint, smiles at Officer Reynolds. He flashes his badge. She nods. Two green-uniformed security guards stand behind her desk, bored-looking expressions on their faces. They barely acknowledge us as Reynolds leads me to a set of shiny metal doors and pushes a round button on the wall.

We enter a small room when the doors open. An elevator! We learn about these in school, but it's my first time in one. He pushes a button labeled 3. I'm disappointed when I can't tell if we are moving. I assume we are because Reynolds stands back with his arms folded, staring at the doors.

"Lydia, I'm going to be honest with you, since you seem like a nice girl. There've been a couple of scampers in the past who've tried to hide storage devices inside their bodies. They put off numbers like you. If you've done something like that, tell me now, because the people in the clinic will find it, one way or another. You won't like their way, Lydia. Trust me."

"I don't have anything to hide, Officer Reynolds. How can I prove that to you?"

"You don't have to prove it to me. You prove it to them." He points his chin at the doors. "All you need to know from me is that we take energy seriously around here. If there's something I should know, you need to speak up."

I shake my head.

The elevator opens. He leads me down a sterile white hall of closed doors to the fourth room on the left, our footsteps echoing around us. Oddly, the door has no knob, just a plastic panel that says *Biolock*. Officer Reynolds places his hand on it and light passes under it from fingertips to palm. With a metal-on-metal grind, the door swings open.

A muffled moan drifts from the room next door. I stare in the direction of the sound and am haunted when it comes again. I can't tell if it's the cry of a person or an animal, but someone or something is clearly in pain.

"Don't mind that," Officer Reynolds says. He gently ushers me into the room, hand pushing gently between my shoulder blades. I balk and swallow hard when I see what's inside. The cold steel of an examination table reflects the overhead light. From a cabinet to my right, Reynolds retrieves a thin cotton tunic and tosses it on the examination table. "Undress and put this on," he orders. "Dr. Konrad will be in to see you in a moment."

I nod. This is a clinic and I'm in an examination room, which means the sound from next door was not the moan of an animal but of another patient. My stomach clenches.

Reynolds leaves without saying goodbye. The lock engages with a dull grind. Only then does the reality that I'm trapped, alone, inside a locked room, fully register.

With shaking hands, I do as I'm told. I undress, folding my clothes neatly on the chair, and don the paper-thin wraparound tunic. I tell myself that the person I'll be seeing is a doctor, like Doc Nelson. A doctor is trained to examine the body. But tears well in my eyes. I've never been sick. This doctor will be the first to examine me. Will he need to touch me? I don't know. I tug the gown over my knees as low as it will go.

I've barely finished dressing when the door opens swiftly, without the courtesy of a knock, and a stoic man enters the room. His mouth is a tight line, his eyes as gray and soulless as any I've ever seen. He is older, maybe in his sixties, and the lines on his face are not smile lines like my father's, but tracks commemorating years of stressful living. I fold my arms across myself.

"I'm Dr. Konrad. I'll be doing your examination today. Please sit." He turns to wash his hands in the small sink.

Ungracefully, I hop up on the cold steel table, smoothing the gown and tucking it under my tightly pressed-together knees. He snaps on a pair of latex gloves and does not make eye contact as he goes about pulling a steel tray to the side of the table and loading it with baskets of needles and tubes. "Arm," he commands.

I extend my right. He swabs the crook of it with a brown liquid. The chemical stench coats my nostrils.

"Hold very still." He ties a rubber band around my upper arm. It pinches my skin, pulling out the tiny hairs. "Make a fist."

I obey. He unwraps a needle and connects it to a tube. Without saying another word, he grabs my arm and jabs the point into my vein. "Ow!" It's a small pain but it catches me off guard.

Dr. Konrad's thin lips grin in response. A tight smirk as if my pain amuses him. He's enjoying this. I've never met anyone like Dr. Konrad. That thin smile makes my soul squirm and my skin prickle. I am afraid. I force myself to hold still as everything within me yearns to be free of his touch. I swallow.

My ruby red blood fills one tube, then another. It doesn't hurt now that the needle is in, but the pressure is uncomfortable.

"Release your fist."

I do. He swaps in a third tube and unties the band on my arm. Finally, he pulls out the needle and presses a square of gauze over the bubble of blood welling up. He tapes it into place. From the wall, he pulls down a black tool that looks like a small hammer.

"Open." The end of the hammer lights up. He points it at my lips. I obey, allowing him to poke a flat wooden stick into every corner of my mouth. My ears and nose are inspected next. Then, he digs his fingers into my hair. From my head, his hands pat down my body, between my breasts, under my arms. Every inch of me. It happens so fast I have no time to protest. When he's through, he unfolds two steel stirrups from under the table.

"Lie back and put your feet up."

"Excuse me?" I cross my arms over my chest, hugging myself through the flimsy gown.

"Lie on the table and put your heels in the stirrups. I need to examine your body cavities."

No! A shiver crawls over me, and I can no longer hold back the tears that stream down my cheeks. "Is there a female who can perform the examination?"

Dr. Konrad's lips return to that sinister smile. "This is

a detention center clinic, not a hospital. We have a very limited staff. I'm the only doctor here today. Now, let's get on with it."

This can't be happening. He pushes me down on the table and lifts first one then the other foot. He pulls apart my knees. I weep as he examines me in places I always thought only my husband would ever see. I want to melt into the exam table, to somehow become invisible and walk out the door. Mercifully, it doesn't last long.

"Okay, sit up."

I do, crossing my legs and tugging the gown down as far as it will go. With the heels of my palms I wipe the tears from my face. It wasn't that bad. Nothing I can't handle. I need to be strong. This will be over soon.

Dr. Konrad peels his gloves off into a garbage pail. "Follow me," he says, not making eye contact.

"Should I get dressed?" I ask the back of his head.

"No."

I follow him into the hall, leaving the door open behind me. I'm relieved no one else is there to see me in the skimpy tunic. I'm curious why there aren't more patients, but then I remember what the doctor said. This is a detention center clinic, not a hospital. Any other patients would be locked inside the exam rooms like I was.

Dr. Konrad leads me to a chamber with a monstrous circular machine at the center that hums ominously. In the corner, a glass room faces the machine. It houses a desk, covered in blinking electronic equipment in various shapes and sizes, and an empty chair. An observation room, I suppose.

"Have you ever had an MRI?" he asks.

"No."

Cold gray eyes meet mine. "We need to scan your body. I didn't find anything during my assessment, which means you must have had the mechanism surgically implanted into you. This machine uses powerful magnets to make images of what's inside your body. I must warn you, if the object is metal, this machine will rip it out of you and I'll be patching you up on the surgical table. Tell me right now if it is."

Every muscle in my body tightens, and pain throbs at my temple. I have been cooperative long enough. I've been violated and treated rudely. "I told you," I rage, raising my voice for the first time, "I am not stealing electricity. I was electrocuted. There is nothing inside of me but me!"

Dr. Konrad looks strangely pleased with my answer. "Lie down on the table."

I comply, hoping this machine will prove my innocence once and for all. With three thick straps, he secures me to the table. The plastic buckles lock over my arms and chest. I turn my head to the side and watch him retreat to the glass room. He sits in the chair and turns his attention toward the blinking equipment.

With an initial jerk, the narrow table I'm lying on slides slowly under the arc of the machine, cutting off my view of the doctor. I'm in a long cream-colored tube. The hum grows into a buzz, a hundred swarming bees but amplified. I try to relax and stare at the dome above me. *Click, click, clickity, click.*

Pain. It starts behind one eye, then spreads through my

body to my fingers and toes. It's sharp and hot. Fire blazes inside my veins, a thousand pins that cut through my skin. Prickle and heat, a sunburn from the inside out.

"Stop, stop! It hurts!" I cry. My voice echoes inside the tube.

Clicking circles my head. "What have you done? Wired it to your bones?" Konrad's taunting voice is harsh and accusing, like I'm getting what I deserve.

Agony, so intense I think I will black out. The pain has gone deeper. I tug against the straps and squirm on the narrow table. Surely my bones are being ripped from my flesh.

"Stop! Please stop!" I scream.

"Highly unusual," trails Konrad's voice, but the machine keeps clicking.

I can't take anymore. I curl and twist, like a dying animal, held in place by my restraints. Silently, I pray to God to take me home, to end my suffering in this torturous machine. I am ready to die. Anything to end this.

Snap. My body jolts on the table, then goes rigid, straightening from its writhing position. My muscles stiffen and seize. My spine is a rubber band that God has stretched to the limit and then let go. All sense of self is lost to the pain. Am I still on the table? Or am I floating in acid? The only things keeping me from hitting the ceiling of the machine are the straps that bind me.

I press my eyes closed. *God help me, please!* I need a miracle. My muscles clench. I turn my head and heave, but there's nothing in my stomach. When I open my eyes again, I moan. Everything around me glows pale blue. Everything. My skin. The air. The machine. I lift my head and try to look down my body out the hole in the tube, but I can't see past my toes. My skin itches as if it's stretched too tightly across my muscles, as if a stronger sensation is waiting to take hold.

And then, just like with Caleb's lamp, lightning bolts of electricity shoot from the machine into me. But unlike in the house, I don't pass out this time. The energy pours in through my heart, my hands, my legs. It burrows along my spine and funnels out my mouth in the form of an exhilarated howl. The straps binding me scorch, then snap. Blue-white streams blaze between the machine and my body, getting brighter, stronger, until the entire thing explodes in a shower of circular plastic, exposed wires, and sprays of sparks. Metal twists and breaks apart. Sections bounce off the bluish-white glow and ping-pong against each other. Parts of the machine fold outward, away from me.

I float up through the destruction until my feet land on a pile of burnt rubble. Hot wind swirls around me, blowing back my hair and making a sound...a sound I've heard only once before. I am in the center of a chugging tornado. The wind howls and the sizzle of power threatens to blow out the walls. This is what I prayed for. This is my miracle.

Dr. Konrad gawks at me through the observation window. He moves for the door to the small glass room. In a panic, I pick up a chunk of machine and hurl it toward him. I only mean to block his exit, but the projectile hits the door with surprising force, throwing him back into the room. Through the glass I see his head slap the desk and his body tumble to the floor. And then I run.

I don't waste time questioning God's way of saving me. The door is unlocked and I scramble into the hallway. The cold reminds me I am effectively naked. Singed shreds of my tunic hang in ribbons from my body. I can't escape in this. I return to the room where I'd been held and snatch my pile of clothes off the chair. Heart pounding in my ears, I clamber for the elevators.

But to get there, I have to pass the room next door, where I'd heard the moan. My conscience grips me by the throat and stops me in my tracks. I check over my shoulder. How much time do I have? I shake so hard my teeth clack together, but the sound of the moan won't leave my head. It's like heaven is tugging at my heart. My brain says to run, but my soul demands I save what's in the room. I can't accept the gift of God's miracle without being His hands, His miracle for someone else.

I push on the door. Locked. The moan comes again. Weak. Pitiful. There isn't even a knob, just a Biolock. I rest my hand on it and make a deal with God. If he wants me to save whoever is inside, then I need a way to enter. Now. The force I'd felt in the MRI machine bleeds down my arm and makes the panel glow. I push with everything I have, and the mechanism clicks.

Plowing my shoulder into the door, I burst into the room then back-pedal when I see what's inside. There is a boy...well, if you can call a body as broken as the one in front of me a boy. One breath away from a corpse, his skin is covered in sores and his lips are ashen blue. Blood stains his thin white tunic and hospital pants folded up above the knee. There are wires hooked to his flesh. Wires run from his arms, his legs, his hands. The entire room is filled with beeping, blinking machines.

I don't hesitate. I fist the wires and rip them from his skin. Without thinking about the consequences, I lift his arm and roll him across my shoulders. It isn't unlike carrying a bag of grain, and I feel strong. Stronger than usual.

"Who…are…you?" the boy groans.

I don't answer. As fast as I can, I carry him on my back to the elevators and slap the button.

"Stop!" Dr. Konrad calls from the end of the hall. Blood runs from a gash in his head and he stumbles toward us with hands extended.

The elevator doors open and I lunge inside, tipping my shoulders to dump the boy in the corner while I hug my clothes to my chest. I hit the button labeled *Atrium*. Dr. Konrad's shoes slap the tile and his face appears between the closing doors.

"Stay away from me!" I snap.

He reaches for me, but it's too late. The doors close him out. The elevator descends.

"Who…are you?" the boy mumbles.

"Thank goodness you're alive," I say, as I dress hastily. "What were they doing to you?"

"Hit the red button," he rasps.

I poke the button marked *emergency*, as I slip on my

shoes. The elevator jerks to a halt. A loud siren sounds overhead. I cover my ears. The lights above me turn red and blink. "What's going on?"

"You need to help me."

"What else can I do? I *am* helping you. I got you out of there, didn't I?" I have to scream over the alarm. His image takes on a jerky quality in the flashing red light.

"The panel," the boy gasps, pointing at the buttons. "Rip it off."

"What? The button panel?"

"Yes! Now!"

I don't like vandalizing the elevator. It goes against everything I've been taught my whole life. But this place is not like home. I've tried to be compliant. I've tried to follow the rules. But these people don't play by the same rules as Hemlock Hollow. I follow the boy's directions because I don't understand any of this and he seems to. I dig my fingers into the place where the metal plate is screwed into the wall and pull. It doesn't budge.

"Unless you have a screwdriver, you're going to have to use the juice. Don't pretend you don't know what I'm talking about. I saw how you got into my cell."

I focus on the panel, trying to call the miracle again. It's harder this time, like the blue glow is deep within me. But it does come. The panel sizzles beneath my touch, the screws melt, and I fall backward onto the floor of the elevator with the panel in my hands. My newfound strength is gone, replaced by an exhaustion just as extreme. I am so tired my skin hurts.

"You scampers just get better and better. What is it,

wired into your hands?"

I part my lips to answer, but I'm too tired to speak.

"Don't worry." He grins slightly. "I've got no room to judge."

"I'm not..." I start to say I'm not a scamper, but my voice peters out in my throat. This is more than exhaustion. I can barely keep my eyes open. He isn't listening anyway. He drags himself to the exposed wires of the panel, grips one, and pries it apart. He laughs in a way that makes me shiver, the sound wicked and dark. From the exposed wire, the blue glow flows into his hand. What I thought was my personal miracle suddenly seems common. The siren wavers and then dies.

"Oh yeah!" he howls.

The blinking lights extinguish, and then the only break in the blackness around me is the glow from the boy. He's still bloody and covered in sores but his pale skin radiates blue. His ashen lips transform to a full, rosy pink and the dark circles under his eyes fade. I have a moment to register that he's around my age. What's he doing here?

He leaps to the balls of his feet and casts a straight white smile in my direction. "What's your name?" he asks.

"Lydia," I mumble.

"Lydia, I have a million questions for you, but there's no time for chitchat. Give me your hand. We need to get out of here."

I barely move, inching one heavy hand in his direction. Impatient, he stretches forward and grabs my fingers to pull me to my feet. But something inside me shifts, and a stringy tickle courses through my palm. My body drinks from the connection, refreshing itself in a way I never knew possible. The blue glow slips from his hand into mine, creeping up my wrist to my shoulder.

The boy's eyes widen. "Oh! Crap. What kind of scamper are you?" He yanks his hand away, as if I've stolen something from him.

My strength returns, and I scramble to my feet, my palm tingling. For a moment, the boy and I stare at each other. His eyes narrow and he shakes his head. I wipe my hand on my jeans but the tingle remains.

Then he touches two wires together and the elevator begins moving again.

Chapter 6

When we reach the ground floor, the boy pushes me aside, wires still pinched between his fingers. In a flash, he squeezes through the opening doors into the atrium, releasing his electric hold. The elevator freezes and the lights go out.

As we exit the elevator, the atrium is complete chaos. People flood toward the exit, but no one is leaving. Instead, they bark into their phones and snap at each other. I glimpse a security guard with his thin plastic phone to his ear. He looks at us, then the elevator, confused, presumably because the elevator shouldn't run with the power out.

"I have them," he says. Then he pulls a gun.

There's a scream from a woman in a yellow suit next to the guard, but the boy is unfazed. With a burst of speed, he charges and kicks the gun toward the ceiling. The weapon discharges, eliciting more screams from the already panicked crowd, then drops and skims across the floor. A second guard rushes from the crowd and thwacks the boy with a club. The boy plows the heel of his hand into the soft spot under the guard's chin and blocks a punch from the first guard with his forearm. *Bam! Thwack!* He spins and plows his foot into the second

71

guard's chest while punching the other under the ribs. His strikes are powerful and true. This boy is a skilled fighter; even I can see that. The officers crumple. Blood sprays from the mouth of one of the men, stark red against the bright white floor. I have to cover my mouth to keep from getting sick. The men don't get up.

Ears ringing from the gunshot, I'm disoriented as the boy grabs my wrist and drags me through total chaos. The glow of his skin lights the darkened atrium, reflecting off the glass of the front windows. We move toward a crowd of people gathered near the glass entrance.

"They can't get out," the boy says to me. "CGEF security. When something goes wrong, none of the Biolocks work. They lock everyone inside on purpose. Down with the ship."

"What? Why?" What he's saying doesn't make any sense to me. Why would CGEF lock their people in? But I can see right away that what he says is true. A woman beats against the glass, arms spread in panic like a bee caught in a storm door. When the others in the crowd notice the boy's blue body shifting ghostlike into their midst, they scramble away in terror. Normally, my upbringing would move me to comfort them, but under the circumstances, I'm more concerned about our freedom.

"No time for explanations. There will be reinforcements." He sweeps me slightly behind him. With a deep breath, he throws his hand toward a break in the crowd. A lightning bolt flies from his palm, thick and white. The air crackles around us. It plows into the glass and the entrance shatters.

Instinctively, I turn to the side and cover my head. A waterfall of falling glass washes toward my feet. It's loud and it keeps coming. New glass breaks and falls, each section shattering and sending a new swell of razor-sharp segments. I expect to be sliced to pieces by the influx, but when the glass comes to rest, I'm unharmed. I look at the floor in confusion and see that the shards have missed us by a fraction of an inch.

"How did—" I start.

"Come on!" he commands. His hand grips above my elbow and moves me forward.

He leads me through the broken window and into the panicked crowd. People race out of the building, darting in all directions in a stampede that closes in around us. We shoulder through the masses toward the streets. A traffic jam has formed in front of the building, drivers gawking through downed windows.

Suddenly, I remember the containment cuff Officer Reynolds placed on me. "Wait," I say, holding up my wrist to the boy, but all that's left is residue.

He tugs me forward, annoyed.

Flashing lights. Sirens. The boy yanks me into the street, weaving between vehicles.

"Stop right there!" a man in a green uniform yells.

Officers pour from the building, pointing metal boxes in our direction. Unlike the security guard's gun, the boxes hardly look menacing. But the boy tenses and grips me tighter like he's afraid for the first time.

"Sorry, pigs, I don't care for your hospitality."

The officer closest to me pulls the trigger and I see two probes shoot from the weapon. The boy sweeps me out of the way at the last second and then squeezes my waist. A surge of power explodes from his hand, and the guards fall to the pavement, twitching. He's taken it—somehow he's pulled the energy from me. Unable to catch my breath, the world tilts and I sag against him.

He half-drags, half-carries me to the railing on the far side of the street. Sweeping me into his arms, he looks me in the eye and flashes me a cynical grin. "How are you at falling?" he asks.

I look over my shoulder and see we are on the edge of an overpass. Does he intend to drop me? "No—"

He jumps and we drop toward concrete. I scream and thrash, but he holds me tight. There's a sharp jerk. He's landed on his feet!

Overwhelmed, I tilt my head up. "How?" is all I can manage. His hazel eyes widen in fear and I follow his gaze over my shoulder to see a truck barreling toward us. The boy thrusts me to the side, straight into the concrete of the underpass. My cheek slaps the wall, and his body presses into mine, holding me there. The truck passes, close enough to blow my hair forward in its wake. After it's gone, he backs off a few inches, and I take my first real breath.

I sweep the hair out of my eyes and get a good look around. We are under the bridge. A ramp circles around from above and then passes under CGEF. It's only a matter of time before more guards come for us.

"What now?" I shout to the boy, but he's collapsed at

my feet. The sores on his arms are bleeding. Traffic races by at dizzying speed. I don't know what to do. I scramble to lift him as green uniforms point at me from the railing above. They are coming for us. *Lord, help me*, I pray again.

As if on cue, a white van with a painting of a desert sunrise rolls to a stop just under the bridge, out of sight of the guards. A gray-haired woman hangs out the window, the buckle of what looks like an apron glinting in the moonlight.

"Get in," she commands. The hatch of the van opens on its own.

I turn my face toward the ramp.

"It won't take them long, honey," the woman says.

For the second time that day, I roll the boy onto my back, and with everything I have left, I move him onto the floor of the van. I'm not strong enough to get him completely in, and his legs dangle off the end. Groaning, I crawl inside and hook my hands in his armpits, digging my heels into the carpeted interior and falling backward to get him completely inside before the doors close. The van lurches into motion even before the hatch is closed.

Panting, I turn toward my rescuer. A steel grate separates us. She doesn't look at me, engrossed as she is in the blinking lights of her dashboard. Soon, the blurring cars speed by in the disorienting way that makes my stomach turn. What did Officer Reynolds call this? Snapping to the grid.

"I'm Helen," she says, turning her seat to face me.

"Nice to meet you, Helen. I'm Lydia. Thank you for helping us."

"Who's your friend there?"

The bruised and bloody boy next to me is still unconscious. "I don't know his name."

She laughs through her nose, her wrinkled face contracting into a kind of smile that I'm not familiar with, a showing of teeth that makes my chest tighten.

"You may not know who he is, but I know what he is and what you are. You're scampers."

I shake my head.

"Don't bother denying it, honey. I'm going to help you, but then you're going to help me." A blinking light on her console makes her brows knit. "We're slowing down. There's a roadblock. They're checking for you two." She frowns at me. "Get into the pottery crate. Him too. Let's hope it's standard procedure."

Mounted to the wall of the van is a coffin-like box. I open the lid and see a large misshaped pot inside.

"Just place it on the floor. I can't sell it anyway."

I remove it and work the boy's dead weight over the edge of the crate. Arm. Leg. Roll. The thin material of his pajama-like tunic leaves nothing to the imagination. I try not to think too much about what I'm doing as I climb in on top of him. I'm thankful that the crate is long enough that I can straighten my legs, but the narrow width means the boy's shoulders don't lie flat. I have to curl my arms awkwardly against his chest and tuck my face into the crook of his neck to get the lid closed. He smells of blood, sweat, and something else. Burning—smoky, like a campfire. It is the closest I've ever been to a boy, even Jeremiah. I don't even know his name.

The van stops. Several minutes pass, and then the vehicle creeps forward for a few bumpy seconds before stopping again. The boy groans softly into my ear.

"Shhhhh." I tip my ear toward the lid of the crate.

Under me, the boy seems to figure out our situation and runs his fingers silently over the lid before settling his hand on my shoulder. I can't fault him for it. There isn't room for him to put it anywhere else.

"Good evening, ma'am. Have you seen this boy or this girl?" a man's voice says. I can feel the night air seep through where the boards of the crate connect. Paper rustles.

"No, sir," Helen says. "What've they done anyway?"

"Scampers. If you see them, call this number immediately." Another rustle of paper. "Don't try to handle it yourself. They are very dangerous."

"Dangerous? How so? Since when are scampers dangerous?"

There is another rustle of paper. "I just relay the information, ma'am. Carry on."

The van begins to move again. The boy turns his face into my hair and inhales. Is he smelling me? He sighs into my ear.

"You can come out now," Helen says. "We're back on the grid."

I press my hand against the wood and flip open the crate. In a series of uncomfortable movements, I lift myself, trying hard not to land an elbow or knee in the wrong place on the boy. I roll over the side and onto the floor of the van. He groans. I help to pull him up to a seated position. Wincing, he makes the effort to climb out, then eyes Helen suspiciously.

"Glad you could join us. Care to share your name with your rescuer?" Helen asks.

The boy crouches behind her, hooking his fingers into the grate. "My name is my business."

"You might as well be friendly. We have the same enemy, after all. I'm a potter from Badlands Province and unfortunately, CGEF is overcharging us for power. Some kind of political mumbo jumbo. I don't give a crap. Between running my potter's wheel and making deliveries, I'm barely getting by." She shakes her curly head. "Factories in Central Province can pump these things out for half the cost. I need your help. I help you, you help me."

"For how long?" the boy asks.

"For as long as I need you."

My stomach twists. I'd thought Helen was helping us. I'd been naive. This is what Jacob had meant about the English world. The people here act like electricity is as valuable as their own blood. Helen isn't trying to save us; she's trying to steal us.

The boy leans his forehead against the grate, frowning toward the floor.

Helen reaches for the dashboard. "We'll be in Badlands in fifteen minutes." She keys something into the blinking panel.

Working his fingers through the squares in the grate, the boy attempts to reach for the back of Helen's head while she's hunched over the dashboard. The palm of his hand is too wide to fit through the hole. The grate is built for industrial purposes, to keep the cargo in the back from hitting the driver. It's not that the squares are so small; his hands are just large. For that matter, *he* is large. Despite being utterly wasted by whatever they did to him at CGEF, his broad shoulders and tall stature are undeniable. He raises an eyebrow in my direction, eyeing my much-smaller hands.

I think I understand. While the van is snapped to the grid, it drives itself. This may be our only chance to get free. If we can incapacitate her, it might be possible for us to safely gain control of the vehicle and escape.

I work my hand through a square while Helen is distracted with the dashboard. He must want me to grab her by the neck while he disables the vehicle in some way. I can't ask without revealing the plan so I just do it. Before I can reach her, she removes her hand from the keypad, and the boy thrusts my arm into her head by my elbow. The blue juice I'd sensed in the elevator stretches like stringy taffy up my arm to my fingers and into the old woman.

Her body twitches and falls to the floor.

"What have you done?" I yell. "Is she dead?" My heart pounds and my breath rattles. I've never hurt anyone before, not by my own hand. The thought of killing someone wrings my throat.

"She's not dead, just knocked out. But we have to get up front before the vehicle leaves the grid. Help me pull off the grate."

"Help you? How can I h-help you? You're the scamper.

I've never done anything like this." My voice breaks with panic. I stare at my hand, clenching and opening it like it was only recently attached to my body. The events of the day catch up with me all at once, and I completely lose my composure, shaking violently.

The boy narrows his eyes at me. "You're denying that you're a scamper now? After the elevator? I pulled electricity from your body."

"But I'm not. It's just something that's in me, like a miracle." Tears rain down my cheeks. "Everyone here thinks I've broken the law, but it just happened." I slap the floor out of frustration.

The boy snatches my hand and wraps his fingers around my palm. The energy drains from my body. I fold forward, too exhausted to hold myself up. A purple bruise has formed between my thumb and pointer finger. With my cheek pressed into the prickly carpet, I watch the bloody pink center widen into a sore.

Using the power he's taken from me, he melts the bolts and then yanks the grate off the frame, maneuvering it behind us. Only then does the boy notice my state of exhaustion. He lifts my hand and stares at the sore in disbelief.

"Who the hell are you?" he asks breathlessly.

All I can produce is a whimper.

"I'm sorry. I'm sorry," he says. "It really is part of you." He gathers me into his lap. The light in the van keeps blinking in and out. Or is that my vision? I can't hold my head up. It lolls to the side, and I slump like a ragdoll, helpless, against his chest.

He pushes the hair out of my face. "I'll take care of you. Don't fall asleep yet. I know you're drained. I'm drained too. We've got to find someplace safe first." He slides us over to the driver's seat. Punching a sequence into the dash, he redirects the van. I drift in and out of consciousness until the van slows and he grabs the control stick. We veer onto a ramp.

On the side of a deserted road near an underpass, he parks. Carrying me, he abandons Helen and limps across the dark highway. I have no idea what time it is but the full moon is the only light. Eventually, he lowers me to my feet. "Just a little farther," he says. We hobble the considerable distance to a narrow hallway beneath the bridge, where an orange door is the only break in the concrete.

The boy touches the knob, and I feel what's left of my strength flow from the place where he holds my waist. The mechanism clicks, and he shuffles us into a small storage area. He collapses to the floor with me in his arms. The door slams shut behind us from its own weight; the room plunges into darkness.

"Get some rest," he says.

I don't have the strength to argue. Curled into his chest, I give myself over to sleep.

Chapter 7

S quares of light filter down from above. I blink, allowing my sleepy vision to adjust and memories of the night before to come back to me like a forgotten nightmare.

"Good morning," the boy murmurs. His voice is deep and smooth with a hint of trouble to it. A voice with secrets.

I push myself up from the concrete. The grate above us casts enough light for me to see him clearly. Surrounded by orange traffic cones and road signs, hazel eyes peer at me from under too-long black hair. The ashen tone and blue lips are gone. His skin is naturally olive, although still pale. His cheeks are gaunt, and the sores on his arms are crusted over in the early stages of healing. They look a bit like the sore on my hand.

Despite his wrecked appearance, I am comforted by his presence and my mind wanders to the night before, when I was stretched out on top of him in the van's storage crate. His breath against my ear. The weight of his hand on my shoulder. I cast the image aside, annoyed at my misaligned reflection.

"Who are you?" I hug my knees to my chest. "Why were they keeping you in that place?"

"I should ask you the same thing," he says. His eyes

bore into mine, like he's trying to read something off the back of my skull. "I'll go first. I'm Korwin, and obviously I'm an electrokinetic, just like you."

"Electrokinetic?"

"Well, you said you weren't a scamper. Were you lying? Are you using some new technology?"

"No. I'm not a scamper. I'm not… from here. I don't even know what electrokinetic means." Uncomfortable under his intense stare, I squirm and shift my gaze toward the floor.

"Huh. I doubt that very much, but I'll play." He frowns. "An electrokinetic is a person who can do what we did last night. I prefer the slang term 'Spark.' A Spark can create, absorb, store, and transmit electricity… in his or her cells. No device required." He wiggles his fingers in the air.

"People here are born like this?" I look down at my hands, remembering how the electricity flowed in and out of me. "Did I catch it?"

He tilts his head, his eyes squinting in my direction. "No, sweetheart. We're *made* like this. Sparks are made, not born."

"Made? I wasn't made!"

"You said your name was…?"

"Lydia."

"Lydia, where exactly are you from?"

I don't answer.

"I don't blame you for being tight-lipped. It's amazing you've stayed hidden this long. But you don't have to be on guard with me. I'm a Spark, and so are you. Scampers don't get electro-scurvy."

I blink at the sore on my hand and then slowly shake my head. "I know this is confusing for you, Korwin, but I'm not what you think I am. My power was a gift from God so that I could save you and myself. Now that the purpose is served, I'm sure it will go away."

One side of Korwin's mouth peels back from his teeth, and he looks at me like I'm insane. "I think after all we've been through together, we should be honest with each other."

"I agree."

"The doctor who chased after you at CGEF, that was Dr. Konrad, yes?"

"Yes."

"And what do you know about Dr. Konrad?"

"Nothing. I met him yesterday. He thought I had scamping equipment inside my body."

Korwin runs a hand through his mop of hair. "Twenty years ago, Dr. Konrad led a secret government-funded study in biotechnology at Crater City University. The Alpha Eight, four men and four women, were injected with a retrovirus designed to make them electrokinetic. Konrad's sponsor, Senator Pierce, thought the technology would boost his political career. But the study ended in disaster."

I lean forward on my knees. "What happened to them?"

"Their bodies became unstable." He held out his arms. "Uncontrollable scurvy. They went insane and eventually died. But there was a pregnancy, and the baby had none of the problems of the first generation."

My head begins to ache. "What happened to the baby?"

"He's sitting in front of you."

I swallow the lump in my throat and press my fingers into my lips.

"See, up until now, I thought I was the only surviving child, but now I wonder. It begs the question... so, again, I ask you, who are you and where are you from?"

The ground shifts beneath me. My stomach lurches like I've jumped from the haymow. I hold my head. "My name is Lydia Lane. I grew up in Willow's Province." The lie rolls clumsily off my tongue.

He squeezes his eyes shut and leans his head back against the concrete wall. "Willow's Province? How is it possible we never found you?"

"You don't understand. I never had any power. It just happened yesterday."

Korwin turns a quizzical eye on me. "And you grew up in Willow's Province?"

The lie burns in my throat. I can't stand it. Korwin saved me. If I don't tell the truth, it's going to eat me up inside. "No," I say so softly, I wonder if he hears me.

He crawls forward and places a hand on mine. "I won't hurt you. You can trust me."

Warmth from his palm infuses the back of my hand. I'm temporarily bemused by the way the olive tone of his skin contrasts sharply against my milky complexion. There's something about him; I'm completely drawn in. I can't pretend anymore. "I'm from the Amish preservation," I say. My voice quivers. "This is my first time to Crater City. I know I didn't come from the same place as you. I know my father. I grew up behind the wall."

Seconds pass as he scrutinizes my face. He laughs. "You're joking."

Out of habit, I lower my eyes but then force myself to meet his gaze again. I shake my head only once.

He winces as if I've played him for a fool. But the longer we stare at each other, my face carefully impassive, the lines of hard skepticism in his expression soften to mild suspicion. "No." He snorts.

"Yes." I put as much conviction in my voice as possible. The drama of yesterday comes back to me and I shake visibly.

His eyes grow wide. "Holy crap, you're serious!" He scoots away from me. "You're an unvaccinated, animal-eating Amish? For real?" He says "unvaccinated" like it's a curse.

I flinch, insulted, but nod.

"How did you get over the wall? It can't be true. How in the world could you get all the way out here? How could you be like me?"

"We occasionally visit in secret. Nothing like this has ever happened before to any of my community. Honestly, like I said, I think God gave me this power to save us. I think this is a miracle."

He snorts derisively. "A miracle?"

"Yes. From God. I've never had such crazy things happen to me. It must have been divine providence that

86

sent me to you, to help save you."

He scoffs. "Wow." For a long moment, he stares at me, the silence growing awkwardly between us. When I think I can't stand it any longer, he rises and extends a hand toward me. "Well, come on, my miracle. I'm hungry, and we still have to find a way home."

"Yes. I'm staying at fifty-four Lakehurst. Can you take me there?" I accept his hand and allow him to pull me up.

"Lydia…" He looks at me with pity. "You can't go back there. As of yesterday, you're wanted by the Green Republic. You broke out of CGEF and aided and abetted a criminal." He taps a finger on his chest. "If you go back, they'll just arrest you again."

"You don't understand. I have to go back. I have friends who are worried about me. People waiting for me. I have to get home," I say.

Korwin holds up one hand. "Where I come from, people are used to keeping secrets. My father will know how to help you, but you need to come with me. I can guarantee the Greens will be keeping close tabs on your friends. It's not safe for you to go there."

I know he's right, I just never thought of it. Fifty-four Lakehurst is where Officer Reynolds found me and most certainly will be the first place CGEF looks for me. I don't have a choice. I need to trust Korwin. "Okay," I say.

He turns away and plants his ear against the door. Cautiously he cracks it and extends his head into the passageway. Stepping out, he motions with his hand for me to follow. We seem to be in an area meant for road service workers. It borders an underpass, but there is no traffic, at least not at the moment. Korwin moves fast, and I have to jog to keep up with his long strides. His head is down, his gaze sweeping over the concrete.

My stomach growls. I fold my arms across it, hoping the noise isn't as loud outside as in.

"Here," he whispers, advancing toward a round grate in the pavement. "I'm sorry to have to do this to you. I'd try hitchhiking but…"

"We don't need another Helen," I say.

"We'll have to go through the sewer."

I nod. I have no idea what exactly I'm agreeing to.

He reaches down and flips a metal bar up from the circle, then cranks it, turning the section in the concrete. Eventually the round grate pops out, exposing a hole in the pavement. A foul odor permeates the hallway, and I cover my nose and mouth with my sleeve.

"I wish there was another way," he says.

I straighten my back and approach the hole. "Let's be thankful that there's a way at all." Positioning my foot on the ladder within the hole, I climb down into the sickening odor.

Korwin follows, closing the cover over us as we descend. "You're brave," he says from above me.

"No. It's prideful to turn down the gift of freedom just because it's disguised as a sewer. It's the same reason I eat eggs, even though they come out of a chicken's butt." I laugh, reaching the last rung and stepping into a gigantic pipe. I have to balance on the raised edge to stay out of the sludge that flows in front of my toes. Only a trickle of light reaches us. The tunnel is a nest of shadows and foreign shapes that leave me twitchy.

"You've convinced me." He positions himself on the ridge next to me.

"Of what?"

"That you didn't grow up in Crater City." He points over my shoulder and to my left. "That way. It's a couple of miles north."

I flatten myself against the wall and allow him to take the lead. "How does eating eggs convince you I'm telling the truth?"

He clears his throat. "Is it true, what you said, that eggs come from a chicken's butt?"

"Sure. Well, technically it's called a cloaca but, you know, the egg and everything else comes from the same place."

"I never knew."

"Where did you think they came from?"

"The food factory, like everything else. Eggs here come pre-scrambled in a carton and the ingredients are mostly chemicals. I just figured they grew the base in a lab, like they do chicken."

"Huh?" I'm completely lost. I know what a chemical is, but the idea that *Englishers* eat them is foreign to me.

"You know, chicken breast. It's never actually a living chicken. They just take a cell and coax it in a lab to become a chicken breast."

"They can do that here?"

"Yeah, they have to because of the animal cruelty laws. Farming's been illegal since the war. I think that was probably a big reason for the wall. The Green Republic couldn't deal with being accused of genocide, and your community was so heavily vested in farming. The Raw Milk trials and everything."

Every citizen of Hemlock Hollow knows about the Raw Milk trials. Before the war, the government tried to make drinking unpasteurized milk illegal. Amish fought the law because we don't pasteurize our milk. The trials went on and on until the war and the wall became a suitable solution.

"It's considered cruel here to kill and eat a chicken, but not to use a human being as a battery?"

"You have a lot to learn about the Green Republic, Lydia."

Homesickness presses its heavy hand against my heart. "I think I've learned enough," I murmur.

For the next quarter mile, I follow Korwin in silence, feeling sorry for myself. Why me? Why, after generations of Amish going on *rumspringa* without incident, do *I* end up getting arrested? But then my father's voice comes to me. "Don't ask 'why me,' Lydia. Ask, 'Why not me?' Who are we to question God's will?"

"How long were you a prisoner at CGEF?" I ask, because the surest way to stop dwelling on your own problems is to think of someone else's.

"What's the date today?"

"September fifteenth." My stomach sinks at the horror of being trapped somewhere without so much as a means to track the time.

"A little over three weeks."

"They drained you for three weeks?"

"Hence the scurvy. I don't think I would've lasted much longer if you hadn't come along."

"Thank the Lord."

He snorts. "Thank *you*."

We come to a cross pipe.

Korwin looks each way into the dark hollow. "I don't suppose you'd know which way was north?"

"How could I without the sun?"

"Some secret Amish way?"

I smile and shake my head. "I thought..."

"You thought I knew where I was going? That I'd been down here before?"

I nod.

"Yes and no. Yes, I've escaped through the sewer. But no, not this section. My knowledge of this area is mainly academic. We need to go north."

"My gut tells me north is to your right," I say. "But it's a guess."

He pauses, scanning both directions. A scraping echoes down the pipe from the left. Korwin rubs his upper arms with his hands as if the sound gives him the chills. I'm not cold at all, but then, I have the benefit of the silver jacket.

"Right it is," he says.

My shoes are caked with filth and squish grotesquely with each step. I'm glad for the darkness because I can't see what I'm stepping in. "Are you sure the police won't search down here?" I ask.

"They don't think we'll risk it."

"Why not?"

"Sewer rats. Since the war, they grow as big as pumas."

91

Korwin rubs his upper arms again, and I realize it is not the cold giving him a chill.

I stop walking and scan the dark pipe. My blood runs cold, my skin crawling.

Korwin turns when he notices I'm not following. "Don't worry about the rats. Most of the time, when they hear us coming, they run away. Even though they're big, they've inherited their smaller relatives' fear of humans."

I catch up to him, walking closer than before. Licking my lips, thirst nags me. I try to think of something else to talk about to distract me from it. "Korwin, was that the first time you've been captured?"

"Yes."

"How did you evade Dr. Konrad as long as you did? I mean, if you never left Crater City after the experiment?"

He sighs. "It's a long story."

"I've got time." My nervous laugh echoes through the tunnel.

"My mother hid me with a stranger she hoped would be sympathetic to my cause. Remember how I told you the experiment was funded by the Green Republic?"

"Yeah."

"Well, there was a man who led the opposing political force to the Green Republic, a grass roots group called the Liberty Party. She left me on the man's property. Turns out it was a good bet. He believed her story and took me in. He adopted me. We'll be safe with him."

"How did you get captured?"

"That…is an even longer story. I've shared enough. Your turn to answer a few questions. Like, what the hell are you doing in Crater City if you're part of the preservation? I thought no one got in or out."

"We have a tradition in my *Ordnung* called *rumspringa*. Before you're baptized, you spend some time among *Englishers*, to make sure it's what you want."

"But that's not how it's supposed to work. My tutor said the Green Republic walled you in so you could have your independence without infecting the general population with your choices. You're unvaccinated. You kill animals and use leather and drive buggies. No offense, but I thought part of the deal was you couldn't come and go as you please. Hell, the rumor is that most of you died off from the radiation."

Now I regret telling him the truth, but there's no going back. "We're not dead, obviously." I spread my hands. "It's not our law."

"What do you mean it's not your law?"

"The Green Republic made up those rules and forced them on us. We never agreed. Morally, we don't need to follow unjust laws."

"But how do you get out?" Korwin glances over his shoulder at me as if I'm completely missing the point.

"I told you. We just leave. It's not like the wall has armed guards anymore and even if there were, we'd find a way. *Englishers* on the outskirts, in Willow's Province, help us and provide safe houses. It's been done for generations." I decide not to give him specifics about the gate in the Outlands. No matter how much I trust him, that is one secret I decide to keep.

"Wow. I never knew. How long do you stay?"

"A few weeks, sometimes longer. Rarely, a person will stay forever."

"That's impossible. You'd need to get a work permit, and there's no way they'd give you that without records of your education and vaccinations."

"We've always had help outside of Hemlock Hollow."

"Interesting. My dad is going to be fascinated with you."

"Is he interested in Amish life?"

"No." Korwin stops abruptly and looks me in the eye. "He's interested in freedom." We've stopped under the squares of light of an access point. He mounts the ladder on the wall and climbs to the grate.

Click-click-clank. My eyelids flutter at the unbroken sunbeam that floods past Korwin's body. He disappears into the light and then beckons me to follow. I crawl out of the hole and join him on a mercifully abandoned stretch of sidewalk. The sun is directly above us, noon. In the light of day, I can see the remnants of our journey smudged across my sleeves and shoulders, where I must have nudged the inside of the pipe. My jeans have dark splotches from cuff to knee.

Korwin looks just as soiled. I say a silent prayer that the sores on his arms won't become infected.

"This way. Usually there isn't much traffic out here during the day," he says, leading me across the street and up a driveway.

On our right, a tall hedge partially cloaks an even taller fence. Korwin approaches a metal box attached to a gate as big as a barn door. A face pops up on a screen inside the box, a tightly groomed man in a bowtie and apron.

"Can I help—Korwin!" The man gasps. The gate beeps and slowly swings open. "I'll tell your father you're here. Thank goodness."

Korwin motions for me to follow. I jog through the gate, fascinated by the automation. Even after everything I've seen, I marvel at the technology.

"How does it work?" I ask, turning toward Korwin. I don't register his answer. I'm too distracted by the house on the hill in front of me. It's five times as large as the largest barn in Hemlock Hollow, with a manicured lawn and flowering shrubs of a variety I've never seen.

Korwin places a hand on my shoulder. "Welcome to Stuart Manor, Lydia. This is home."

Chapter 8

"This is your home?" I gawk at the mansion, with its ivy-covered walls and gigantic wooden door.

A bald man with coffee-colored skin similar to my friend Mary's strides out of the manor toward us. He sweeps Korwin into a hug, his eyes wet with unshed tears. "I thought I'd never see you again."

"You might not have. I thought I was dead. I was as good as dead," Korwin says.

The reunion is warm, even loving, but there's something missing. It hovers on the edge of emotional but never crosses the line into the type of family intimacy I'm used to. I wonder if it's an English thing.

"How did you escape?" his father asks.

"This is how." Korwin points at me.

His father extends his hand in my direction. "I'm Maxwell Stuart. Thank you for bringing Korwin home."

"I did less than you might think," I say, shaking his hand. "To be honest, it would be fairer to say we saved each other."

Korwin clears his throat. "This is Lydia, Dad."

The smile fades from Maxwell's face. His eyes sweep over me from head to toe. "Should I ask how you ended up in CGEF's detention center?"

"She's like me."

Maxwell laughs. "What do you mean, like you?"

"She's a Spark." Korwin grabs my hand and holds the crusty sore in his father's direction.

Korwin's dad stares at the sore then lifts my hand and inspects it from all sides. His Adam's apple bobs with the effort of a strong swallow. He drops my hand as if I've burned him and meets my eyes, cupping his mouth for a few tense moments. "Where did you come from? I have so many questions." He scans the sky, as if to check for God's own prying eyes. "Let's go inside. You must be starving, and Korwin, those sores on your arms need treatment."

The man from the gate, in the suit and apron, holds the big wooden door open for us. Once inside, metal grinds against metal as the heavy door locks itself. I perch on the edge of the welcome mat, trying my best not to soil the wood floors that go on and on across the gigantic room. The place is so large, I wonder if my footsteps will echo.

Music plays from Maxwell's person and we all pause inside the door while he pulls a thin piece of plastic from his pocket, identical to the one in my treebox. He pokes at the front. "I have to take this," he says to the man in the apron and abruptly leaves the room.

"Master Korwin, the healing room is prepared for you in the training center," the man says.

"Thanks." He turns toward me. "Lydia, I'll see you later. I'll help you with your hand when I'm through, okay?"

I nod. What's a healing room? And why does he need

to help with my hand? All I need is a small bandage.

"Jameson will take care of you." Korwin disappears down a flight of stairs to the left.

I fold my hands, hoping beyond hope that Jameson will offer me a place to get cleaned up. He turns his full attention on me, his eyes widening at my appearance.

"Lydia, is it?" he asks softly.

"Yes."

"It is a pleasure to make your acquaintance."

"Thanks. Nice to meet you, too."

"If you'll follow me, I'll show you to your room."

My room. Thank goodness. I slip off my shoes and pad after him in my relatively clean socks. He leads me down the same flight of stairs Korwin descended and through an entryway that maintains the home's charm, but with muscle—a foot-thick, shiny metal door. Unlike upstairs, there are no windows. But the carpet under my feet is plush and the art that hangs on the walls woos me with its captivating array of colors and textures.

"This is incredible." I stop in front of a floor-to-ceiling-sized painting of palominos galloping through a glade. The horses themselves are fairly ordinary, but the colors—blues, violets—pull me in. I've never seen art like this; my fingers reach for it before I catch myself and return my hand to my side.

"Painted by Master Korwin. One of my favorites as well."

"He painted this?"

"Yes. He's an accomplished artist. It's unfortunate that his fate and genetics have dealt him the hand they did. I've always felt his talents should be shared with the world."

I nod. Jameson continues down the hallway but I lag behind to absorb the artwork for one moment more before following him. At the end of a maze of hallways, Jameson opens a white door.

"Here you are." He extends his arm into a room that is something out of a dream.

As large as the first floor of my house in Hemlock Hollow, the room features a bed swaddled in white downy linens. On the far wall, a window reveals a large green yard. The window confuses me because I thought we were in a basement. I walk to the glass and watch a butterfly flit behind the panes. Only, halfway across the glass the orange and black colors of the monarch morph to pink and blue.

"Oh!" I take a step back. The sky out the window is cloudless. This isn't right. This isn't the world I left outside the door.

"It's a hologram, Miss Lydia," Jameson says. He taps on the windowpane. "It's an artificial window."

I understand what he's saying but I gape at him, dumbfounded. How can this be? Turning, I take in the rest of the room. There's a small sitting area at the end of the bed that looks cozy and a frame on the wall holding a classical painting of *Water Lilies*—Van Gogh, I think, or maybe Monet. I only recognize it from a book I read once. Based on Jeremiah's description, I think the art might actually be a television. The material, slightly luminescent, is too thin to be an actual canvas.

"Through here is the bathroom," Jameson says, passing

his hand inside a doorway. The lights come on, presumably from his movement.

The room is pearly white with a tub, separate shower, and a toilet fancy enough for me to question whether I can figure out how to use it.

"Your bathrobe is there on the hook. If you would kindly leave your soiled garments outside the door, I would be pleased to see to them for you."

"Oh Jameson, I can wash them myself. I'd hate to be a burden."

Jameson relaxes into a genuine smile. "This is my job. I'm happy to do it, and it makes me feel useful."

I don't want to offend him. "Of course. I'll leave them outside the door."

"Good." For a moment, he stares at me expectantly and I wonder if there is some *Englisher* custom I am forgetting. Shifting from foot to foot, he finally breaks the silence. "I'm sorry to be so forward, but you look familiar to me. Have we met before?"

"No. I'm not from here."

"Where are you from?"

"Willow's Province."

"Oh." He sighs and shakes his peppered gray head. "I must be mistaken." Regaining his formal composure, he points back into the bedroom. "The refrigerator is stocked with water and snacks if you need something to tide you over until next meal." He steps over to what looks like a wardrobe and swings open the door. A tiny kitchen is concealed there: a basket of fruit and bread, a small sink, and a half-sized refrigerator.

My eyebrows shoot up. I cannot comprehend the opulence.

He gives a slight bow and turns on his heel, closing the door behind him.

Turning circles in the gleaming white of my guest room, I finally allow myself to cry. I have no idea where Jeremiah is or what he must be thinking. I wonder if I can safely visit my father now that I'm a fugitive. I am an entire world from home, covered in grime. The filth of this world is sinking in, penetrating my skin and burrowing straight to the bone. My empty stomach heaves, and I rush into the bathroom.

But it's too late for me to expel what this new world has done to me.

Chapter 9

A person can only get so empty before their instincts, raw and primal, demand attention. One moment I am on my knees on the white tile floor of the bathroom, and the next, I am frantically foraging in the pantry Jameson introduced to me. I eat like an animal, hand to mouth, not bothering with the plates provided. A piece of bread, a slice of cheese, peanut butter straight off the spoon. I guzzle from a bottle of water I find in the tiny refrigerator. I eat so fast, I don't taste any of it.

Sated, I leave my mess of clothes outside the door and walk naked into the bathroom. It takes me fifteen minutes to figure out how to use the shower. Out of frustration I start sobbing again. But through trial and error I finally get the temperature and pressure right. I step in. Warm water sprays my face, mixing with my tears before washing the stench of dung and disappointment down the drain. About the time I finish scrubbing, I knit myself back together. My tears dry up in the final rinse, and I turn off the water with the same torque as I close off my self-pity.

Stepping from the shower, I find everything I need and some things I don't in a basket on the counter. I brush my teeth and hair and wrap the fluffy white bathrobe around me before exiting into the main bedroom chamber.

Apparently Jameson has let himself into the room while I bathed. A gorgeous swath of colorful material stretches across the bed. Resting on top is a note written in painstakingly neat handwriting. I capture the paper between my fingers.

Lydia,

I thought this dress would be appropriate. If it doesn't suit you, the other items I've obtained for you are in the closet.

In your service,

Jameson

Tenderly, I lift the dress. It's cerulean blue with tiny white flowers. When I pull it on over my head, the silky fabric skims down my body, clingy at first then adjusting to my size as if it were tailored for me. Sliding my feet into the silver slippers next to the bed, I twirl in front of the mirror. The hem of the skirt hits just above my knee, an inappropriate length if I'd been in Hemlock Hollow, but expected, I'm sure, in this world. Given the circumstances, I put all misgivings aside. Until I find my way home, I need to fit in.

Something is missing. Per the note, I check the closet. Racks of clothing fill a room that could house a small family. One wall is nothing but shoes. A cabinet at the center holds rows and rows of shallow drawers. Who needs all this? Overwhelmed, I search until I find undergarments and tights. I finish dressing and set out to find the others.

Retracing the path back upstairs proves challenging, maybe because I'm exhausted from the events of yesterday or because this part of the house is a maze of hallways. For a good twenty minutes, I am lost until the blue palominos provide a visual anchor. I drink in the texture of Korwin's painting, the way the shoulder of the largest horse bunches like the animal is bucking the sky itself.

Inexplicably, my attention wanders from the painting to the door next to it. There's this hum that calls to me from beyond. It's a feeling in my gut like a hunger, like my mouth is watering for what's inside. A hollow, empty feeling—*a wanting,* not unlike my instinct to eat—urges me forward.

The room is unlocked. Inside, music plays softly. Huge machines with blinking lights line all four walls, and in the middle is a square tub of water that bubbles and glows electric blue. Flashbacks of the room I saved Korwin from fill my head, only no one is restrained in here. The room isn't menacing at all.

The technology fascinates me and I scan the machines, the knobs, the lights, the grids of measurements I don't understand. My silver slippers creep across the room to the edge of the tiled tub, and I lean over to look into its depths.

There's a body. My mouth opens on a gasp and my hand goes to my heart. Someone is in there, at the bottom, masked by the ripple and refraction of the blue water. I glance at the door and then into the water again.

"Hello?" I call.

No response. The body is motionless. I can't see the face because there's a current, a constant bubbling across the surface. What if the person has drowned? Is drowning?

Without thinking, I thrust my hands into the water, grasping for the victim at the bottom of the tub. No sooner have my fingers broken the surface than two things happen at once. First, a current of electricity flows into my body through my hand, the intensity making my experience in the elevator seem like child's play. And second, the body's eyes open beneath the water.

"Holy mother of God," I yell. It is an exclamation I've never used before, but it rolls off my tongue like a veteran curse.

I try to retract my arms but the person grips my wrists. I squeal and yank harder.

The body sits up in the tub, a dark head breaking the surface with a splash that spills across the front of my dress and onto my shoes. When the spray settles, I am mute with disbelief. Korwin stares at me from the tub, very much alive. In fact, the arm holding my wrist is completely healed of sores, the bruises and swelling gone. Silky smooth olive skin stretches over tight muscles. My eyes travel from his arm to his face, his dark hair slicked back and tucked behind his ears. He is... stunning. Full lips, dark lashes, bright hazel eyes and a nose carved like artwork, like a sculpture that belongs with the rest of the art in the hallway. I cannot look away.

"Lydia!" he sputters, releasing me.

I take two giant steps backward. "Are you killing yourself?" I demand. Although somewhere deep inside, I know he's not.

"No!" he says, shaking his head, positively offended. "This is a healing tank. The water is supercharged and

105

oxygenated. It works at the cellular level."

I shake my head.

"I don't need to breathe under this water. The oxygen is delivered with the electricity directly into my cells to speed healing." He holds up his right arm. His smooth olive complexion is peppered with dark hair. "It's like recharging my battery. Check your hand."

I do, and he's right.

"Completely healed and juiced to a subtle blue glow," he says.

Juiced. Right. I'd forgotten the term for this feeling. "It's a miracle."

"This one, I can fairly say, is science."

I tiptoe back to the edge and peer into the blue water. I want to stick my hand back in, to experience the rush one more time. But he scoots to the far side of the tub, his arms diving beneath the surface.

"Um, Lydia..."

"Yes? Does it hurt you when I touch the water?"

He laughs, his face flushed. "No. Uh... I'm naked in here."

I stumble backward, almost tripping over my own feet. "I'm sorry," I blurt. A nervous laugh bubbles up my throat as I find the doorknob and work my way into the hall. I close it behind me but can't bring myself to leave. My skin tingles and there's still a pull from behind the door anchoring me to the spot. My only question is whether the force I'm drawn to is the electricity or Korwin.

Either way, despite my hunger and feeling lost in a strange world, I am smiling. Smiling at the painting of the blue horses.

* * * * *

I don't have to wait long. Korwin emerges from the healing room, wearing a gray sleeveless tunic and drawstring pants.

"I'm very sorry if I embarrassed you," I say, my face warm again. "I saw nothing."

"Don't worry about it. No harm done." He straightens his tunic. I've never seen clothes like his before. The material has a metallic sheen and moves like it's alive.

He notices my fixation. "It's woven from talimite. The mineral conducts electricity. It's, um, soothing to new skin." He holds out his arms.

"At home, I'm a seamstress. This fabric is fascinating. How is it stitched together?"

Korwin shrugs. "I'm not sure. You can look at it more closely if you want." He tucks his arms behind his back.

I can't help myself. My fingers creep forward toward his collarbone. An inch away, I can feel the buzz, the spark coming alive in my fingertips. On contact, the material has the texture of miniature chain-link but gives off zaps of electricity. I flatten my hand against his chest, stroke down the material and around the side of his torso to his hip.

"There's no seam," I say.

"No? I never noticed before." The husky tone in his voice causes me to lift my face to his. He's not smiling anymore. Instead, his eyes look hungry and the expression sends a flood of heat through my body. Convinced it's the juice, I force myself to back away. When I pull my hand from his chest, the tunic follows the pads of my fingers, billowing beneath my touch until my hand is far enough away to break the connection. It settles back against his body.

I clear my throat. "They must have made it on a round loom."

Blinking, his eyebrows knit as if he's trying to understand what I'm talking about. "It's one of a kind," he finally says. "My dad had it made for me."

"Your father's gone to great lengths to keep you healthy."

He tips his head. "He needs to if we're going to succeed."

"Succeed at what?"

He opens his mouth as if to answer but closes it again and smiles. "Dinner first. You must be starving."

I'm about to agree but then I notice something odd. "You know, I was hungry until I stuck my hands into your bath. Now I'm…okay." I look down at my palms. Flashes of blue dance under my skin. Juiced.

"Yeah. It does that, but if you don't eat you won't be able to hold your charge for long. We have to eat, too."

"Oh," I say. It surprises me how comfortable I've become with this newfound ability in such a short time. Part of it is my faith. My heart is open to the unexplainable. I accept that I can manipulate electricity as a gift, like my ability to run fast and to cook.

"Your dress is wet," he says.

I run my hand down the damp section near the hem.

"It's okay. Just a little water."

"Let me help you with that." Korwin reaches for my skirt, his hand glowing bright enough to make me blink. Heat blooms over the wet material, steam rising between us. "There," he says, retracting.

My dress is dry. "Thank you."

He leads me to the base of the stairs but stops before going up. His hazel eyes find mine and I can see the glow flickering beneath his skin extend to his irises. Blue light washes over my face. As I look at him, I have the most intense feeling of connection, like two pieces of a puzzle fitting together. I sigh deeply, and the place where his hand touches my elbow tingles. He must feel it too because he looks down at the spot before speaking.

"Lydia, meeting you this way..." He shakes his head. "I finally feel like there's someone else in the world who understands. Someone just like me. Do you know what I mean?"

I step closer. His tunic moves, shifting with the zaps of electricity that jump between my skin and his. Blue light arcs between us, drawing us closer, until I have to crane my neck to maintain eye contact. We are chest to chest, but I feel a compulsion to move closer.

"I do know," I say. It's true. A little piece, a hole in my soul I'd never realized was there, is suddenly filled. I don't know why God sent me the miracle that lives beneath my skin, or how long it will last, but in that moment, I am standing next to my *other*. A person from an entirely different world who connects with whatever this is.

Korwin lowers his face toward mine. Tiny blue

lightning bolts zap under his skin, concentrating around his lips. Without a doubt, I know he intends to kiss me. I inhale deeply; he smells like our field right after a thundershower. Energy swirls between us. I close my eyes and wait for his lips to brush mine.

"Master Korwin," Jameson calls down the stairs.

I jump back, my face hot. I can't believe I've almost kissed a boy I hardly know.

"Yes, Jameson?" Korwin growls.

"Your meal is served."

"Thanks," he says, then mumbles, "for nothing."

I roll the toe of my slipper over the carpet.

Korwin smiles at me and makes a sweeping motion with his hand toward the stairs. "Dinner is served," he repeats pompously.

"I'll beat you to it," I tease, as much to break the awkward moment as because I am hungry again. I give him a wry grin and bound up the stairs. He chases after me, laughing when I just barely reach the landing before him. We cross the massive great room, where he takes the lead because I have no idea where I am going, then burst into the dining room side by side, panting from the run.

"Glad to see you two are getting to know each other," Maxwell says. He gives a tight smile, all business. "We've got trouble. Come and eat. We need to talk."

Chapter 10

Dinner looks like beef stew but tastes like paste. My appetite has returned and I'm hungry enough that even if it were paste, I would eat it. While Korwin and I shovel it in, Maxwell presses his fingers into a painting of a woman in a large hat on the wall. The canvas melts away, replaced by a moving picture. Television.

He taps a box that says *news*. Music plays and then the camera focuses in on a blond woman sitting behind a desk. *Good evening. I'm Alexandra Brighten and this is Channel 12 News, the official news station of the Green Republic. In top news tonight, terrorism at CGEF.*

The picture changes to Korwin and me escaping from CGEF's atrium. I drop my fork and swallow what's in my mouth. I'm on television? How did they record this? The video is from the outside of the building at the moment Korwin shattered the glass. People run from us screaming as we exit CGEF.

A man in a wide-lapelled blazer turns his concerned face toward the camera. *The destruction is senseless. The public will end up paying for the damages if we can't find these monsters.*

The scene replays in the background as another bystander speaks to the camera, an elderly woman in a mauve jumpsuit. *It was a horrific brush with crime. We are all lucky to be alive. The two scampers were crazed. I thought they might kill us all.*

"That's not how it happened. I don't even remember her being there," I say, looking toward Korwin for support. "They were torturing us. We had to escape." I turn to Maxwell but he's fixated on the screen.

Then the video skips to when Korwin blasted the officers and jumped over the side of the bridge with me in his arms. They replay the jump again and again, each time ending with the focus on the officers writhing on the concrete.

Clearly, these killers are armed and dangerous, Alexandra says.

I gasp. Killers? I am not a killer. I flash on Helen seizing beneath my touch and am flooded with guilt. No, I didn't kill her, but I did hurt her, as unintentional as it was. Please, Lord, forgive me. I bow my head but keep my eyes on the screen. Korwin must sense my inner turmoil because he reaches over and squeezes my hand. His touch sends electric ribbons up my arm and makes my breath hitch. I move my hand away so I can concentrate.

The clip finishes with a close-up of our faces. Under my picture, the name Lydia Lane blinks in bright yellow letters. Korwin's name is also there, although no last name is included. *Citizens should report any sightings of these two immediately. CGEF is offering a one thousand-unit reward for any information leading to the arrest and conviction of these two terrorists. Authorities want to remind everyone that these fugitives are deadly. Do not try to apprehend them yourselves.*

Our faces leave the screen, replaced by a video of a panda bear. *In other news—*

Maxwell taps the screen, and it returns to the canvas painting of a woman in a large hat.

"We had to. We had no choice," I whisper, shaking my head. "Terrorists!" My voice rises. "That's not how it happened at all." I look from Korwin to his father, desperate for an explanation. I can't make sense of this.

"The truth doesn't matter," Maxwell says. "You are now Crater City's most wanted. And they know who you are."

"But they arrested me for no reason and tortured Korwin. We were escaping. We didn't mean to hurt anyone. Terrorists? Who are we terrorizing, and for what? We're the ones who were terrorized!" My head pounds along with my heart. This isn't right. I expected they'd be after us for escaping, but terrorism?

"Both of you are on lockdown. High security, high alert."

Korwin nods next to me. I'm not sure what "lockdown" means but I have a feeling I won't be visiting my father or seeing Jeremiah anytime soon.

A tear escapes the corner of my eye, and I bury my face in my hands. "This isn't how it was supposed to happen."

"Lydia, I'm prepared to shelter and protect you, but I need to know the entire truth. Where do you come from, and how did you end up at the CGEF detention center?" Korwin's father threads his fingers together and leans forward.

I look at Korwin.

"You can trust him, Lydia. He won't tell anyone."

I start from the beginning, explaining *rumspringa* and the house in Willow's Province. He doesn't flinch, as if Amish people show up on his doorstep on a regular basis. I explain about the light, how the electricity flowed into me. I skim over Dr. Konrad's exam and thankfully Maxwell doesn't ask for details. The MRI machine I describe in detail, as well as our escape. I end with our trip through the sewer. The conversation is cathartic, as if telling my story releases some built-up pressure. "So, you see, I have to reach Jeremiah and get home. This is all a mistake. I don't belong here."

"And you've never had anything like this happen before?"

"No."

"I don't mean to hound you about this. Korwin's power came on at fifteen. Before that, if we hadn't known better, we'd have thought he was the same as everyone else." Maxwell purses his lips. "Korwin is a product of the Alpha Eight, the second generation result of Operation Source code. You, Lydia, are a mystery. If what you say is true, if you've developed this power without implants or bioengineering, it truly is a miracle. I have no explanation for it."

I fold my hands in my lap and shrug my shoulders. "I'm telling the truth."

"What about Jeremiah? Did anything similar happen to him? Maybe it's environmental. The preservation is close to the Outlands. A mutation from the radiation?"

114

"I don't think so, but he wasn't standing as close as me."

Maxwell rubs his forehead. "As much as I can understand your desire to get home, you can understand why that is currently problematic."

My face tightens and I hold my breath, trying not to cry.

He waves his outstretched hands. "I'm not saying we can't help you, just that I need some time. Give us some time."

I nod.

"While you're here, I'd like to run some tests to see how similar or different you are to Korwin. Can I have your permission?"

My mind reels. A day ago, I was at home, living a normal life. And now everything has changed. It's too fast. But what else can I say but yes? Korwin's father is the authority in this household and knows the workings of the English world. I have nowhere else to go. I'm completely at his mercy.

"Yes, Max—" I remember that *Englishers* use the last name and a prefix to address elders. "Mr. Stuart," I say.

He takes a deep breath and smiles. "Wonderful. We'll take some blood and tissue samples after we finish here."

A muffled squeak bubbles up my throat. Blood and tissue. I think back to Dr. Konrad's assessment. Will it hurt? Will I have to take off my clothes? I'm afraid to ask.

Maxwell's eyes lock on my face. "It won't take long and afterward, Korwin can show you around Stuart Manor."

Korwin nods. "Sure." But he doesn't look sure. Behind his smile are the telltale signs of worry.

I stand to clear the table, lifting my bowl and reaching for Korwin's. Gently, he places his hand on my wrist. "You don't have to do that here. Jameson will get it."

"Oh, I wouldn't feel right. Not after he made the food."

Jameson sweeps to my side, seemingly out of thin air, and lifts the bowls from my fingers. "Please."

I allow the man to take the dishes, noticing the way he smiles like it's his honor and duty to serve. He'd fit in perfectly in Hemlock Hollow.

"Okay," I say weakly.

Maxwell stands. "Good. Let's get started."

* * * * *

The size and complexity of Maxwell's examination room makes my stomach clench. But he takes my blood so gently I hardly feel it, and the tissue sample comes from the inside of my cheek. I don't even have to change my clothes.

He explains what he's doing as he mounts the tissue on a glass slide and transfers my blood to a test tube. He feeds both into a machine attached to a computer.

"Let's take a look," Maxwell says, donning a pair of thick black glasses.

The viewer is red, with octagonal shapes that bubble and dance. Sparks of light ignite between them when they collide. My blood is beautiful, filled with shadows and light, life and mystery. Without thinking, I touch the screen. The cells grow beneath my fingers and I retract my hand, hoping I didn't damage his device.

Maxwell laughs. "It's touch-sensitive," he says. He places his fingers on the screen and the cells grow larger. When he removes them they shrink again. "It magnifies the cells so you can see them better."

I nod. I try it a few times, fascinated by all the moving parts within my blood. "So, can you tell by looking at this what is different about me?"

His dark eyebrows sink over his glasses. "You've never seen a normal cell?"

Too embarrassed to answer, I glance at the floor. In fact, we did touch on the basics of biology in school but I hated it and rarely paid full attention. He keys something into the corner of the screen.

"Here are normal human erythrocytes, er, red blood cells. These are my cells." He points to the left side of the viewer.

Red and round, the chubby disks float in their sector of the monitor. No blue sparks light up the edges. The cells have no corners. Next to the jittery ricochet of my cells, the human ones seem positively fat and lazy.

All of the air is sucked from the room. I take shallow breaths but my pulse races anyway. I compare the two screens in confusion, my brain buzzing uselessly. My power is not just a miracle. I'm different. My cells are different. I have so many questions I don't know where to start. If these are "human cells," does that mean I am not human? Am I some new species? *Homoelectrokenis*?

"How did this happen?" I ask once I've caught my breath. "Was it the radiation from the Outlands?"

Maxwell raises an eyebrow and tips his head. "Here are Korwin's cells."

He types another code into the screen, and more cells pop up. These look the same as mine. "Your cells are identical to Korwin's, but the DNA analysis shows you aren't related. When Korwin was left with me, there was a note that explained everything we know about Operation Source Code. It said there was only one child—Korwin."

My breath is shaky. I lean forward, fingertips hovering over the monitor's display of cells.

"I don't know how you became a Spark, Lydia. I wouldn't think radiation could do this to a human cell but...I don't know. I don't know how a girl who's born and raised in an Amish community comes to have electrokinetic abilities." He throws his pen down on his desk and rubs one hand over his lips.

"Maybe it *is* a miracle," I whisper toward the monitor.

Maxwell spreads his hands and shakes his head. "Is it a miracle to be what you are?"

I don't answer, but inside I wonder. Maybe it is.

Chapter 11

"Let's start with the training room." Korwin leads me from the lab into a maze of corridors. He's giving me the tour of the Stuarts' facilities. I'm hopeful that it will get my mind off the image of the sharp edges of my supercharged cells. We start in a gym as big as our hay barn, maybe bigger. A section of odd machines lines one wall across from a thick mat and rack of weapons.

"What are those machines?"

"What? The cardio equipment?"

"Cardio equipment." I think back to my book but can't remember anything that looked like this.

"Wait. Are you serious? You've never seen a Holotread?"

I step onto the mat and press a button on the console. The belt makes an odd sound and jolts backward. I trip to the floor.

"Easy." Korwin steadies my shoulder. His mouth forms a tight grin, like he's trying not to laugh. "Here, let me show you." He stops the Holotread and climbs onto the one next to it. "Step on up," he says, slapping the console.

I get back on the strange machine and fold my hands in front of me.

"Here, start slowly. One is the slowest and twenty is

119

the fastest." He punches a one on his keypad and starts walking forward. I do the same and quickly grow accustomed to the feel of the machine shifting beneath my feet.

"I use it to exercise. I can't go outside anymore because they know about me, so I have a training program to stay strong."

I smile. "This makes you strong? Walking without going anywhere?" My silver slippers fall rhythmically on the belt. "I run faster catching our chickens."

"Oh ho ho! That sounds like a challenge. Let's add a scenario." He punches a code into the keyboard and suddenly I'm walking on a path through a forest.

"How?" I reach for an oak tree and my hand passes right through. I trip.

"Careful. It's a hologram. You have to keep your feet on the treadmill."

"I understand." I center myself on the revolving belt.

"Take it up to five." He pokes his console.

I grin and press the five on my keypad. The belt speeds up, and I break into a light jog. It feels good.

"How are you doing?" Korwin asks. With longer legs, he's able to keep up at a fast walk.

"Piece of cake," I say. The expression is considered prideful in Hemlock Hollow, but given the circumstances, I indulge my will. As Jeremiah says, when in the English world, act English.

Korwin laughs and hands me a long plastic rod from the front of my treadmill. He unhooks his own and punches another code into the keyboard. "Don't let them hit you."

"Don't let what hit me?" He doesn't have to answer. A spiky ball sails toward my head. I use the rod to slap it away. The hologram responds to my swing, and a blue number one pops up in the corner of my vision.

"Good! Faster." He punches ten into my keypad. I lurch back, laughing, and have to run to stay on the platform. I reach over and punch the same number into his, sending him sprinting forward. We fall into a rhythm, running side by side.

A barrage of spiky balls attacks me. I swat at them without breaking my stride. My head knows they can't hurt me, that they'll pass through me like the tree did, but I can't stop my heart from pounding. It seems so real. I fight like my life depends on it.

"How fast can you go?" I ask.

"Right now, we're running ten miles per hour. Most people can't keep this up very long, but being a Spark gives me more energy and endurance. I usually run an hour at fifteen."

I punch fifteen into the keypad and sprint forward, pumping my arms to keep up. Korwin does the same. The scenery changes and the forest is no longer filled with spiky balls but men with guns.

"Hit away the bullets," he says.

We have guns in Hemlock Hollow, but they are only used for hunting and look different from the ones in the hologram. The bullet is small and fast. I miss, and it passes through my belly. A red number one appears next to the blue forty-three in the corner of my screen. I've missed one and hit forty-three.

"Aw. Come on, kid. You can do this. Focus!" Korwin says.

The way he calls me *kid* sounds condescending. I want to put him in his place so badly it makes my chest ache. I close my eyes and for a second I'm running through the fields of Hemlock Hollow, touching the prairie grass. My whole body buzzes with energy. The silver slippers I wear can't keep up; my toes threaten to rip through the material. Without missing a step, I kick them off, my bare feet landing on the belt with surety. I open my eyes in time to whack a bullet before it hits my head.

"*Bam!* Nice work!"

I look at his score. Sixty-eight blue. Mine is forty-four.

"Let's go faster," I say. I feel strong, like I can do anything. I up my speed to twenty, as fast as the machine will go. At this speed, my arms and legs move like pistons. I whale on bullet after bullet. Sixty, seventy, seventy-five. My blue numbers grow and I'm running faster than I've ever run. If I had wings, I would fly.

"Lydia…" Korwin slaps the red button on his console and stops running. He stares at me, wide-eyed.

My arm passes in front of my face on its way to intercept a bullet and I notice why he's staring. I am glowing like a star, neon blue, a light so bright it shines through my dress. It startles me enough to lose my footing. I fly off the back of the Holotread into the wall behind me.

"Are you okay?" Korwin jumps off his machine and runs to my side. Gently, he rubs his palm over the back of my hair, where my head connected with the wall.

Stunned, I blink at him a few times. Nothing hurts, so I sit up. I'm not glowing anymore, but I'm not injured. "I'm okay." I stand, smooth my dress, and slip my shoes back on.

"You are full of surprises," Korwin says.

"It would seem so," I whisper, staring at my outstretched hands. I wish I could see into my cells without the microscope. I wish I understood how this was happening. But my own body is a mystery to me, a puzzle where none of the pieces fit. At least, not yet.

* * * * *

Korwin offers to continue the tour of the compound. Although I'm exhausted from the day and my experience with the Holotread, I tacitly agree. As he reaches for my hand to lead me down the hallway, tiny bolts of electricity touch me before he does. I allow his fingers to slip into mine, enjoying the tingle against my palm. I don't even register where he's taking me. I'm too distracted by the heat that runs from our coupled hands up my arm to where it makes my scalp prickle.

I've held hands with boys before and with Jeremiah almost every day for the last year, but this is different. Korwin's hand makes every cell in my body perk to attention. My stomach flutters and hovers, like I'm jumping from the haymow or diving into the river. I can smell him, too. His scent is familiar, like the air after a thunderstorm.

All of this comes to me naturally, without effort or decision. It just is. My body, my senses, are fascinated by Korwin, from the shift of his muscles under his tunic, to the tone of his voice, to the protective way he keeps one eye on me. I wonder if my touch does the same thing to him as it does to me. He doesn't seem as affected, but then his skin is darker than mine, harder to see a blush.

The cream-colored walls give way to glass panels and what's inside takes my breath away. There is an underground garden, as sculpted and colorful as any I've seen above ground. We step from the hall onto a cobblestone walkway. For a moment, I think we're outside, and I lift my face to check. I have to squint, but there is a ceiling high above us made to look like the sky. The dim blue and purple aura gives the illusion of twilight.

"Does it imitate the sky outside?" I ask.

Korwin nods. "Even the rain. The lights are ultraviolet. Artificial sun. You can get a tan in here during the day."

I find the thought of Korwin having to settle for fake sun depressing and try to focus on the positive. "I can't even name all the plants and shrubs."

"That's because they're from all over the world. We have perfect growing conditions."

He leads me into a labyrinth of tall green hedges that wall us in. Besides our footsteps on stone, I notice other sounds that add to the feel of the outdoors. "You have birds!" A goldfinch rests on the hedge near our heads.

"A few," he says.

The rush of falling water greets us as, hand in hand, we

turn another corner. Korwin leads me from the maze of trees into an opening I assume is the center of the labyrinth. The source of the sound is a fountain, a marble sculpture of a woman pouring water from a jar into a pool at her feet. The water babbles and splashes a soothing symphony.

"I could stay here all day," Korwin says into my ear. His breath warms my cheek. Have I leaned into his shoulder, or has he stepped against my back?

"It's so peaceful," I say, enjoying his closeness.

There's a long pause while I sink into Korwin's slow breaths. "My dad will want to do more tests tomorrow, to compare your abilities as a Spark to mine."

"Will the tests hurt?"

"If you're like me, Lydia, it won't hurt to use your power. It'll hurt to stop. The hard part is the control. It's like today on the Holotread. You tapped into your spark. If I hadn't interrupted you, you'd probably still be running."

It's true. When I'd been in the thick of it, I didn't feel tired. I felt invincible. I swallow hard. Invincible is a deceitful, dangerous feeling.

From behind me, Korwin's hands rub the outside of my shoulders. "I'm sure you'll do fine. How could you not? As far as I know, Dad has no expectations, he just wants to see what you can do." His smile flashes in my peripheral vision.

Maybe it's the way my shoulders relax at his touch or the fact I internally quiver at the contact, but our closeness triggers my sense of propriety and I force myself to take a step away, toward the fountain.

He clears his throat and rubs his chest as if my distance is making him uncomfortable. I can't say I understand why, but I feel it too, a stark emptiness at the heart of me.

"You must be exhausted," he says.

The goldfinch flits overhead and my eyes feel heavy just watching it fly. I'm relieved when Korwin takes my hand and leads me back to my room.

Chapter 12

"Just relax, Lydia. This isn't going to hurt a bit." Maxwell connects wires he calls electrodes to my head, chest, and limbs. We're back in his lab and this time I'm sitting on a padded examination table next to a machine with a dozen different gauges and blinking lights.

"I'll try," I say.

"Did you sleep well last night?" He adjusts his glasses on his nose before continuing his application of wires to my skin.

"I think so." In truth, I woke not knowing where I was from a deathlike sleep. I might still be sleeping had Jameson not roused me for the noon meal. "In all my life, I've never slept so long or so soundly."

"You're in the inception period. Korwin experienced something similar."

I arch an eyebrow. "You mentioned last night that he became a Spark at fifteen. So, he wasn't always able to throw lightning bolts from his hands?"

Maxwell smiles. "No. Before his inception, we had the note but no proof it was true. Everything about him appeared...average."

"How did it happen...for Korwin?" I wonder if Korwin's change was as dramatic as mine.

"Struck by lightning," he says. He states it clinically, without a hint of emotion. "Korwin went through a period of intense pain afterward, followed by an exponential increase in electrokinetic ability over the following several weeks."

I roll my lips together. I'm familiar with the intense pain. "So, the lightning helped him change into what he is. Do you think I might have been normal without the lamp?"

He laughs. "Who is normal? If you are asking if you might not have become electrokinetic if you'd never left the preservation, the answer is, I don't know. It's possible. The DNA analysis shows that you and Korwin have the same gene, latent for both of you as children. We don't completely understand how it works. Would it have eventually triggered the change whether or not you were exposed to electricity? I'm not sure. In your case, it just as well could have been lightning."

The sheer randomness of it all overwhelms me. Could I have escaped this fate by staying in Hemlock Hollow, or was my change divine providence? My faith tells me both. I was called to be this way so that I could save Korwin.

Maxwell adjusts his glasses again and flips a switch. The screen on the machine flashes numbers and letters, then graphs.

"What does that mean?" I ask.

"It means, I'm surprised the Greens weren't harder on you. The voltage you're putting off is almost as high as Korwin's."

"You can tell all that from this gibberish?" I squint at

the display, completely at a loss.

"The miracle of modern science." He bends over to adjust the placement of an electrode on my foot and his glasses fall off.

"Seems the miracle hasn't extended to your vision," I say, laughing. "Don't the *Englishers* have a way to fix what's wrong with your eyes?"

He straightens, glasses firmly in place, and frowns at me. "In fact they do, but curing my specific condition requires a period of several days without vision and my current responsibilities make that impossible."

"You mean, because you're a scientist and a politician?" Korwin said he led the opposing political party to the Green Republic. I am not learned about how the *Englishers'* political system works, but I figure it must be a pretty demanding job.

Maxwell busies himself with his notebook and doesn't elaborate. I don't push the subject. Strictly speaking, it's none of my business. "I'd like you to try something for me. Korwin says you used the spark on the Holotread yesterday. Can you try to show me? Draw it down into your hand."

I try to find that thing inside of me that I used at CGEF. Without time to think, I'd acted on instinct that night, simply trusting it. This time, my slow introspection reveals the source. I turn my attention inward, toward the tickle that has lived at the back of my brain since the MRI machine. I try to stretch it to my fingertips. It's difficult. I don't have a target like I did with the Biolock or the panel in the elevator. Still, with some concentration, the spark obeys me, stretching to my elbow, then to my palm. I grunt, and a small arc of white light travels between my thumb and forefinger.

"Very good, Lydia," Maxwell says, clapping me on my shoulder. "How did that feel?"

"Like threading a quilting needle with yarn," I say with a laugh.

He shakes his head.

"It was difficult," I say. "Draining."

With quick fingers, he peels the electrode off my arm and moves on to the next one. "Enough for today. Let's get you out of this. More tomorrow?"

I think about that for a moment. "Not that I don't want to help, but I need to find a way back home. My friend, Jeremiah, is still in Willow's Province. I'm concerned for his safety."

Maxwell buries his hands in his pockets and gives me a long look. His yellowing eyes seem tired behind his glasses, and the lines around his tight mouth age him. "Hmm. Give me a day or two to see what I can do."

* * * * *

"How do you find your way here? I keep losing my sense of direction." I'm back in the maze of hallways with Korwin, done with testing for now.

"You noticed, huh? This place is designed to be confusing, in case the enemy ever made it this far. You'll get it, eventually."

Will I? How long will I be staying? Clearly, Korwin

130

thinks this will be an extended visit. I'm not ready to admit I'm a prisoner here or to take issue with the help the Stuarts are giving me, but homesickness plows into me when I think about staying. All I want to do is go home to Hemlock Hollow. I miss the simple thrill of diving off the haymow with Jeremiah. I'd give anything to share a glass of lemonade on Mary's porch swing. Where will I go to church on Sunday? I desperately need Bishop Kauffman's sage advice. My father! Oh, I need to see my father.

"Are you okay?" Korwin asks.

"Just homesick," I say. I hide my distress by taking interest in the artwork on the wall and square my shoulders in front of a painting of a pack of wolves in purple hues. It's breathtaking, and for a moment, I forget what I was worried about and just take it in, not just what I see but how it makes me feel. A scrollwork K is painted in the bottom corner, a symbol I remember from the palomino painting near the stairwell.

"Did you paint this?" I ask in amazement.

"Yes."

"But I thought you didn't go outside much. How do you know what these animals look like?"

"Internet. Television. Sometimes books."

"There are videos of animals?"

"Living and dead. Every one since video was invented. I can tell it's not exactly how it would look in real life, but I don't know what's missing. The color is my way of filling in the missing pieces. Well, what I imagine them to be." He rubs the back of his neck like the thought is ridiculous.

"Oh, I think I get it. You've captured their relationship with the color."

"Huh?"

"They're pack animals. I've watched them before, at the edge of the wood where I live. See how you've made this one bright? I think you could tell that he was the alpha, the leader. This dark one, this is the submissive. Look how you used the different shade in the snow. You can tell they just finished playing. It's a very good likeness. Very real." I correct myself. "The colors aren't real, but the relationships are. Maybe more real than if you'd painted them in their natural colors."

Korwin steps closer, peering over my shoulder at his artwork. His brow furrows. "None of that was on purpose. I just painted."

I pivot, realizing when my shoulder brushes his chest just how close he is to me. I look up into his eyes. "I've seen wolves, Korwin, in real life. Your paintings are very good. They're amazing."

A cynical grin forms on his lips. "I wish I'd seen what you've seen. It's too bad the English don't have the opposite of *rumspringa*. I'd like to visit Hemlock Hollow."

I search his face for any sign of insincerity. The irony is that I've spent my life longing to taste the wonders of the English world, and here is a boy who aches for a taste of mine. "Maybe some day I can show you."

His hazel eyes play over his wolf painting, taking in his own work in a new way. I can see I haven't satisfied his curiosity about the wolves. In fact, he seems agitated by the revelation of their relationship.

"Do you have more to show me?" Casually, I run my fingers down the outside of his wrist to get his attention. The contact reignites the electricity inside of me, sending a hot current through my body. *Whoa.* Heat creeps up my neck to my ears.

The hard lines of Korwin's face soften. If he notices my blush, he doesn't say anything. "Yeah. Come on. There's more."

"Where are you taking me?"

"A part of the compound I didn't get a chance to show you yesterday. I think you'll find it interesting." He leads me a bit farther down the hall to a set of French doors decorated with stained glass panels. "The library."

I am struck speechless as I enter a room with shelves of books floor to ceiling. At the center, a table is stacked with clear plastic panels, electric tablets if I remember correctly from my studies. "There are so many."

"A little of everything. If it's not here in paper, you can download anything you want on the tablets. We've got an entire section of fiction if you're interested, besides the ones you would expect about politics and electrokinesis."

Turning in a circle, I scan the titles around me. "Can I stay here for a while?" The books in Hemlock Hollow are few and far between. Each one has to be approved by the *Ordnung.* I am overwhelmed by the knowledge contained in this room. The sheer number and diversity of the titles astounds me.

Korwin steps in close. "Sure. I can come back to get you before dinner."

"Thank you," I say. The intense pull is back and I have

to force myself not to close the small distance between us.

He leans forward, and for a moment I think he might kiss me. I'm tempted to give in to it too. But I lower my chin and turn away, suddenly overcome with guilt and thoughts of Jeremiah.

Korwin's kiss lands on my forehead, leaving a tingle in its wake. "See you later."

I nod, because I can't speak, and watch him leave the room.

Chapter 13

Lightning. In Hemlock Hollow we make up loads of stories about how it came to be. God fighting angels. God playing baseball. Mary and I sometimes lie in the attic and watch out the window in wonder as fire sliced through the sky. But I never understood it. Not really.

I sit at the table in the library of Stuart Manor in front of a stack of open books, riveted. If I retain a quarter of what I'm reading, I'll count myself lucky. Here's what I've learned. Far above me, particles of ice and water tumble around inside the clouds. When these particles collide, they build up an electrical field. Electrical fields can be either negatively charged or positively charged, and the ones in the cloud are negative. I think of them as looking for trouble.

Meanwhile, on the ground, invisible particles spin and dance, causing a positively charged electrical field. Mutual attraction draws the particles on the ground toward the particles in the sky and when they touch, *crack!* The collision creates lightning. Lightning travels at sixty-two thousand miles per second and is hotter than the surface of the sun. I have a hard time believing what the books say. How could anything burn so hot or move so fast?

Electrokinesis, this thing I have, works in much the

same way. My cells bump into each other, building up a charge. The atoms buzzing around everything else do the same. Even the air. When I want my electrokinesis to work, the books say I can move my charge to the outside of my body and flip it to either positive or negative to connect with objects around me. In theory, it's mutual. The electrokinetic individual "asks" the object to accept the charged particles, and *zap*.

It's so much easier to believe what happened in CGEF was a miracle from God. A miracle has a purpose. But seeing my strange cells and learning about my electrokinesis makes it feel like one giant accident. It frightens me to think that everything that's happened has been a product of my genetics and nothing more. How did I get like this?

All this questioning leads me full circle. My mutation must have been a miracle. There's no other explanation. Which leads me to the ultimate question: why did God make me this way? And what about Korwin?

Korwin. I hardly know him but every time we're together it's like an invisible hand is shoving me in his direction. It's too fast and entirely inappropriate. But just like the particles between the cloud and the ground, I suspect our attraction has more to do with science than affection. As I flip the page of the book I'm reading, I wonder if I have any control over my attraction to him or if, like lightning, it's simply a matter of time before it strikes.

"Have you had enough yet?" Korwin stands in the doorway. Funny, I didn't hear it open. By the way he leans against the frame, it appears he's been there for some time.

"I think so," I say, closing the tome in front of me.

"Good, because it's time for dinner."

"Give me a minute and I'll clean up this mess," I say, walking the book in my hands to its space on the shelf.

"Leave it, Lydia. Jameson can do it later," he says.

I close another volume and return it to the shelf. "I prefer to do it myself. I'm sure Jameson has better things to do than pick up my books."

"Like what? This is his job, and my father pays him very well for it."

Retrieving another book from the table, I scowl at him. "Many hands make light work. Caring for a home is a burden to be shared. Everyone should pick up his or her own mess." Geez. I sound like an old Amish *maam*. Why does the thought of Jameson picking up after me bother me so much?

Korwin laughs and grabs a book from the table. "You said you're a seamstress on the preservation, right?"

"What does that have to do with anything?"

"How would you feel if one of your customers demanded to help sew her own dress?"

I finish shelving the book and rise to my full height, hands on my hips. "That is completely different."

"Is it?"

"Yes. I'm trained as a seamstress. The buyer might do more harm than good."

Korwin raises an eyebrow. "Jameson trained to be a butler at a professional school. He's an expert who keeps this library in tiptop shape. Frankly, I hope we've put these books back in their proper places or there might be hell to pay."

"I… Uh…"

"He's not my mother. He won't give me a hug if I fall down and skin my knee. He's a butler and this is what he's paid to do. Why not let him do it?"

I return to the table but there are no more books to shelve. Gripping the back of the chair, I toss the idea around in my mind. Is this my way of clinging to Hemlock Hollow? "Maybe you're right. This world is different. We don't have servants on the preservation." I grin. "Instead, people have children. We're the servants."

"Well, it's time to put down the broom and go to the ball, Cinderella," Korwin says.

"Who's Cinderella?"

His face falls.

"I'm kidding. Even I know that one."

He hooks his fingers into mine. "Speaking of Jameson, he's going to kill me if I don't get you to dinner on time. Come on."

I let him lead me from the library, my hand in his. I know I should fight it. Holding hands is a promise I'm not ready to keep. But I can't. I can't bring myself to let go.

Chapter 14

I wake in a cold sweat. It's pitch black and the pounding of my heart is audible in the stillness. Or maybe it's an internal noise punctuated by the thumping inside my chest. I'm in bed. A bed that is not my own. It's comfortable enough but has the muffled walls of a cellar. In Hemlock Hollow I fall asleep to the sounds of the night, the howl of the wind or the chirp of crickets under the moon. It's too quiet in this room and too loud inside me. Nightmares of giant rats and officers in green uniforms plague my dreams.

Surely my anxiety is due to the questions riddling me. Is Stuart Manor a safe house or a different kind of prison? Will I ever see Jeremiah or my father again? What will Maxwell expect from me tomorrow? When can I return to Hemlock Hollow?

There's a Bible verse in the book of Matthew that says, *Therefore do not worry about tomorrow, for tomorrow will worry about itself. Each day has enough trouble of its own.* I've heard Bishop Kauffman preach on it often enough. Dwelling on these thoughts isn't right or helpful, but casting them aside is nearly impossible.

I decide to take a walk to try to calm my nerves. The lights in the hallway are on. It's three a.m. I guess they never turn off. I wander toward the gym and beyond, with no particular goal but to wear myself out so that I can sleep. I end up lost in the maze of hallways, finally finding a landmark in the blue palomino painting. The door to my right is the healing chamber, and the staircase behind me leads to the main level of the house.

On my toes I jog up the stairs and cross the wood floors to the wall of windows at the rear of what Korwin calls "the great room." The night calls to me through the glass. Pale moonlight guides my way, and stars poke pinholes of light in the late summer sky. I need to be outside, to be under the same moon as my father, Jeremiah, and Hemlock Hollow.

I trace my fingers along the cool glass until I reach a pair of French doors and, after some experimentation, figure out how to unlock them. Stepping out into the warm night air, I jog across the enormous white deck to the railing. There is a stark drop and then miles of lawn blend into ever-thickening woods.

"Makes you want to run to the Outlands and never look back, doesn't it?"

Startled, I pivot toward the voice, gripping the rail of the deck to steady myself. Jameson sits in an Adirondack chair pressed against the side of the house, a place he'd be impossible to see through the windows. He swirls a glass of something brown and syrupy in his hand, the ice clinking with each rotation of his wrist. Striped pajamas hang off of him like loose skin. They age him. Or maybe it's the moonlight that gives his face the quality of parchment.

"Jameson. You scared me," I say, adding a breathy laugh. "I didn't see you there."

He lifts his drink to his lips and gulps. When he lowers it again, the ice clinks to the bottom and he sets the empty glass on the deck next to his chair. "Maybe, you *should* be scared."

What? "I think I have enough to be scared about already," I say. Why is he staring at me like that?

He stands and approaches me. "If it would make you take your security seriously, I could pretend to be a threat."

"Because I came outside? Is this not allowed?" Maxwell said we were on "lockdown" but what harm could come from being on the grounds in the middle of the night?

Jameson doesn't answer me. "Where did you come from, Lydia?" he asks.

I have no idea how much Jameson knows or understands about my plight. How much of my conversations with the Stuarts has he overheard or been told by the Stuarts? I decide right then I won't burden him with the details. "Willow's Province."

Jamison grunts. He steps closer, close enough that I can smell the alcohol on his breath. By the reek of it, I'd guess that wasn't his first drink. "Willow's Province, huh? They have good schools in Willow's Province?"

"No. The schools are horrible. The energy is inconsistent, as is the record-keeping." Even I know that. There's a reason we're told to say we are from Willow's Province. As an *Englisher,* he must know the answer. So, why is he asking? He's prying. I force my expression to remain impassive but inside I'm suspicious of his interest. I've already shared my secret with two *Englishers.* I'm not

141

willing to expose Hemlock Hollow any more than I already have.

He steps next to me and rests his hand on the railing. When he does, the sleeve of his pajamas stays crumpled at the elbow, exposing a bandage like the one Maxwell used on me when he took my blood. Jameson catches me staring and tugs his cuff into place. "You look just like her," he mumbles.

"Like who?" I ask. It's the second time he's mentioned it. "Who is this twin I have in Crater City?"

Jameson blinks rapidly and clears his throat. "Someone I used to know. A friend. You look incredibly similar. Of course, if she were alive today, she'd be my age."

"Do you have a picture?" I ask.

He shakes his head and steps in closer to me.

"It's interesting when people look alike. I've always been fascinated by twins and doppelgangers." My voice is abnormally high and my skin crawls with discomfort. What does he want from me?

"Likewise." He stares at me as if I will bloom an explanation. It's unnerving. I can feel him willing the truth from me.

I turn away and stare across the lawn.

"You shouldn't be out here," he says abruptly. "If someone sees you, it could cause hardship for Mr. Stuart."

I'm perplexed by the trace of venom I hear in his voice and turn my head to look at him again. His eyes are dark and intense. He's too close and I inch down the railing to avoid touching him. I glance down at my tangled fingers and remind myself that Jameson is an employee and I've

G. P. CHING

disturbed his personal time.

"Of course. I—I'm sorry. I'll go inside now." I step awkwardly around him and jog toward the door.

"Take care of yourself, Lydia from Willow's Province," he calls over his shoulder.

I close the French doors behind me, anxious to put distance between us.

* * * * *

Head swimming from my strange encounter with Jameson, I pass the blue palominos and pad down the hall, trying to find my way back to my room. I get lost again and wind up wandering aimlessly near the gardens. A door on my right catches my eye. Although it looks exactly the same as any other down here, I can't take my eyes off it. My heart aches to know what's in this room, and an invisible tug moves me to place my palm on the wood. It's warm beneath my touch. A hum reaches me through the barrier, a kind of music that eases my soul. I release a deep sigh.

The door opens. I lower my hand and tilt my chin up to Korwin's confused face. He's dressed in plaid cotton pants and a gray T-shirt. I pull my robe tighter around me, suddenly feeling naked again.

"I'm sorry," I say. "I can't sleep. I was trying to be quiet."

"I didn't hear you," Korwin says, raising an eyebrow. He rubs a circle over his heart and lifts one corner of his mouth. "I felt you. Here."

Blink. Blink. I swallow. I know what he means but I

can't say it. There's something wrong about the connection I feel to Korwin. I hardly know him. "Um, I guess I should try to go to bed now," I say, but I can't move.

Korwin seems just as riveted. "Would you like to come in? For a few minutes? Until you can fall asleep?"

All I can do is nod. He backs into his room and I follow. The bed is plain, with a gray wool cover that reminds me of home.

He crawls in, pats the opposite side. "Keep your robe on—I mean, if it makes you more comfortable."

I lie down next to him, stretched out on my side so that we are face to face. He reaches over and strokes my hair. It's not until he pulls his hand back that I even consider that the touch might be presumptuous.

"I keep having these dreams that officers in green uniforms are chasing me with those...weapons," I whisper.

"You mean, the scramblers?"

"Is that what they're called? I knew they weren't guns."

"Your subconscious must know that they are nightmare material. Scramblers were invented to stun human criminals by pumping voltage through their nervous systems. Believe it or not, scramblers are more dangerous to us than guns. When we're fired up, our energy will absorb a bullet, but the technology behind the scrambler interrupts the transmission of electricity between our cells. They're as incapacitating to us as they are to humans."

"Avoid scramblers," I say to myself. My eyelids grow heavy, and I allow them to close. Despite the talk of guns and scramblers, I feel safe here next to Korwin. As safe as if I were home. "We don't have weapons like that at home. I miss it so much. You would like it there, Korwin. There's no fighting. No officers." A tear escapes the corner of my eye, and I feel Korwin cup my cheek and wipe it away with his thumb

"No wonder you want to go home so badly. It sounds... too good to be true."

"But it's not." I nuzzle his hand.

"Lydia?"

"Mm-hmm?" The question wakes me from my almost sleep. His eyes are wide. The heat from his palm seems to travel through me like a gathering storm. He runs his thumb across my bottom lip and the ribbons of electricity return, as does the faint blue glow. Just like at the bottom of the stairs, when I thought he might kiss me, blue sparks ignite at our touch.

"We're glowing," I say.

"Yeah."

"Has that ever happened to you before?"

"No."

"Me neither."

He clears his throat. "Lydia, you know the day you saved me from CGEF?"

"How could I forget?"

"There's something I want you to know." His eyes drift away from me and his brows knit. "I'd given up. I'd reached a point...I was as good as dead. When you walked through the door, I thought you were either a hallucination or death coming for me."

"Honestly, I was afraid you might die," I say. "You looked so sick. But I couldn't leave you there."

"You took care of me that day. I'll never forget what you did."

"Any decent human being would have done the same."

"After weeks inside that cell, I can tell you there aren't many decent human beings in this world."

I cover his hand with my own, holding it against my cheek. "I'm sorry."

"You're the only one who doesn't need to be. You know what's funny? Before I met you, I thought Amish women were historically timid."

"Well, we are supposed to be plain and modest. I try to be, but to live like we live, you've got to be brave."

Stroking my face one last time, he retracts his fingers and lowers them to the bed. The glow from our contact gradually fades. "This one time, let me be brave for you. Close your eyes. I'll watch over you while you sleep."

My lids flutter closed again and I slip off, feeling completely at ease for the first time since coming to the English world.

Chapter 15

Singing birds and a brightening light usher me into consciousness. Of course, it isn't the sunrise or actual chirping. Both are artificial. Korwin has the same fake window as I have in my room, complete with computer-generated butterfly.

He sleeps like an angel next to me, his olive skin a tempting contrast against his white pillow. Full lips part slightly, and a strand of his black hair sweeps across his forehead. Everything about him is peaceful. For a moment, I just lie there, smiling for no good reason whatsoever. But then, like a slow leak, my joy drains from me, and reality seizes me by the throat. I am in bed with a boy I hardly know. What would my father say?

I creep from the bed, careful not to disturb Korwin, and slip into the hall. Halfway to my room, a sharp tug at my ribs pitches me forward onto my toes. My distance from Korwin. I've broken some unseen physical boundary, torn myself from the force of gravity surrounding his person. I rub circles over the sharp pang beneath my sternum but can't dull the ache.

Convinced I can wash this feeling away or at least suppress it, I strip down when I reach my room and start a shower. Under the warm spray, I have time and quiet to think about my actions. I've spent the night with Korwin.

Nothing happened, of course. Still, my brain pummels me with excuses for my misaligned guilt. In Hemlock Hollow there is a tradition called bundling, where courting couples spend the night together in the same bed. Parents bundle the girl in blankets or hang a sheet between the two. It's a way of showing they trust the boy and also a rite of passage. One more stop on the journey to Amish marriage.

I compare what happened with Korwin to bundling and try not to think about the fact that we aren't courting and my father isn't here to approve. I'm in the English world, after all, and this behavior might be commonplace. Only I don't think it is, even here. Desperate for self-forgiveness, I tell myself that my actions are due to my new abilities. My blood is different, my cells are different, and I've just met the only other person in the world with the same condition. However it came to be, Korwin and I share something unique.

This last excuse sticks. I forgive myself for spending the night with Korwin. After all, I have more than enough to feel guilty about. I've participated in injuring a slew of people. Yes, it was in self-defense, but in the Amish world, violence is never the answer and self-sacrifice is not only encouraged but demanded. Then there's Jeremiah. Technically we aren't courting yet, but that doesn't mean promises weren't made. He'd promised to court me, and I hadn't given him any reason to doubt that I'd accept. From the time we could walk, we've done everything together. Everyone in Hemlock Hollow expects us to marry.

But never, not in all the times I've stretched out in the

hay next to Jeremiah, have I felt the kind of attraction I feel for Korwin. I'm not sure it's solely because I'm a Spark. Maybe, like the lightning, my cells are drawn to Korwin's in some scientifically explainable way. Maybe Maxwell can make me understand with a series of charts and graphs.

Here's what I can't deny. If God gave me this power—made me a Spark—for the purpose of saving Korwin and myself, then he also gave me this attraction to Korwin. And if he did, this is more than a human connection. Who am I to deny fate?

All this thinking doesn't give me any answers. Not how to get home or what Korwin will do when it's time for me to leave. It doesn't answer what to do about my father or Jeremiah. I finish showering, resolved to face the future as it comes.

From the closet, I select a pair of jeans and a long-sleeved black shirt with a clever design I've never seen. My thumbs fit through holes in the cuffs and the neck is cut at an angle to reveal one shoulder. I apply some makeup from the basket on the counter, imitating the picture on the kit, and brush out my hair until it falls in waves down my back. The person in the mirror is not Lydia Troyer but an *Englisher* named Lydia Lane. For now, that's how it has to be.

A knock startles me. I don't have to open the door to know who it is. I rub my chest, noting the way my heart pounds, as if it has just noticed there's blood in my veins.

"Korwin." I open the door. The connection snaps into place. "Good morning."

His mouth drops open, his eyes searching my face. "Good morning."

Whoa. His stare is intense. I lower my eyes.

He rubs his chest in the same spot I did. "I felt you leave and now…do you feel this?"

"Yes." My cheeks warm as I say the word. I'm flustered by the intimacy between us. "It's getting stronger. I felt it the first day, after seeing you in the healer and last night. Every time I see you it's stronger."

"What do you think it is?"

As if I would understand it. As if I was the one who grew up with a science lab in my house rather than milking cows and baking bread. "I don't know."

We stand in the doorway, staring at each other until the silence becomes awkward.

He shrugs and smiles weakly. "Well, maybe there will be some answers at breakfast." He holds out his hand to me.

I lace my fingers into his, and we walk to the stairway. He stops me at the landing, the same place where we almost kissed my first night here. "By the way, you are… beautiful, really beautiful."

I play with the hem of the black shirt. "Thanks. I'm still getting used to your manner of dress."

He sighed. "I wasn't talking about your outfit."

I smile. "Thank you, Korwin. I find you… where I'm from, we would say handsome. What's the word here for an attractive man?"

He laughs. "Scorching hottie."

I lift an eyebrow. "Really? Then I guess you are a

scorching hottie."

"I'm kidding, Lydia. We say handsome too."

"I'm sticking with hottie." I grin. "Thanks for helping me last night."

"Any time."

We climb to the top of the stairs and enter the dining room, hand in hand. I stop short when I see who is sitting at the table.

"Well, it's good to see you're okay after all." Jeremiah's somber face stares at our coupled hands.

"Jeremiah," I gasp. I drop Korwin's hand and spring around the table. His stony expression warms as I approach and by the time I reach him, he's out of his chair and receiving my hug.

"How? How did you get here?" I grip his shoulders to make sure he's real.

"Maxwell Stuart sent for me," Jeremiah hisses. There's nothing happy about his tone. He looks terrible. His blond hair is matted and there are dark circles under his eyes. But worse, his disposition, usually bright and sunny, feels like a gray cloud in my arms.

Maxwell clears his throat. He's sitting at the head of the table. I'd walked right by him to get to Jeremiah and hadn't noticed. "May I suggest we eat before the crepes get cold? I'll explain everything."

I frown, not knowing what to make of this turn of events. But Jeremiah definitely needs to eat. He looks worn and thin. I give a curt nod.

Jameson pulls out the chair next to Jeremiah for me. As he begins doling out breakfast, I remember our odd conversation from the night before. The butler doesn't make eye contact even though I make a point of staring in his direction. Korwin seats himself across the table from me.

Jeremiah's hand finds mine under the table, and he rests our threaded fingers on his thigh. "Lydia, there've been officers at the house since they took you. Your face is all over the television. They're calling you a fugitive and a scamper. What is going on?"

I open my mouth to answer, but I don't get a chance.

"Jeremiah, I know this must be confusing for you," Maxwell says.

"Confusing?" Jeremiah says angrily. "That's not the word I might have chosen."

"I'm sorry I had to take you the way that I did, but there was no other way of getting you out of there. The house is under constant surveillance."

"How did you get him?" I ask.

"They came into my room this morning before sunrise, put duct tape over my mouth and a bag over my head. That's how." Jeremiah drops his fork and squeezes my hand beneath the table.

"How awful!" I eye Maxwell incredulously.

"I can explain—" Maxwell starts but Jeremiah speaks over him.

"I didn't know what was going on. They dragged me through an underground passageway." If his cornflower blue eyes had their way, Maxwell would be dead, struck down by the daggers in them. I've never seen Jeremiah so upset.

Maxwell takes a deep breath and blows it out. "You said you were concerned for Jeremiah's safety. I promised to help you with that. This was the only way we could get him out of there alive." He removes his glasses and returns my scathing look with a point of his finger. "If we didn't take him, someone else would have, Lydia. They would use him to get to you. We couldn't have that."

"What about Caleb and Hannah?" I ask.

"Those two can take care of themselves."

"Meaning?"

"Hannah and Caleb work for me."

Korwin's head snaps toward me and his eyebrows sink over his nose. "Fifty-four Lakehurst... You were staying with Caleb Hunter?"

"Yes, why?"

"That's how we were able to get to Jeremiah. There's a tunnel to the house."

Jeremiah exchanges glances with me, but I can't offer an explanation. I shake my head. I'm as confused as he is.

"Stop, Dad. She doesn't need to know this." Korwin seems angry. "Why did you bring him here?"

But Maxwell ignores his son and looks directly at me. "Caleb and Hannah are scampers. They keep their energy usage below normal and their house full of renters like you. Increases their units. We skim the difference off the top, sell it on the black market, and pay them ten percent. That's how they support themselves."

"But it's illegal," I say.

A flash of disbelief wrinkles his face, and he stares down his nose at me, as if my concern for the illegality of the matter is a sign of my ignorance.

Korwin's fingers are splayed on either side of his plate. No one is eating.

"How much have you told Lydia about our mission?" Maxwell asks Korwin.

He answers through his teeth. "Nothing. She doesn't need to know."

"Of course she needs to know. She's a part of this now." Maxwell's eyes bore into me.

Korwin's expression hardens. "She doesn't have to be."

Crossing my arms, I glare at him. "What's he talking about?"

He shakes his head and turns away.

I look back at Maxwell. "What exactly is your mission?"

"To overthrow the Green Republic," he tells me. "To take back the government by force."

Everything stops. My mouth drops open. I can't organize my scattered thoughts long enough to form words. Next to me, Jeremiah takes a deep breath and runs a hand through his mess of blond curls.

Korwin is around the table in a heartbeat and tugging on his father's bicep. "I need to speak to you. Now!"

Chapter 16

Korwin's voice ebbs and flows like a wave, as if he's trying to whisper but the volume keeps getting away from him. I can't hear every word from the dining room where Jeremiah and I wait, but the wood floors and high ceilings do a good job of carrying the general tone of the argument from the kitchen.

"... think you're doing? ...Classified...no choice..." Korwin's smooth voice cuts in and out.

"...Greens will never let her go. Impossible," Maxwell answers.

"You promised..."

"...only way."

"...pacifists...deadly game... Almost killed me!"

"Too late. Can't risk...only way."

I train my ear toward the kitchen but the voices have quieted again. Jeremiah nudges me under the table. "Let me do the talking when they come back," he says.

"What? Why?"

He raises his eyebrows at me as if the answer is obvious. Of course, it's obvious. He's a boy and thinks he's more capable than me. But he doesn't know. He doesn't know what I can do, what I have done.

"No, Jeremiah, listen—"

I'm interrupted as Korwin and Maxwell plod back into the dining room. Neither looks happy.

"I've promised to help you get home, Lydia, and I plan to keep that promise," Maxwell begins. His eyes flash to Korwin's. "But the question is timing."

"We need to go back now," Jeremiah says. Korwin nods.

"It can't happen. It won't happen. You don't understand the stakes." Maxwell straightens his glasses and buries his hands in the pockets of his shawl-collared cardigan. The man looks like a schoolteacher, not the leader of a revolution.

"Then make me understand," Jeremiah says.

At home in Hemlock Hollow, we go to school until eighth grade in a one-room schoolhouse. The older kids help the younger kids. We learn math and how to read and write. We also learn about the English world, especially how it relates to our community's history and our needs. Even before Maxwell tells us about the Great Rebellion and the history of the Green Republic, I am aware of most of it.

The pollution that brought about the rebellion reached us too. But the Amish community accepted the resulting hardships with passive rebellion. We didn't try to fight the outside world, except to promote our own independence. The Green Republic claimed to clean up the environment, a change that would have benefited the Amish as well as the *Englishers*. But the war itself took a horrific toll and did nothing to curb the *Englishers'* energy addiction. Maxwell claims there could be enough power and food for everyone, but that the Greens use political influence to maintain control of the masses. "The rich stay rich and the poor stay poor."

I shake my head. For the Amish, this history lesson is a warning to keep our focus on God and on simplicity. Our way of life is to stay separate. It's why we don't use electricity, because then we'd be dependent on a sinful world. We've been living more or less the same way since our ancestors arrived during the early eighteenth century in what was then called North America. It's not my place to tell Maxwell what to do, but war is never the answer. The look in Jeremiah's eyes says it all. This is not our fight. We are visitors here, nothing more.

"Max, er, Mr. Stuart," I say. "Jeremiah and I can't become involved. It's against the law of our community."

Jeremiah nods and nudges me under the table again. "We don't believe in using violence to settle our differences."

"What about how they treated you? What about what they did to you and Korwin?" Maxwell asks.

I can't meet his eyes. Instead, I look to Jeremiah for support.

"What did they do to you?" Jeremiah asks me under his breath.

"They tortured her," Maxwell chimes in. "The Green Republic is corrupt to its core."

"I'm sorry. But we can't help you," Jeremiah states firmly.

But Maxwell doesn't quit. "I don't think you're grasping how bad things are here. Imagine your factory makes shoes and your competitor is favored by the Green Republic because he lobbies his customers to support Green Republic programs—like the recent one that established random home inspections. Pretty soon, you notice that your competitor is making twice as many shoes as you. And you realize that it's because he can run his factory for ten hours instead of eight. Your business fails, and they have the nerve to tell you it's because of poor business practices when you know, without a doubt, the chips were stacked in your competitor's favor. But if you complain, well, then your house is selected for a random inspection—and what do you know, they find you've been scamping energy. You're never heard from again."

"How can they do that?" Jeremiah asks. "Wouldn't people eventually figure it out?"

Maxwell spreads his hands. "Yes! We've figured it out. We've formed our own rebellion, the Liberty Party. Across the continent, we have houses scamping energy, draining the grid."

"Why would you do that?" Jeremiah asks. "Isn't scamping like stealing? Wouldn't it make it worse for everyone? Less to go around and tighter security?"

Maxwell holds up one hand. "We've been rerouting energy for years, evening the score. Who do you think we give it to? The wealthy? No. We use it to help the poor. And now we have as many supporters as they do. We could free the continent from energy tyranny. If Lydia joins forces with us, we'll be unstoppable."

Across from me, Korwin leans against the wall, distant and statuesque. The revelation that his father expects me to join the Liberty Party seems to eat at him.

Jeremiah locks eyes with me; their intensity speaks volumes.

"Mr. Stuart," I say, "I can appreciate your cause, but Jeremiah and I have to return to the preservation. We never intended to get involved."

Maxwell braces his long fingers on the table in front of me, two brown spider-hands that flex against his weight. He lowers his face to be level with mine. The action is quiet but somehow threatening. "Sorry, kid, but it's too late. You're as involved as a person can be, and unfortunately, there's no going back." He pushes off the table and taps the canvas painting on the wall.

Alexandra Brighten's face smiles at me. A sign above her head reads WJDC News. *This just in. Progress in the CGEF terrorism case we reported yesterday. Authorities believe sympathizers of the terrorists are hiding in Willow's Province after a sting operation uncovered their plan to bomb the energy facility.*

A photo of fifty-four Lakehurst Drive plasters the screen. Hannah's, Caleb's, and Jeremiah's faces pop up in the corner. *Whoa!* Jeremiah really is involved. "How did they get your picture?" I ask.

"I don't know." Jeremiah pales, eyes fixated on the screen.

I rest my forehead against my coupled hands, consumed with guilt. Maxwell is right. Jeremiah is involved because of me.

Troops will occupy Willow's Province until these criminals are found. The investigation continues into the histories of the two terrorists still on the run.

As a clip of Korwin blasting the CGEF officers repeats in the background, close-ups of all five of our faces display under the action.

CGEF would like to remind everyone that a ten thousand-unit reward is available to anyone providing information that leads to the arrest of these fugitives. Call the number on your screen to report any information about these two or their three accomplices."

The screen goes black. I continue to stare at it. This can't be happening. I exchange glances with Jeremiah. "I'm so sorry."

He says nothing. I think he's in shock.

"Ten thousand units. That's a fortune," Korwin says softly. "Now everyone on the continent will be looking for us. Green Republic sympathizers will want to report us for the reward. We can't get you home because Willow's Province will be crawling with troops and bounty hunters."

A tide of panic rises within me. "My father!" I say. "How do I keep him safe? He's in a hospital, here in the English world."

I see Jeremiah's eye twitch and then he seems to come back from somewhere far away. "No one knows you're related. He has fake identification, remember?"

After a beat when I realize he's right, I take a different angle. "But he must be terrified for me. If he's seeing this on television or reading it in the paper, he's probably beside himself."

Maxwell leans across the table and places his hand on

top of mine. "I can help you, Lydia. If you do what we need you to do, if you train and get stronger, you can help us overtake the Greens, and then I can get you home. No strings attached."

I cross my arms over my chest and sit back in my chair. Maxwell shifts his gaze to Korwin's closed expression, and then to Jeremiah, who looks more confused than ever.

"Jeremiah, you're part of this too," Maxwell says. "We need to test your blood to see if you have the same condition as Lydia."

"What condition is that?" Jeremiah narrows his eyes and curls his lip. He doesn't know the truth. He still thinks this is all some kind of horrible mistake—which it is, but not in the way he assumes.

"Show him," Maxwell says.

I face Jeremiah, who looks nothing but concerned for me. Suddenly, I'm ashamed to be what I am, as if I'm about to show him a rotting, leprosy-laden limb. Opening my hand, I concentrate on the glow that sleeps somewhere inside, that tiny tickle at the back of my brain. I manage to cause electric blue ribbons to flash beneath the skin of my palm. It's enough to make Jeremiah scoot away from me, his chair legs scraping the wood floor. The way he looks at me... it's like I'm a demon, the devil himself. He's repulsed.

"I'm a Spark, Jeremiah." My voice cracks and my eyes sting. "They call it electrokinesis. We think I developed it from the radiation from the Outlands, which means you might have it too."

He shivers and bites his lip. As long as I've known

Jeremiah, he's always had a smile for me, even if it was only in his eyes. Not now. I've never seen him look this way, like every ounce of sunshine has been squeezed from his soul.

"We need both of you," Maxwell says. "Will you agree to help us in exchange for our help getting you home?"

I fold my hands in my lap and wait for Jeremiah to say something. Will he completely reject me because I'm a Spark? Demand to leave immediately and not take me with him?

"We'll do it. We'll join the resistance," Jeremiah says slowly, out of the blue.

What? We'll do it? I jerk backward. Where did that come from? My guilt at dragging him into this mess transforms into anger at his presumptuousness. How dare he answer for me after reacting like I'm some sort of freak?

Jeremiah pins me with a paternalistic glare and like a trained animal I find myself unable to speak. But I don't look away as I should. Instead, I meet his gaze with fiery aplomb. Surprised, he turns away first.

"And then we'll go home," Jeremiah says. "In return, you promise to get us there."

The sigh Maxwell releases sounds like a cheer.

Of course, Jeremiah is right. We don't have any other choice. My anger ebbs. He's just taking care of me, like always. I blink in Jeremiah's direction and answer without looking at Maxwell. "I agree with Jeremiah. We'll stay. We'll help. Then we'll go."

Maxwell claps his hands together. "Alleluia!" he says. "It's a deal. We'll start training today."

Behind me, Korwin punches the wall and knocks into a chair in his haste to leave the room. He's gone before I have time to say a word.

Chapter 17

"I need to speak with you privately," Jeremiah says. He hooks his index finger into my pinkie.

"Later." I yank my hand away. "Let's get this over with first." I've never talked to him like that before. How this world has changed me.

He scowls. "What's wrong with you?"

"You shouldn't have decided without checking with me first. You committed both of us."

Jeremiah looks totally confused. "What choice did I have?"

"We," I whisper. "What choice did *we* have? It was *our* decision, not yours."

He frowns at me like I'm not making any sense.

Maxwell leads us to the basement. I search the hall for Korwin but he's disappeared; I assume he's somewhere recuperating from the revelations of this morning. I don't blame him. I wish I could go to bed and sleep for a week.

"I want both of you to know, you're safe here. The mansion is a bunker," Maxwell says. "From the outside, the house looks like a typical Tudor, but inside, everything is reinforced. The glass is bulletproof. Steel shutters slide into place at the touch of a button. In the case of an emergency, the basement entryway to the compound can be sealed and appear as a solid wall. If we ever need to evacuate, there are multiple routes out of the mansion through the sewer."

"Why didn't Korwin bring me in that way when we escaped CGEF?" I ask.

"There is a Bio-Tech membrane that only goes one way. You can leave the mansion through the sewer but to get back in, you need a biological key. Even Korwin doesn't have it."

I don't understand what a biological key is, but it seems strange Maxwell wouldn't give it to his own son. "Why doesn't Korwin have a key to his own house?"

"He used to, but when he was captured by the Greens it was too dangerous. We had to change the locks. Protocol."

"Why is all this necessary, anyway?" Jeremiah asks.

Maxwell smiles. "Most directly because of the data. Stuart Manor is the intelligence hub of the Liberty Party. Not to mention Korwin. Seventeen years of unique research on the only electrokinetic human ever studied is here. It can't ever fall into enemy hands."

Maxwell's words nag at me like a splinter in my skin. "Until now. I will add to that data."

"Yes. We will find out how alike or different you are to Korwin. And your results will become part of history."

And just like that, I understand why the way Maxwell talks about Korwin affects me. He talks about both of us as if we are prized animals. Trick ponies. Maxwell talks about his own son like some kind of secret weapon. Not as a human being. Not as a child of God.

"We'll test you first, Lydia, and then I'll take

Jeremiah's blood."

I nod. I will do what he wants, but I don't fully trust Maxwell. Who could trust someone who talks about their son in terms of years of data?

He ushers me into a large open room with padded gray walls labeled Test Room A. Maxwell and Jeremiah appear a moment later on the other side of a thick observation panel. I'm surprised when Korwin enters the room behind me.

Our eyes meet. "You're back."

"I need to show you what to do." He doesn't explain where he's been or why, but he gives me a reassuring smile that relieves some of my mounting anxiety.

Jeremiah's face twists into a grimace behind the window. I'm not sure why he's so upset. I think he's worried for me and probably still trying to digest the news that I'm a Spark and he could be too.

On the table in front of us are metal bins. One is filled with lightbulbs, the other blocks of fresh cut wood.

"Shall we start with the LEDs?" Korwin asks the window.

"Please proceed." Maxwell's voice comes from a speaker above me, even though he's standing in front of me. It has a muffled quality like he's talking through a wall.

Korwin picks up one of the bulbs, flips it in the air, and catches the base in one hand. He raises an eyebrow at me and without breaking eye contact, the bulb slowly glows to life. The corner of his mouth turns up, and it's as if it's me he's lighting up. A swell of joy rises from deep within me. I can't help myself. I giggle and glance away.

"Now you try," he says, handing me the bulb.

I wrap my fingers around the base and repeat what I've done before. I concentrate on a tickle deep within my head and move it down my arm to my hand. The best comparison I can make is to say it's like stretching a piece of elastic or taffy from my head to my fingertips. I stretch the power into the waiting bulb. The clear bubble of glass glows ever brighter. After a moment of pride, my push turns into a pull. It's easier than I expected to let the elastic out. It feels good, almost a relief. But I know it's too much. I try to retract the energy, grunting with the effort, but it doesn't help. I can't control it.

The bulb shatters, spraying glass across the room. Korwin turns his back to shield his face.

"Are you both okay?" Maxwell's muffled voice calls over the speaker.

Korwin scans me from head to toe while he brushes his hands over his hair, his T-shirt. "You get cut?"

"I'm okay." I glance down my body. Incredibly, the bits of glass missed me.

Jeremiah's worried expression appears behind the thick pane of glass. I can see his lips moving but can't hear what he's saying to Maxwell. A moment later, the little door at the back of the room opens. Without even looking at Korwin, Jeremiah hands me a pair of protective glasses. He hugs me and whispers in my ear, "You don't have to do this."

"I don't mind," I say. "I'm okay. I want to know what I can do."

"She's a Spark. When she uses her power, it produces an electromagnetic field that protects her. The glass can't hurt her," Korwin states smugly. I give him a harsh look and he makes himself busy straightening the equipment.

"Thank you," I say to Jeremiah, holding up the glasses.

Jeremiah backs out of the door and returns to his spot behind Maxwell, who is writing feverishly. I place the goggles over my eyes. Curious, I pick up another lightbulb without being asked. This time I barely stretch the elastic to my fingers when the pull threatens to take control. This time, instead of attempting to reel it back inside, I simply picture a knot forming at my wrist. I mentally tie off my power. The bulb glows, gently pulsing while I adjust the flow from that place in my brain. Eventually, I smile at the constant light. I've done it! I ignore the drip of sweat that starts at my temple and works toward my chin.

"That's awesome, Lydia! Great control. It took me weeks to learn to hold back like that," Korwin says.

"It's harder to keep it inside than to let it loose," I whimper. I drop the bulb onto the table and let out a huge puff of air.

Korwin scoops me up in a hug that takes my breath away. He twirls me around in a circle, laughing, before placing me gently back on my feet.

"Good job, Lydia." Behind the window Maxwell scratches some notes on his pad, smiling like a child with a new toy. "Let's try something else."

Rolling my shoulders, I stretch my neck and back. My muscles ache with fatigue. My skin is too tight, and I scratch the backs of my arms until the itch goes away.

In the bin next to the lightbulbs, fat wooden logs like we use in our fireplace back home are stacked in a pyramid shape. The green ring under the bark tells me they're freshly cut.

"What do I do with the wood?" I ask.

Korwin answers. "The wood is to test if you can throw the juice. Observe." He pulls a log from the stack and places it on an unused section of the steel table. "You may want to stand back."

I recede a few steps from the table.

He takes a deep breath and blows it out. Circling his arm, he flicks his fingers like he's tossing a ball and a blast of electricity leaves his hand and plows into the log. A cloud of steam rises up. When it clears, the log looks dried out, ready to burn.

"Take a new one. This one will start on fire," Korwin says, as he removes the used log.

I do as he says, setting a new green log in the same place as Korwin did.

"Blast it, Lydia. Let it out fast and then pull it back in, but don't actually touch the log."

"I'll try." Taking a deep breath, I stretch the elastic tingle to my hands again, but it's a much different thing to move the power from my fingers to the wood without physically touching it. I try a few times to let it out, but fail. It feels like I'm forcing the cord into something thick and dense. The stretch stops before I can reach the log. I mop my forehead with the back of my hand.

"It's okay," Korwin says. "This is hard. Remember when I broke the glass at CGEF? And just now, how I threw it forward?"

I do remember—he'd tossed his hand toward the log. The way he moved wasn't just mental. It was physical. In the book I'd read, it said air was a poor conductor of electricity. I needed to communicate with the wood, which meant leaping over the uncooperative air.

Instead of a ball, I picture a yo-yo in my hand because a yo-yo comes back. I center myself, concentrating on the wood. Stepping forward quickly, I swing my hand, directing all my momentum on the invisible yo-yo. The elastic stretches and catches on the wood. But it doesn't come back to me as I planned. More and more moves out. *Ahh.* I let it go. I don't even attempt to tie it off. It unravels from my body into the wood faster than fishing line, out and out and out.

BOOM! The explosion sends splinters to every corner of the room. The force blows me back into the padded wall. Before I can process what's happened, I'm flat on my back, staring at the fluorescent lights in the ceiling.

Korwin is the first to reach me. He crawls to me from the place he was thrown and shakes my shoulder. "Did you break anything?" he asks, laughing. He seems to know I didn't.

Out of nowhere, a hand shoots between us and grips Korwin's shoulder, yanking him back. Jeremiah's deeply worried face comes into view. "Lydia? Lydia, speak to me."

Maxwell is the next on the scene. He beams down at me with a smile that goes all the way to his eyes. "Are you injured?" he asks, but I can tell he's sure I'm not. His tone is how a parent might talk to a child who's fallen down and is about to cry. His tone is both reassuring and slightly condescending.

I move my arms and legs experimentally and then sit up, adjusting my neck. When everything works, I fold my feet underneath me and stand. "I'm a little sore but I'm okay."

Jeremiah lets out a deep sigh of relief.

"I know it looks bad, Jeremiah, but she can take it," Korwin says.

"You don't know that." Jeremiah pokes a finger toward his face. "Your father said he doesn't know if Lydia is the same as you. If you're not the same, then you don't know for sure that this won't hurt her."

"It's okay, Jeremiah," I say. "I'm okay. He's right. Not even a bump on the head."

"But you said you were sore." Jeremiah rubs my shoulders.

I wrap his hands inside my own. "I am, but on the inside. Like when you run farther than you're used to and your muscles hurt. On the outside, I'm fine."

"I don't like this."

"I know."

Maxwell clears his throat. "That's enough for today. I don't want to wear you out."

"Yeah, maybe you should spend a few minutes in the healer," Korwin chimes in, "just to aid your recovery."

I shake my head and follow him out the door. "I think I just want to rest."

"Of course, Lydia. We'll try again tomorrow. I'm very pleased. Very pleased." Maxwell jots more notes in his notebook, then turns toward Korwin. "Can you escort Jeremiah to the examination room in ten minutes?"

"Sure," Korwin says. "I'll show Lydia back to her room and then bring him down."

Jeremiah frowns but gives a reluctant nod.

Maxwell wanders off, his nose buried in his notes.

I follow Korwin back to my room, shoulder to shoulder with Jeremiah, who walks abnormally close. Too close. I let it go because I know today has been hard on him.

"Your father seems happy about how I did," I say to Korwin.

"Um, yeah. You're really strong. In order to make the log explode, you had to heat it to over sixty thousand degrees Fahrenheit. That's hotter than the surface of the sun."

I laugh. "That can't be right."

"You brought the beads of sap to a boil so fast that it forced the wood molecules apart. All in under a second." He stops in the doorway to my room.

Even with Jeremiah standing right next to me, the connection when Korwin's hazel eyes meet mine is something palpable and powerful. I don't want to feel it, not with Jeremiah right beside me. But it isn't a decision. It just is. An internal shiver runs the length of my body.

"I don't have your control," I say, stepping slightly behind the doorjamb.

"It took me a month of daily practice to be able to master the skill. I'd say you did pretty well for day one." He's distracted, as absorbed in our connection as I am.

Jeremiah clears his throat, and I nod in such a way as to break eye contact. "Thank you, Korwin. I think I need to rest now."

"Okay. Jeremiah, are you ready to go?" Korwin asks.

"No," I say too fast. "I need to speak with him." I squeeze my eyes shut. "Plus, the examination room is just down the hall, and we have a few minutes. Can you come back for him?"

Korwin sighs. "Sure. I'll, uh, see you later." He doesn't leave. He stands there, eyeing Jeremiah and me long enough for the moment to feel awkward.

I understand why he's struggling. This thing between us tugs at my ribcage. I force myself to look away and walk inside the room, pulling Jeremiah in behind me.

Not until I close the door do I feel Korwin turn to leave.

"What was that about?" Jeremiah asks.

"It's hard to explain," I say, crawling into bed. "Whatever causes this electrokinesis also makes me…"

"Makes you what?"

"It's like I'm … connected to him or something," I say honestly. Tears gather in the corner of my eyes. I'm so overwhelmed. It feels like I'm being torn in two.

Jeremiah reaches forward and wipes a tear from the corner of my eye. "Don't cry. Everything that's happened is really confusing. This disease—"

"It's not a disease, Jeremiah. It's me. The electrokinesis is in my cells." The words come out slurred. My limbs are half-ton concrete blocks. Without even bothering to take off my shoes, I bury my head in my pillow and close my eyes.

Jeremiah pulls the comforter over me and tucks me in. "Don't worry, Lydia. You can tell me all about it when you wake up. Besides, I have a blood test to take. Maybe I'll understand firsthand."

I want to stay awake, to tell him the truth about how confused I am about these feelings I'm having for Korwin. I want everything out in the open. But I'm so tired.

His fingers lace into mine. "Just rest. I'll be here when you wake up."

Chapter 18

I rouse in the way you do when you know you've overslept—with a start. My fingers are still laced into Jeremiah's but he's attached to my opposite hand. A bandage on his left arm tells me he's kept his appointment with Maxwell. He's asleep, his head and shoulders hunched next to me while the rest of him sits in a chair near the bed. Poor Jeremiah. I wonder how long he's been in the awkward position. Carefully, I pull my hand from his.

It's midnight. I've slept for almost eight hours. I'm wide awake and ravenously hungry. Climbing from the bed, I wrap my arm around Jeremiah's shoulders and coax the covers back from under his head.

"Into bed, sleepy head," I whisper into his ear.

He doesn't fight me. Rolling out of the chair, he stretches out, his wavy blond halo finding the pillow. As I tuck the comforter around his body, I know for sure he's returned to peaceful slumber. For a moment or two, I watch the rise and fall of his chest in the silence of the room.

All I can think is that he is the embodiment of everything good in the world, everything pure and right and loyal. I love him with an old love. A love that comes from knowing someone before you understand why boys and girls kiss or get married. What a fool I've been. I can't explain this new attraction to Korwin, but surely I should ignore it. He won't be coming home with me. Jeremiah will. Jeremiah is my true future.

Unexpectedly, a heavy weight settles over my chest at the thought. I need to walk. I need to think.

I slip out the door and into the maze of hallways. The tile is cool under my bare feet. Jeremiah must have removed my shoes while I slept, but I'm still wearing the black shirt and jeans from yesterday. I'm glad he didn't try to completely undress me.

Last night, I ended up in Korwin's room. I turn in the opposite direction, not wanting a repeat of that confusing experience. I must be getting better at navigating the compound because I find the gardens without any trouble. Days ago, when I was here with Korwin, ultraviolet panels lit the room to imitate the sun. Now the gardens are dark, simulated stars scattered across the black ceiling. I can see enough though. Along the path near my feet, small square lights bathe the shrubbery and flower blossoms in a subtle glow. The heady smell of roses mixes with the tang of juniper trees. I can almost forget that I'm underground.

I find the labyrinth of hedges Korwin showed me and get lost in the twists and turns. My mind wanders, and a welcome numbness enfolds me. The patter of running water in the distance keeps me moving forward, and the brightly colored flowers, delicately opening in the darkness, enthrall me. The roses don't care if anyone enjoys their beauty; they simply are beautiful. They are beautiful for themselves, because of what they are. No one made them that way, and they are not dependent on any outsider's affirmation. How would it be to have such self-confidence?

Distracted, I find myself in the center of the garden, the marble fountain of the woman glowing on her pedestal. As I approach it slowly, I take it in again. Carved from white marble, she's dressed in a Greek toga and lifting the lid off a curved jar. Water and light flow out and tumble into the pool at her feet. I've never seen anything like it. She glows like an angel.

"It's Pandora." Korwin's voice makes me jump. I turn to see him standing in the shadows, next to the hedges. "Do you know the story of Pandora?"

"Oh, hi. I didn't think anyone would be up," I blurt, noticing he's wearing nothing but a pair of gray cotton shorts. I divert my eyes to the fountain in an effort to avoid the smooth skin of his chest. "I didn't wake you, did I?"

"No, I couldn't sleep. I like to come here when I can't. The sound of the water is soothing."

"Oh." My cheeks burn and I hope he can't see my blush in the poor light. "Um, Pandora, I know she's Greek, but I don't know her story. We don't learn much about art or mythology in Amish school."

Korwin steps into the light of the fountain. His olive skin gives off its own blue light as he draws nearer. "It's back," he says, holding out one glowing limb.

Extending my hands, I see they have the same blue aura as Korwin's. "Do you think it happens during the day too and is just harder to see with the lights on?"

He raises an eyebrow inquisitively. "Strange, it seems to be getting stronger. Last night, I had to touch you. Now, I'm just close to you and glowing."

I sigh. "Everything about this experience is strange."

He folds his arms across his chest and turns his attention toward the fountain. "Yeah," he says absently. Whatever he's thinking about must be disturbing.

"So, you were saying, about Pandora?" I prompt, hoping to pull him out of his mood.

He blinks twice, as if he's waking up, and turns a smile toward me. "The story of Pandora goes like this. Zeus, the head honcho in Greek mythology, ordered Hephaestus, the blacksmith of the gods, to make Pandora, the first human woman." He points a hand at the statue. "To celebrate Pandora's creation, the other gods gave her some gifts. Aphrodite gave her beauty, Athena, curiosity, and Hermes, the art of persuasion. Everyone loved her. But later, two human brothers angered Zeus when they stole fire from Mount Olympus. To punish the brothers, Zeus gave Pandora a jar full of every evil thing and told her never to open it. Then he sent her to the two brothers, knowing that her gift of beauty would make her irresistible. One of the brothers, Epimetheus, fell in love with her and took her as his wife, even though the other brother, Prometheus, warned him she came from Zeus. As expected, Pandora couldn't resist her curiosity and opened the jar. Every type of evil escaped into the world. Of course, she tried to put the lid back on, but it was too late. The jar was empty."

"So she's a symbol of things we do that seem harmless

but have big consequences."

"Yep. You've got it."

"Depressing. Why on earth would your father have a statue of this in his garden?"

"He thinks the Green Republic has opened Pandora's box. Everything they've done started with good intentions. They wanted to save the earth from environmental destruction. They wanted to legislate sustainable living. But the power they had to gain to change people's behaviors corrupted them. There aren't enough checks and balances. And now, no one can put what happened back in the jar."

"Oh. The statue is a reminder of the weaknesses of the current government."

"Yes. But more than that, it's a reminder of what we need to move forward. Part of the legend says that Zeus allowed one good thing in the jar, something that could counteract the evil."

"What was it?"

He looks at me out the corner of his eye and smiles. "Hope."

I stare at the constant flow of water from Pandora's jar. The splashing in the pool at the statue's feet is soothing. It's easy to understand why Korwin comes here when he can't sleep. "How does your father know what should be done? I mean, what if the cure is worse than the disease?"

He rubs his palms together. "Dad is a good person, Lydia. Sometimes he has to make hard decisions, like keeping you and Jeremiah here, but it's only because he wants what's best. He's not out to advance himself, like the Green Republic. He's got a conscience. He's leading the Liberty Party to reestablish a real democracy, like there used to be. The majority will decide their own rules."

"And he's willing to make war and potentially kill people to do that."

Korwin shakes his head. "He'll try to do it without spilling blood."

"There's no such thing as a bloodless revolution," I say. "Even I know that. My ancestors chose life behind a wall over bloodshed."

"You've seen the evil that is the Green Republic. Even you must agree we need to do something."

"In many ways, my community wanted the same things as the Liberty Party, freedom to continue to live as we always have. But we made a choice to separate ourselves from the evil of this world rather than make war. It's what sets us apart."

"But what if the wall wasn't enough? What if the Greens found out you were alive behind the wall, coming and going as you pleased? How would your life change? Sometimes there are things worth fighting for." The light from the fountain makes his hazel eyes twinkle.

I chew my lip. "If the Liberty Party succeeds and forms a democracy, that means the majority rules, right?"

"Yes."

"Well, what happens to people like Jeremiah and me? The way we live, we're definitely in the minority. Would they tear down the wall? Register us as citizens?"

"I don't think anything would have to change for you. Not really. Why would it?"

"But you don't know. Not for sure."

Korwin steps closer, reaching for my hands. His touch sends tiny shock waves up my arms and down my body. "I won't let anything happen to you," he says, his hazel eyes drilling into me. I can tell he means it.

Snap. The elastic feeling from the test room starts at the top of my head, a tickle that shivers through my torso and rushes down my arms to my hands. My spark is coaxed out by his closeness, by his eyes. Electricity pours into Korwin like it poured into the wood, an uncontrolled flow that I struggle to tie off.

But stranger still, I feel his power flow into me. Clearly it's his and not mine, because I can taste it. I can smell it, that post-thunderstorm scent he carries. The warm velvet current caresses up my arm from my fingers.

We glow bright enough to put the fountain to shame.

I don't register either one of us taking a step, but abruptly there is no space between us. Our hands flatten palm to palm beside our shoulders. Korwin, taller than me, bends his neck to press his forehead against mine. My neck cranes from the place I'm pressed into his chest.

"What is this between us?" I ask. "My brain is telling me to stop but my body won't let me. It feels...it feels like—"

"Like we're connected. Two parts of the same whole." He slides one arm behind my back so we're hip to hip, and raises our coupled hands to face level. Pulling his fingers away, blue lightning dances between our palms. It's beautiful. Our own electrical storm.

"We're a complete circuit," he says. "I'm charging you

and you're charging me."

"I hardly know you," I whisper.

He laughs. "True. But every cell in your body knows me. I'm the only one on the planet made out of the same stuff as you."

I close my eyes. Tingling volts pulse through my veins, course down my abdomen, through my heart, to my toes, up to my face. His heartbeat, audible with my ear pressed into his chest, pounds in time with mine. I give myself over to it, sighing in contentment. Our link magnifies every sound, every sensation.

"I want…" He releases my hand.

I open my eyes and tilt my head back to meet his gaze. "What? What do you want?" Tiny blue bolts of electricity grab on to my face as he moves to cradle my cheek. I shift my hand to the bare skin of his chest and feel him jerk beneath my fingertips. His eyes widen.

"Are you okay?" I ask.

"Yeah." He sighs, thumb tracing my jaw. He lowers his full lips toward mine.

I should stop him. I should back away. But every cell in my body is at the mercy of his gravitational pull. I don't understand the science behind it, but I am not strong enough to deny it.

His lips brush mine. Soft. Warm. Wanting. Zaps of electricity travel from my mouth to low within me. Pressing against me, his kiss grows harder. Hotter. His fingers thread into the hair at the base of my skull. *Ahh. Yes.* I part my lips, welcoming his tongue as it darts between my teeth. Hot. Deep. I drink in the burning tingle. Lightning courses down my throat and it is ecstasy. I trail my hand up his chest and around his neck, pulling him to me, but we can't get any closer.

It's my first kiss and it is electric. Korwin crushes me against him. All I want is for him to press harder, to be closer. I feel my way from the base of his neck to his shoulder, under his arm, up his back. Something is building inside of me: heat and energy. Longing. An ache I don't have a name for but know without a doubt he can cure.

I want more. I need more. His lips part from mine, and I'm afraid he might stop. But no, he trails them from my ear to my neck, his fingers stroking my long hair down the length of my back and lower. My heart pounds, fast as hummingbird wings.

Suddenly, there is nothing but blue light.

We are thrown apart in a shower of glass, dirt, and wood. The square lights and the trees that line the periphery lay in tattered and burnt remnants around us. Pandora looms over me, safe on her marble perch, her jar providing the only light.

"Wow," he says, the corner of his mouth lifting. "Are you hurt?"

Eyeing the destruction around us, I run my hands over my arms and inspect myself. My shirt is shredded but my skin is intact. No blood. Like before, the energy has protected me. "I'm fine."

A voice comes from the other side of the charred evergreens. "Well, that's a relief." Jeremiah steps into the wreckage around the fountain. His expression matches the destruction around us. "I'd hate to think you'd been hurt. There's too much hurt in the world as it is."

The way he says it, I'm sure he's seen us. The sting of betrayal is all over his face.

"Jeremiah, I—"

"Don't say it. Just don't say anything." He turns on his heel and walks away. I scramble to follow him.

Korwin grabs my wrist. "Lydia, trust me. If it were me, I'd want to be alone."

I hang my head.

"What is it between you two, anyway? How bad should I feel about kissing you?"

I try to put it into words. What *is* between Jeremiah and me? "We've been best friends since we were children. I guess lately it's been more. In Hemlock Hollow, everyone thought we'd end up together. You know, married."

"So, you guys have, um." He makes a gesture with his hands that is easy to understand.

A hot blush creeps across my face. "Ah, no. We wait for that until marriage."

"But you've, like, kissed and stuff."

"No. Not yet. I mean, we've come close."

Korwin sits down on the rim of the fountain, rubbing his chin. "Is kissing something you usually wait until marriage for, too?"

I think about that. Kissing is something you do in private in Hemlock Hollow, but plenty of girls my age have been kissed, courting or not. "No. Girls and boys kiss, mostly when they're courting."

"Courting... That's like dating, right?" he asks.

"Yes. Stronger though. For us, very few people court who don't get married."

Korwin runs a hand through his hair, flexing the muscles in his arms and chest in the process. I become hyperaware that he's not wearing a shirt. "And you and Jeremiah were courting?"

"No. We weren't yet."

A puff of air escapes his lips. "So, what you're telling me is, I came between you and an almost kiss and a someday, maybe, courting?"

I fold my arms across my chest and turn my head in the direction of Jeremiah's exit. "Yes. I guess that would be accurate."

"Good. I'm done feeling bad about this. And I hope you are, too. If he wanted you, really wanted you, he should have staked his claim a long time ago."

Truth can be a hard thing to hear, a jackhammer across my heart. He's right. Jeremiah had multiple opportunities to court me, and to kiss me. True, he's made his intentions known, but what did that really mean? It certainly wasn't a vow of exclusivity.

I reposition my arms to cover the more provocative rips in my shirt. "Sometimes the unsaid in the Amish world is as important as what's said. I know Jeremiah would have courted me eventually. I regret hurting him. But the truth is that I am still free to do as I please. I enjoyed kissing you, Korwin. You were my first." I turn in a tight circle. "And I can safely say that if I ever kiss anyone else, I'm sure it will be... different."

Korwin chuckles, low and breathy. "You were my first,

too."

I gape in his direction. I don't believe it. How could a boy who looks like Korwin, living in the English world, not have been kissed?

"I've had opportunities. There are some girls who come to the house regularly, daughters of the Liberty Party founders. But they've never... we've never... connected."

"Oh." In many ways, Korwin's childhood sounds more cut off than mine. I grew up behind a wall but Korwin's walls are just as real and follow him everywhere.

"But I agree, Lydia." He meets my eyes. "If I ever kiss another girl, it could never be the same." He hugs himself like he's trying not to touch me. "I think we'd better call it a night."

"I agree. I'm not sure..." I hold my hands out toward the destruction.

"Yeah. I think we should take it slow until we have more control."

I nod.

"I'm going to go find Jeremiah and show him to his own room. He's gonna need some space," Korwin says. When I shake my head, he holds up a hand. "Don't worry. If he's angry or if I think he might lash out, I'll get Jameson to do it."

"He won't lash out. That's not Jeremiah. But it might be embarrassing to him to have to face you."

"Jameson, then. Goodnight, Lydia." He flashes me a conspiratorial smile and steps over the rubble to exit the garden. I follow, but not until I tip my chin toward the ceiling and thank God for freeing me from CGEF and introducing me to Korwin. Then I follow it up with a prayer that somehow all of this will work out and I'll make it home again.

But as I enter the hall, a small thought takes root in my brain and sprouts questions that go unanswered. If I go home again, will I have to give up my power? My freedom? Korwin?

Chapter 19

I dream of thunderstorms that night. Lightning rips across a silver sky. It flattens everything in its path. I'm in the dream but I can't tell if I'm the sky, the lightning, or the scorched earth. In the morning, I'm covered in sweat.

After a long shower, I dally in my closet, unable to make the simplest decision of what to wear. Eventually I decide on a stretchy pair of jeans, a sleeveless blouse, and a long orange blazer that reaches the back of my knees and is covered in buckles and straps. Orange, blessed orange. I relish my chance to wear the color we don't have in Hemlock Hollow. I slide my feet into a pair of strappy orange sandals with three-inch heels. I've never worn heels before and take a few practice strides across the room before ascending to the main part of the house.

With how late it is, I hope I've missed breakfast and with it, the need to face Jeremiah after what happened last night. I'll ask Jameson for a small bowl of cereal and eat it alone in the kitchen. But when I walk toward the dining room, voices drift across the house: Korwin, Jeremiah, and Maxwell in heated conversation. I can't make out everything they're saying, only the sharp edge of Jeremiah's words. They stop talking when the *click-clack* of my shoes on the hardwood gives me away.

"What's going on?" I ask.

"Nothing," Maxwell says.

Jeremiah shoots him a defiant look.

Jameson pulls out a chair for me. Without asking if I want it, he brings me a cup of coffee and a yogurt parfait.

I glare across the table at Maxwell. "I heard you fighting. What were you talking about?"

Jeremiah folds his hands, knuckles whitening. "I was suggesting to Mr. Stuart and Korwin that they help us visit your father." His blue eyes drill into mine.

I stiffen. "I thought we'd settled this yesterday." I take a deep breath and blow it out in a huff. "When we are done here, Mr. Stuart will return us to Hemlock Hollow."

"But you have to visit him, Lydia. It's why we came."

Maxwell leans back in his chair and shakes his head. "It's out of the question. If anyone sees you, it would be disastrous. I'm sorry, the risks are too great."

"Right," I say. "Like we talked about yesterday, it's too risky. I wouldn't want to put him in danger." Guilt squeezes my heart like a vise.

"I've changed my mind. I'm willing to take the risk," Jeremiah says. "He's ill. He needs us." The pointed look he gives me tells me everything I need to know. After last night, Jeremiah can't stand to be here any longer.

"No, Jeremiah. What if you're like me? You need to stay until we're sure."

Maxwell clears his throat. "His blood is normal."

The news doesn't surprise me. He didn't react to the lamp like I did, and I haven't felt the connection with him I have with Korwin. I mourn the loss of the leverage to make him stay.

"You can't go. The risk isn't your own," Maxwell says, glancing between Jeremiah and me. "If you're captured, they'll torture you. They'll kill you, Jeremiah, and drain Lydia like they did Korwin. And they'll take her father, too. They'll use him to manipulate you, if they don't kill him first."

I drop my fork. It clanks against the glass and flips berries across the table. Red splatters the white tablecloth. I bury my face in my hands and can't stop the tears from coming. My sobs are the only sound in a room full of suddenly silent men.

An arm slips around my shoulders. I know it is Korwin's by the way the tiny hairs on my neck react to his touch.

"We'll figure something out." Korwin's voice coaxes me from behind my hands.

"Don't make promises you can't keep, son," Maxwell says.

A sharp look passes between father and son.

Jeremiah glares at Maxwell through narrowed eyes. "Are you saying we're prisoners here? Are you saying she doesn't have a choice to leave if she wants to?"

Maxwell shakes his head. "No. You're not prisoners. Any of you can leave whenever you wish. I'm just asking you to please think about the consequences. The entire rebellion hinges on Korwin and Lydia. Decades of planning and posturing. If you throw yourself to the wolves, please don't take us all down with you."

"Of course we won't," I say. I turn toward Jeremiah,

balling my hand into a fist on the table. "I miss my father. You know I do." My voice sounds high and tight. "But I have to consider the big picture. CGEF thinks I'm Lydia Lane. I can't let them know who my father is. You didn't see what they did to me—I never told you what happened. They're evil."

With a curt nod, he stands from the table. "As long as that's the only reason." He bumps into Korwin's shoulder as he leaves the room. Accidental? Maybe. But he doesn't apologize.

"Jeremiah, come back! We need to talk," I call after him.

"Later," he barks. He doesn't even look back.

I can't help it. The tears come in great sobs and I bury my face in my hands again. Should I go after him? Maybe he wants to be alone. Am I doing enough to protect my father? He must be so worried but what choice do I have but to stay away? I'm so confused. Oh, how I miss Hemlock Hollow, where there are clear expectations and common rules.

Korwin pours me a glass of water from a pitcher on the table. I wipe my face and take a shaky sip, pulling myself together by force of will.

Maxwell watches me, his jaw tight. The wrinkles in his forehead are more pronounced than usual. I can't tell if he's worried about me trying to leave or unhappy with Jeremiah's outburst. "Now that that's settled, I need you to know I've invited the leaders of the Liberty Party here tonight to meet Lydia," he says. "I'll need both of you to be prepared."

"What about her father?" Korwin asks. "What can be done? Can we bring him here?"

Maxwell's gravely serious eyes search my face. "I'll see what I can do."

"Thank you. Thank you, Mr. Stuart," I say, clasping my hands in front of my chest.

"Now eat, Lydia," he says. "You'll need your strength."

* * * * *

"For you, Lydia," Jameson says, handing me the swath of gauzy blue fabric through the door to my room. He's strictly formal, and I can almost forget our awkward confrontation on the balcony. I would prefer to forget.

"What is this?"

"Your dress for the party tonight. A full length is appropriate."

I wrinkle my nose. "I don't understand. I thought this was a political meeting, boardroom-type stuff."

"Mr. Stuart prefers gatherings of the Liberty Party to be jovial occasions. You will be the main event. It's important you fit the part."

I pull the rest of the dress from his hands and the fabric rustles in my grip. It's shiny and layered and long. I can barely tell which end is up. "Okay." I wonder for a moment if it will fit and then remember that clothes here adjust to the wearer. Nanofibers.

"Good. Be in the great room in one hour. Mr. Stuart will want you in the reception line as guests arrive." Jameson drops a large paper bag lined with tissue paper just inside the door.

I nod and he slips from the room.

When he's gone, I strip out of my clothes and don the dress. Dark blue silk stretches across my bust, held in place only by pressure and the boning that is secured around my waist. The dress is sleeveless and strapless. My shoulders are completely bare, as far from plain as a dress can get. From the waist down, layers of glistening fabric and netting trail to the floor. In fact, they heap on the floor until I open the bag and find a pair of silver heels to give me some height. I also find a necklace and bracelet of sapphires. There are no earrings but my ears aren't pierced anyway. Jameson must have noticed. I look at myself in the mirror, my honey brown tresses sweeping down from my brow to my waist and think there is something missing. Something doesn't fit.

Carefully, I walk to the nightstand, pick up the thin plastic telephone, and dial zero.

"Jameson," he answers.

"I need your help."

* * * * *

I'm late. On unsteady feet, I climb the stairs to the great room, all my focus on staying upright on the strappy silver heels I'm wearing. At the top, I notice Korwin first. My eyes snap to him like an invisible string has tugged me in his direction. He's in a sharp gray suit that wraps around his waist and buttons down the side. A silky blue scarf that matches my dress twists around his neck and is pinned in place.

"Lydia," Korwin says. The word is charged and breathy. Without even thinking, I ball my gloved hands in the skirt of my dress and clip-clop across the wood floor toward him. It's where I'm supposed to be.

"You cut your hair," Jeremiah says, sharp and accusing. I'm embarrassed that I didn't notice him at first, waiting near the windows. With his hands coupled behind his back, he joins us near the top of the stairs.

"Yes." My honey brown hair is now layered, falling only to my shoulders and parted to the side. The hairdresser Jameson found for me has brushed it to a shine and curled it. The waves are pinned up with pearl clips. I think it's beautiful and very English.

Jeremiah scowls.

I consider blaming my circumstances. We have to blend in. My hair was one of the few traits that still set me apart. But then I narrow in on his disapproving expression. Who is he to suggest I can't? He chooses when to cut his hair, even in Hemlock Hollow. I feel unfairly judged and so I look him in the eye and repeat what he said to me in the buggy on the way to the wall, "When in the English world, always act English."

He balks as his own words slam into the space between us. I stare at him, challenging him to respond to me. And then I notice he is dressed in a garishly fuchsia suit with a braided gold sash. His appearance disturbs me, as I have never seen him wear fuchsia, nor does he appear to like it. Undoubtedly, Maxwell provided his clothes, which means Korwin and I match intentionally. This bothers me, partly because it makes me feel like a show pony, a doll Maxwell dresses up to serve his purposes. Mostly though, I think it's cruel. Jeremiah is being forced to watch Korwin and me thrust together by the forces here. A stiff dose of guilt makes me want to eat my words. I am the reason he's here. I am the reason both of us are here.

"I'm sorry," I murmur.

We both turn as Maxwell descends the stairs from the second floor, clapping his hands slowly. "You all look amazing." He grabs me by the shoulders and ushers me next to Korwin. "Places, everyone. Our first guests have arrived."

Places, like we are actors in a play. I glance at Korwin, but he is intent on Jameson opening the door. A flood of people enter, dressed in suits and gowns. Old women with fur stoles, men with flashy gold rings, and families with children who look too young to wear the stiff clothes they have on. They form a line and I shake their hands one after the other.

I have no idea who I'm meeting. Jameson calls out each of their names as they enter the house, but by the time they've waited in line to reach me, I forget who they are. I feel rude and overwhelmed. I am a child in dress-up clothes pretending to be an adult.

"You must be Lydia," the man shaking my hand says. He's gray haired and dark skinned, darker than Maxwell, with large, warm eyes and an expensive-looking wristwatch that flashes with each pump of my hand.

"Yes, I am. It's nice to meet you." I smile sweetly to cover my ignorance of his name.

"Jonas Kirkland," he says.

"Come on, Daddy," a lanky and sophisticated woman with a bridge of freckles across her nose says to Jonas. "There are people waiting." She places a hand on his shoulder and guides him down the line. "It was nice to meet you, Lydia. Welcome to the Liberty Party."

I shake her long fingers and nod as she works her way down the line.

Mercifully, the door closes and I run out of hands to shake. Still, everyone is staring at Korwin and me, and I don't think it is in admiration of our clothing. We stand there awkwardly for a moment until Maxwell leans over and whispers, "Why don't the three of you get something to eat? We won't start the demonstration for another hour."

"Demonstration?"

"The Liberty Party is going to want to see you in action, Lydia. The hope of a revolution hinges on convincing the people in this room that you are strong enough."

I gape.

"Remember why you are doing this," Maxwell says through a smile, then walks away before I can formulate a response.

I turn toward Korwin. "Did you know about this?"

He sighs. "You give me too much credit," he mumbles. "Apparently there are lots of things my father doesn't share with me."

Music begins to play and guests take to the floor hand in hand. It's like a ball. A grand reception for a new secret weapon. The thought makes me shiver.

Jeremiah clears his throat. "This is madness. We shouldn't even be here," he whispers. "Can you imagine what Bishop Kauffman would say about the vanity of it all?"

The thought of using my electrokenisis in front of this crowd makes me uncomfortable for more reasons than vanity, but I nod in agreement. My heart quickens, and I can feel it in my throat as my eyes skip over the nameless faces.

Korwin tilts his head, eyes boring into Jeremiah. "Don't make it harder than it is. Lydia will get through this. You both will. And then you can both be free of this."

There is hopelessness in his words. My gaze shifts between the two boys.

"Korwin, will you excuse us for a moment?" Jeremiah asks.

With a curt nod Korwin drifts toward the table of food and drinks Jameson has set up near the windows.

"Come on. Dance with me," Jeremiah says.

My eyebrows shoot up. We have never danced. Dancing is seen as worldly and immodest in Hemlock Hollow.

"It's *rumspringa*, remember?" he says.

With a nod, I take his hand and allow him to lead me to the edge of the dance floor. I glance at the other dancers and try to imitate what they do. One of his hands lands on my waist and I use the other to form a stiff frame, hand in hand but holding several inches between us.

He leans forward to bring his lips to my ear and his

blond curls brush my cheek. "I think we should try to escape."

I pull back. "What are you talking about?" I whisper. I glance around to make sure no one is listening but between the music and the boisterous discussion, we are alone in a crowded room.

"We could sneak out while Maxwell is distracted with the party and find a way to call Bradford Adams to take us home."

"We can't. What about my father?"

"He's safe. Nobody here knows who he is. You and I can go home and when he's better, Doc Nelson can bring him back just like we planned." We sway and turn, blending into the crowd.

"You saw the news program," I whisper in his ear. "Willow's Province is crawling with Green Republic soldiers. We'd never make it home."

"First of all, how do we know Maxwell Stuart is telling us the truth about all that? For all we know, that program was faked."

"Can he do that?"

He shrugs. "Look at all the technology they have here. I don't trust him, Lydia."

"I don't trust him either. But what if it *is* true?"

"They don't know about Bradford Adams. He could help us. If we're careful, we could be home in a couple of days."

I don't think it would be as easy as Jeremiah thinks, but arguing the point is futile. I take a different tack. "But we promised the Stuarts we would help."

He shrugs. "It's *rumspringa*. Their rules are not our rules. This is a sinful world. We don't have to keep our promises here."

I shake my head. "I can't." My whispering is getting louder. I make an effort to lower my voice. "It wouldn't be right."

Jeremiah squints at me, his mouth thinning. "Is it because…?" He stops mid-question and looks me in the eye. "I'm sure you would forget over time."

"Forget what?"

"About your abilities. That's what you're afraid of, isn't it? That people will know you are different when we go back."

Forget I could shoot lightning bolts out of my hands? I seriously doubt it, but he is right about one thing. I am afraid of being different, not because of what others will think as Jeremiah suggests but because everything has changed. My future life, what used to be a clear picture of a two-rut dirt road that led straight and triumphantly to heaven, is now a mystery to me. It is a winding trail leading into the fog.

"I'm not afraid of going back," I say.

"Then what is it? Why can't we leave? Mr. Stuart is treating you like he owns you. It ain't right, Lydia."

"I just…" My eyes flick away from Jeremiah's and stare at the floor. "Can I ask you something?" I return my gaze to his.

"Yeah." He nods.

"Why didn't you ever kiss me? In Hemlock Hollow? All the time we spent together. All the hints and promises to court me, you never stole even one kiss. Did you want to?"

Jeremiah turns his head, his lips parting slightly so that I can see his tongue curl over the inside of his lower lip. "Of course I wanted to," he says. "But, you know, it never seemed like the right time."

I pinch my eyebrows together over my nose. "We've spent hours diving off the loft in the haymow and lying side by side in the hay. Entire days fishing in the river. Long walks in the woods. Evenings climbing my tree and sitting in the branches. When would be the right time?"

He tilted his head. "Think about what you're saying. All of those things, they aren't exactly… romantic. I might have done any one of them with a boy."

"Huh?"

"You were young. We were best friends. It made sense for us to act like children. I was just waiting for a moment when I felt we were both ready for something more."

"You mean, when I acted more wifely and less like your equal."

He smiles and breathes a sigh of relief. "Exactly."

I don't blame Jeremiah for thinking this or saying it. In our *Ordnung*, the man is the head of the household, and his family is as submissive to his will as our community is submissive to God. We have clear gender roles, and diving off haymows and climbing trees is not something married Amish women do. His thinking is normal in the Amish sense. Still, my heart feels heavy. I've always thought Jeremiah liked how I was different. Sure, he teased me about allowing him to be the man, but I thought it was just that, teasing. I thought, even when we were married, he would always respect that I could run faster and jump higher. The married life I pictured with Jeremiah was one of shared winks and knowing smiles where we went through the motions of Amish expectations and wifely submission, but in private we were the same friends we'd always been. No, it is not wrong or odd for Jeremiah to feel the way he does, but it is the first time I truly accept and understand those feelings. They disappoint me. I'm not sure I can live like a good Amish woman. Will it be enough for me? Or am I too selfish and vain to give myself over to that calling?

We sway back and forth in silence for a few beats, both of us far away in thought. We pause when Korwin taps Jeremiah on the shoulder.

"Can I cut in?" he asks.

A glower is all Jeremiah gives Korwin in response. Rude. I release his hand and reach for Korwin's. "Of course," I say politely.

With nothing but contempt, Jeremiah backs away from us, slowly drifting toward the buffet table.

"Sorry about that," I say. "He's very protective of me."

"You don't say." Korwin's hand finds my waist and instantly, my body responds. Unlike the strict frame I made with my arms to remain a proper distance from Jeremiah, I close the space between us and release his hand to snake both arms around his neck.

I'm close enough to hear him swallow. "My dad says we're supposed to meet him in Test Room B in twenty minutes."

"Okay," I say. I chew my bottom lip.

"I know this makes you nervous, but it will be over before you know it. We will make a few lightbulbs glow and zap a few logs and the Liberty Party leaders can go away happy."

"And plan an offensive attack," I say. "This is far from over."

"I suppose. Yes. It will take some time for them to come up with a plan and execute it. Do you think you can last here that long? It must be difficult to be so far away from home. I'm sure this is a much different life than you're used to."

I search his face. "How long do you think I'll be here?"

"I don't know. A few more weeks, maybe. If my dad says he'll get you home, he will. As much as I question his means, if he says he's going to do something, he does it."

"A few weeks," I repeat wistfully.

"Lydia, there's something I need to tell you," Korwin says. "But I might be out of line."

"I guess we won't know until you say it."

"I don't want you to go." I don't just hear the words; I feel them. A thrum of energy hums into me from where his hands touch my hips. I sigh. This boy who I've saved, who I have known for only a matter of days, makes music in my very soul. Who and what he is speaks to the heart of me, without expectation or judgment.

With both hands, he pushes me away. "Lydia, stop," he whispers suddenly. "People will notice." I glance downward and I realize I am glowing.

Fitfully, I try to pull the energy back inside. I back up a

fraction of an inch and wipe a bead of sweat from my brow. To my relief, no one seems to have seen me. The music stops and the dancers break apart.

Korwin takes my hand. "Come on," he says, tilting his head toward the stairwell. We escape the busy room to the basement, past the blue palominos, and the garden, to Test Room B. "We'll have a few minutes to talk privately before my dad arrives."

Like Test Room A, Room B is insulated, but more than lightbulbs and wood await me there. The room is twice the size, with a ceiling as high as the one in the gardens. A level above me, a half circle of mirrors lines the space.

"What's that for?" I ask, pointing at the mirrors. My voice echoes in the large room.

"Observation booth. Like the other one but bigger."

"Oh." Three metal rods are mounted on the wall. Sand is heaped on the floor near my feet.

"I thought you said there would be more lightbulbs and wood," I say frantically. "What am I supposed to do with this?"

"I assumed it would be. My father must be confident in your abilities. This is an advanced demonstration."

"What? What if I can't do it? What if I fail?"

The corner of Korwin's mouth bends upward. "You won't fail, Lydia. You are as capable as I am."

His words strike straight to my heart. He believes in me. Genuinely and truly admires my abilities. Coming from Hemlock Hollow, where I was always second, always presumed to be the weaker sex, a follower, submissive, his words mean more to me than he can possibly know.

"Besides. If you fail, the worst that can happen is the Liberty Party loses confidence in Dad's leadership and decides against an offensive."

And Jeremiah and I will never make it home, I think. Jeremiah already wants to leave. He'll never make it to Hemlock Hollow safely on his own. For his sake, I cannot fail.

"Show me what I need to do."

"This test is about control. Can you control the heat you produce? The goal is to turn the sand into glass."

"Okay," I say, remembering how I'd poured my power into the logs.

"But Lydia, he'll want you to do it with control. Don't just heat the sand. Try to create a rod. Manipulate the melting glass. Observe."

Korwin faces the sand and throws his hands toward the floor, palms up, with a snap that straightens his fingers. Blue fire crackles to life and then lightning connects to the pile of sand. Awestruck, I watch as he melts the sand, forms it into a rod, then bends it into a pretzel shape. When he's done, he pulls the power back into himself and looks at me. "Have fun with it. Think of it as art class."

"I never had art class," I whisper. As I say it, I realize it's not entirely true. My mind flashes back to my lessons with Martha Samuels, when I learned how to cut and stitch fabric. She always said my quilts were the most beautiful in Hemlock Hollow. I could create if I wanted to.

He flashes that ornery half-grin I've grown to adore.

"Give it a try." Moving a few steps back, he motions for me to take his place.

I turn toward the pile of sand. They've certainly given us enough to work with. Even after Korwin's pretzel, the pile is almost as tall as me.

Firing up isn't as easy for me as it was for Korwin. I coax the elastic ribbon from my brain and move it to my hands. It's an awkward push and pull as I try to maintain control of it. When I feel it burning in my palms I throw my hands toward the sand and the familiar pulling starts.

I understand now what the book in the library meant about the molecules in the sand dancing with my molecules. Just like yesterday with the logs, it is a mutual attraction at the most basic level, a dance of competing energies. I see that now, or more accurately, I *feel* it.

To maintain a steady flow into the mound, I mentally tie off the elastic.

The sand forms a hollow tube where I zap it. I experiment with moving my stream of energy to a different part of the sand and back again. Control is key, but how do you control lightning? I might as well harness the wind. I pull my power back inside, then loose it again in an effort to manipulate the glass I've already made. But I only succeed in creating a bumpy, bubbling mess.

"It's okay," Korwin says from behind me. "Keep trying. Don't think about it so much. Just go with what feels right."

I try again. While I play with the electric blue taffy, my mind wanders to last night in the garden when Korwin kissed me, how our energy flowed between us. How when we'd danced, I'd felt alive in his arms. Even now, I feel his presence behind me and feel stronger for it, as if I could take on the world as long as he was there.

But then Jeremiah's face drifts into my thoughts. Last night, a shadow darkened his eyes and his shoulders slumped when he saw me kiss Korwin. He's asked me to go home. I have a vision of us growing old, with me baking bread and sewing quilts and never ever thinking about taking on the world again. Do I owe Jeremiah that? Do I want that? What social contract does our history commit me to? Do I still have a choice?

The melted glass sifts between my electric fingers. I step closer to get the right leverage without actually touching the sand. My mind is a storm of questions. Clearly, Jeremiah wants me to return to Hemlock Hollow with him and expects me to court and marry him as a proper Amish woman. But if I do go back with this power awakened within me, will I even be able to kiss him? If my power accidentally flowed into Jeremiah the way it did into Korwin, would it kill him? Would I accidentally blow him up like the wood or the garden? Do I actually have a choice to go back, or has fate made the choice for me? It isn't safe for me to be with Jeremiah, is it?

I tunnel the glass into a tall vase, and I don't quit there. My forehead drips with sweat, but I like the heat. I like the effort. It makes everything clear. These last few days I've been in denial that anything has really changed. I'd thought and believed that I could return to Hemlock Hollow and continue my life as if nothing had happened here. But unleashing like this, pouring myself into the sand, is therapeutic. I see now that I was wrong. Even if I go back, I will always know this boundless power is just under my skin, waiting to be released.

My thoughts return to Korwin. I have to stop making excuses. It isn't fate and it isn't this power that's kept Jeremiah and me from moving forward in our relationship. It is *me*. The old love we've always shared can't evolve to become something more passionate. If we'd stayed in Hemlock Hollow, maybe I could have changed. We'd probably have gotten married and would have been content, as happy as we'd expected to be. But here, in the greater world, I have tasted a heat, a passion far beyond what Jeremiah and I could ever produce. The more I work the sand, the clearer it becomes. Korwin is the wind, and I want nothing more than to open my sails and see where he can take me.

The truth is, my heart's desire is Korwin. I want to stay with Korwin.

The glass in front of me takes shape. I've used the entire pile of sand to create a replica of Korwin, carved in black glass. I pull the ribbon back inside, panting with the effort, and rest my hands on my knees. The room starts to sway. I lose my balance and fall.

Korwin catches me before my head can hit the floor. "Whoa. I've got you. I've got you," he says, cradling me in his arms.

I smile up at him, dizzy and weak. The rest of the world melts away.

"You were supposed to attempt a pretzel, not create a full-sized sculpture of me." He grins, and my heart does backflips. He pulls me completely into his lap.

"It just happened," I say honestly. "Oh no, your father. The demonstration! I'm tapped. I don't think I can do any more."

"Let me worry about my father," he says. His face is very close to mine as he holds me in his arms, close enough for me to feel my skin pull toward his. He shakes and sighs, fighting the invisible force. And then he gives in. His lips drop onto mine, harder than they did last night, more completely.

Energy flows over my tongue and down my throat. Unlike last night though, I don't immediately give it back to him. I've felt this before. When we were in CGEF, and Korwin reached for my hand to help me up, I'd pulled energy from his body. He'd juiced me from the wires in the elevator. And later, he'd borrowed energy from me to fight off the Greens.

This is so much better. This isn't just a tug of war between us. This juice is my flavor. The perfect current and amperage to make every cell in my body leap up and do jumping jacks. The longer we kiss, the hotter I feel, like the power within me is limitless. It makes my head spin.

Snap! My body starts feeding his. I am a cup, overflowing with power. He completes the circuit and the tingle of exchange sweeps through me, from my fingers, which have tangled in his hair, to my toes that curl within my silver shoes. I am lost to it. Totally and utterly owned by our connection.

Until a strange metallic sound disturbs us.

We pull apart, breathless, invigorated, and turn toward

the sound. The metal poles in the wall are bent over like popsicles left in the sun, and my sculpture of Korwin has melted into a pool of glass.

A series of claps turns into a roar of applause from above. The staticky sound of Maxwell's voice breaks over the speakers, "...imagine the implications." I don't think he's talking to us. I gather my feet under me and allow Korwin to help me up. We stare at the mirrored glass.

"Did I drain you?" I ask Korwin. My hand glows blue as I raise it to his cheek.

"No," he says, lifting an eyebrow. "I don't know why. I get that we can share energy but you were on empty. I shouldn't feel like I just stepped out of the healer."

The door opens and Maxwell bursts into the room, beaming. "I think you two melted the wiring in here. The speakers cut out. Did you see the lights flicker? You juiced her from the walls, Korwin, without a direct connection!"

We exchange confused glances.

Maxwell's eyes dart around the room with Christmas-morning wonder. "Look, Korwin. Look at the way the poles are bent toward you two. There's an electromagnetic quality. That's probably what fried the speakers. That one—" he points at the last rod, "—that was tungsten carbide, the toughest natural metal known to man. You guys plied it like putty."

I shrug. I don't understand the science behind what happened between Korwin and me, only that I want it to happen again. Our eyes meet and I know he wants more, too. He inches his hand closer to mine.

"Oh no," Maxwell says, placing himself between the

two of us. "I don't think you two are getting the seriousness of this situation. You've got to calm your hormones or you're going to burn the place down."

Korwin shakes his head. "Dad, no. I want… I want Lydia to be my girlfriend." He whispers it to me, for his father to hear.

"Me too. I want that too," I say. The words make my pulse race. Courting him feels right. Destined somehow.

"Son." Maxwell places his hands on his hips. "Look around you. You two almost melted an insulated room. If you are going to be in the same vicinity, we need to have a talk about safety, and I don't mean condoms."

Korwin's eyes lock on his father's. "Dad," he hisses.

"What are condoms?" I ask.

Maxwell looks at me incredulously and shakes his head. "Oh, hell no!"

"What?" I ask.

"She grew up on the Amish preservation, Dad," Korwin says, tilting his head to the side.

What am I missing?

"Come on, both of you. The council is going to want to discuss this, and then the three of us need to have a talk."

Chapter 20

I don't fully understand. I'm beginning to think I never will.

It's the next morning before Maxwell has time to talk. His meeting with the council took most of the night. But after a few hours of fitful sleep, I sit in a conference room with Korwin as his father draws us a picture on the whiteboard.

My body is like a machine, as is Korwin's. I burn glucose from the food I eat and make energy called adenosine triphosphate, or ATP. But everyone else's body does that too. Korwin and I are unique in our ability to transform ATP into electricity. Our cells can also work in reverse and make ATP from electricity. That's what he calls "getting juiced." Like every machine, if I use up my fuel, my ATP, I'll eventually stop working. In Korwin's case, when CGEF pulled electricity from his body, using him like a battery, it gave him scurvy. His body didn't have enough ATP left to repair its cells. The sores on his arms were caused by his body eating itself to fuel other cells. If I hadn't saved him, he would have eventually starved to death.

"But here's the interesting thing," Maxwell says. "When your body touches Korwin's body, your cells flip their polarization. You, Lydia, might build a negative

211

charge, which attracts Korwin's positive charge."

"Like a circuit," Korwin interrupts. "We pass energy back and forth like a battery." He glances at me. "We figured that much out."

"Yes, yes, but that's not all. Your cells are like magnets, constantly flipping their polarity when you're…connected. Um, kissing and so forth." Maxwell clears his throat and flashes a tight smile. "When you share energy, the push and pull of your cells is similar to the particles in an atom. They continually charge each other. You two become the world's strongest atomic generator."

"That's impossible. If we're adding energy, it has to come from somewhere. If it's not from our cells, where is it coming from?"

"That's the fascinating part. Somehow, without your knowledge, you two are drawing from the energy around you—directly from the atoms. You didn't need a direct connection in that room. The power within you found the nearest energy source and took it."

Korwin wrings his hands. I know how he feels. A dark worm is writhing in my stomach, a question I am afraid to ask. Korwin is braver.

"What does this mean for us?"

Maxwell sighs. "It means you best be careful when you touch. Holding hands is probably okay, but a kiss could start a fire. A deep kiss could incinerate the people around you. Having sex could produce the same energy as a nuclear blast."

I stop breathing. The room suddenly seems too small and hot, like there isn't enough air. I glance toward

Korwin. His skin has taken on a greenish hue and his eyes are wide.

"That can't be right," he says, but the words come out one by one, like they're struggling for the surface.

Maxwell removes his glasses and cleans them on the corner of his lab coat. "It's an untested theory, to be sure," he mumbles.

The thought that touching Korwin could be dangerous, even deadly, rocks me to my core. I stand, knocking the chair back from the table. "Please excuse me. I need some air." The words are hushed and breathless. I run for the door.

"Lydia!" Korwin calls.

"Let her go," Maxwell mumbles.

The door swings shut behind me.

I navigate the maze of corridors like the lab rat that I am. Some I remember. Some I don't. What I want is to find Jeremiah. I don't deserve his friendship, not after the way I treated him, flaunting my feelings for Korwin. But I need it. I need to talk to someone, to sort this out.

I wander for the better part of thirty minutes, bumping into Jameson near the gardens. "Have you seen Jeremiah?"

"I have not," he says, dusting the portrait in the hall.

"Can you show me where he's staying?"

Jameson sighs deeply, as if I'm inconveniencing him, but leads the way. I question Korwin's theory about the butler liking his job. At the moment, Jameson seems quite put out.

"Here you are," he says, pointing at a door to our left.

He's gone before I can say thank you.

I knock twice. "Jeremiah? I need to talk to you."

No answer.

I turn the doorknob and slowly let myself into the room. He's not there. Odder still, the place is a mess, ransacked. Clothes are strewn everywhere and the bed isn't made. The suit from last night lays strewn across the floor. Jeremiah is usually disciplined and tidy. Am I the cause of this?

I wait for another ten minutes before giving up and returning to my room. My limbs weigh me down. All I want is to throw myself on my bed and have a good cry. I want to sleep for the rest of the day, maybe the rest of the week.

But when I reach the bed, a piece of paper on my comforter chases away any hope of sleep. It's a letter from Jeremiah.

Lydia,

I'm going to finish what we started. I found a way out of here, and I'm leaving. I'll make sure your dad is okay. Then I'm going home. I know who I am, and I don't belong here. When you remember who you are, I hope you will join me. I'll leave the door open for you.

Love,
Jeremiah

I reread the letter. My legs feel weak and I plop down on the comforter, rolling onto my back. Jeremiah is gone.

Or maybe not? Maybe I can catch him.

The note slips from my fingertips. I bound off the bed and burst from the room, moving through the maze of hallways, checking every door, every room. Considering the security in this place, Jeremiah didn't leave through the front door. Maxwell mentioned tunnels out of the mansion. What if Jeremiah found one?

I listen for footsteps behind me, but Jameson is nowhere to be found and Korwin and his father are still in the conference room. I search the compound but don't find Jeremiah. What I do find is one room with the door conspicuously left open. Every other door in every other hall is neatly shut.

What did he say in his note? *I'll leave the door open for you.*

Inside, the room is empty. Four white walls. There isn't any other way out aside from the propped door. I question my intuition. Maybe the door has nothing to do with Jeremiah. But then I ask myself why there's a room here with no purpose. I walk to the far wall, sliding my hand across the paint. It seems solid. About to give up, I hang my head and notice scuff marks on the floor. Hardly worth a second glance except that it means someone has been here—and people don't come into an empty room for nothing.

And then I find it, a ridge under my fingers. It could be an imperfection in the drywall or a chip of paint, but it isn't. Jeremiah has always been a problem-solver. This is the way out; I can feel it. The wall slides open to expose a circular threshold and the sewer beyond. Jeremiah isn't there, but he couldn't have gone far. I step forward. The space in the circle presses against my leg, and I remember Maxwell explaining about the membrane and the bio-key. If I leave, I can't come back. I retreat into the white room and the wall slides closed in front of my nose.

I consider telling Maxwell. Maybe his resources could bring Jeremiah back? But on the way to the conference room, I flip the idea over in my brain. Maxwell says I'm not a prisoner, but he won't let me leave. I've never gotten a straight answer about why he didn't try to save Korwin from CGEF. The truth is, I don't know anything about Maxwell Stuart except that he scamps electricity and for the last couple of days he's tested me like a rat. Can I even prove the news transmissions he's shown me are real?

I'm shocked to come to the conclusion that Jeremiah is right. Of course, I must make every effort to see my father. My dad always told me my mother and brother died in a car accident in the English world. I'm sure my father wouldn't lie, but I need to know if there's something he might remember about me, some early clue that I was different. I long to find him and ask him about my mother and my birth.

And there's something else.

I've become too wrapped up in the English world. This thing with Korwin is unnatural. *Nuclear bomb*. If it's true, I can't ever be with him. No marriage, no babies, no future. How could we have anything together when any physical manifestation of our affection could mean utter destruction? No. It's better if I go. The temptation, the longing, will fade in time once we are far enough apart. I have to find my father and then return to Hemlock Hollow. As much as it hurts, Jeremiah is right. I don't belong here.

With a sense of purpose, I return to my room. A gigantic purse with straps like a backpack hangs on the wall of the closet. I suspect it's meant to be fashionable, but for me it will be functional. I choose three outfits, a cap, sunglasses, and a comfortable pair of shoes, shoving them into the bag. Then I slip my feet into a pair of rubber rain boots. I slip a shiny black coat over my jeans and T-shirt and tie my hair up on the top of my head. Thinking fast, I pack some small towels from the bathroom, water, and nutrition bars from the mini-fridge.

Stealthily, I return to the small chamber but my caution is unnecessary. I'm alone. Running my fingers along the periphery of the far wall, they catch in the upper right-hand corner again, in the place I noticed before. The passageway opens and I step through. Sure enough, as soon as I'm through, the wall snaps closed behind me and I'm plunged into darkness.

What am I doing? A gaping hole is torn through my chest. I pat my T-shirt, surprised to find I haven't been stabbed or shot. The pain is as acute. *Oh good Lord, what have I done?* I'm too far from Korwin! I try to turn around, to reenter the house, but bounce off a field of energy that's formed behind me. There's no going back. Still, I can't bring myself to leave. Can Korwin feel this too? Pacing, distraught, it seems forever before the discomfort fades. Eventually, though, I regain my earlier resolve.

Positioning my bag on my shoulder, I find my footing

on the ledge on the side of the channel. I spend a little energy to light up my hand, enough to guide me forward. It will have to do until I reach the main sewer and its intermittent light from the street grids. I don't know where I'm going, but I pray for God to guide me in the right direction.

Chapter 21

For an hour, I travel east, until the sounds of traffic and footsteps above fade to silence. When all is quiet for several minutes, I tentatively climb one of the shafts and peek through the grate. All clear. I crank the cover and crawl out, relieved to emerge on a corner of sidewalk between two buildings with foreclosure signs and dirty windows. They look abandoned.

Closing the cover, I scramble to the dumpster in the alley and toss my bag behind it. Then I remove my boots and jacket and the remnants of the sewer that cling to them. I throw the soiled clothing away and tighten my ponytail.

"Don't move," comes a gruff voice from behind me.

I smell him before I see him, a strong chemical smell, stronger than alcohol. Slowly, I turn toward the voice. The man is tanned to the shade of leather, with a prickly beard and patchy gray hair that looks like he cut it himself with a knife. His eyes are hidden behind dark sunglasses. His clothing is either gray-colored or dirty, I can't tell which, and a red handkerchief is tied around his left bicep. He takes a step toward me. I flatten my back against the dumpster to keep my distance.

"You're in Red Dog territory, girlie," he says, tapping

the red cloth tied on his arm. "You best crawl back into that hole and move along."

"I—I just need to find Oakdale Rehabilitation Center," I stutter.

He cocks his head to the side and slides his lips back from his yellow teeth. "Huh. See, I find it hard to believe a person takes the sewer to the *deadzone* in order to visit a sick relative in the heart of Crater City. You're plenty far from Oakdale Rehab and no one comes here unless they're a vagrant or a scamper. Judging by the label on those jeans, you ain't no vagrant."

"I'm lost."

"I'll give you five seconds to get back into that sewer or—"

"Or what?" I say defiantly. I can't go back. It's too late for that. The tickle wakes and stretches at the back of my brain, it snakes its way to my shoulders. *No!* What happened with Helen and the Greens when we escaped CGEF was Korwin's doing. I've made my peace with it, but Korwin has more control. He knew he wouldn't kill anyone. If Maxwell is to be believed, I could kill this man, fry him like an ant under glass. I can't risk it. Violence is wrong. I don't want to hurt anyone.

A flash of steel passes by my face and then a knife is at my throat. "Your five seconds are up." His face juts forward until his wrinkled lips are less than an inch from me. The blade presses into my neck. "I'm sure someone in the pack could use a new bitch."

And then his calloused hands have my wrists. He binds them with a cord that cuts into my flesh and pushes me forward by the neck. I tremble at the feel of the knife pressed into my back. The tickle cascades down my arms of its own accord and lingers near my fingers.

He leads me to a warehouse across the street. The door opens before we get there, and a man in patchwork clothes limps toward me, laughing. He looks just as sinister as the man who has my neck, with the same red cloth tied around his arm.

"Where'd you find this one, Hambone?"

"Walked right into our territory," my captor says with a laugh.

Patchwork chuckles darkly. "Finders keepers." They usher me deep into the building. It smells of urine and something else—the chemical smell again. Hambone walks me to the middle of the concrete expanse. By the time my eyes adjust to the dim light, I'm surrounded. There are filthy men everywhere. Twitchy, shifty-eyed men who close in around me. They seem to smell my fear, laughing and taunting me.

"Please, I beg you, I need to get to Crater City," I say. "I didn't mean to come into your territory. I'm lost."

"Riiight," Hambone says. He pushes my hair off my shoulder.

A man I can't fully see presses against my back. Patchwork limps toward me, his smile a window into the trouble on his mind. He's got a red leather dog collar in his hands and he's looking at my neck.

I need help, but no one is going to come to my rescue. No one even knows where I am. For the first time in my life, I am absolutely alone. "I don't want to hurt you," I mumble.

Laughing erupts all around me.

"Haven't you heard, darling? Love hurts," Patchwork says, jingling the collar.

A hand grabs my hip, pressing my back into a man's body. I can't stop shaking. My breath freezes in my throat. Rank breath warms my ear. Not the same man. Another at my side. There must be six of them. All I can see is their leather skin and yellow teeth.

"Who claims this woman?" Patchwork asks, holding up the collar, as if I'm a dog they found in the street.

There are too many hands, too many voices. Panic brushes aside my logical mind.

"*Get off me!*" I yell, but it's not just my voice that comes out. The elastic ribbon stretches down my body, branching into every hand that touches me.

The men fall to the concrete, twitching, leaving me wobbling from their sudden dropped hands.

I shuffle my feet and spread my arms to regain balance. The cord that bound my wrists is burnt to ash. The gray flakes scatter with my movement and snow down over the bodies of the writhing men. With a detached fascination, I back away from them. Did I do this? Did I hurt them? I have a second to think about it before I notice that the balcony of the warehouse is full of Red Dogs. Scrappy men and women in red collars stare at me from above. They do not look friendly.

I bolt for the door. The Spark ignites inside me. Glowing blue, I snatch my bag from near the dumpster and race behind the buildings, pounding feet closing in. I dodge down alley after alley, a mouse in a maze. I run faster than I did on the Holotread, scaling a fence and then another, until I'm sure I've run longer and farther than any Red Dogs. Then I duck inside the first open door I can find, panting hard and raw with fear.

Thankfully, the room is empty. I lock the door behind me and check each of the windows but there's no one outside. I'm alone.

Breath shaky, I throw my bag on the floor and rip a bottle from its belly. The cool water etches down my throat. I'm still hot and glowing blue. Hastily, I pull it inside, extinguishing the spark. Scorched holes pepper my clothing—my thigh, my hip, my back, my chest. I change, wishing I could shower. Wishing I could scrub the memory of that warehouse from my mind.

What would they have done to me? I shiver, thinking of the red collar. Then a more insidious thought barrels into me. What have *I* done? I've never hurt anyone before. Violence of any kind is forbidden in Hemlock Hollow. I have no idea if the men are dead or alive and the scary thing is, I don't care, not really. A part of me, deep inside, believes they had it coming.

Dear Lord, am I losing my soul? My conscience?

I fall on my knees on the cold, gritty floor of the abandoned building, and I pray with everything I have in me for forgiveness. I have strayed too far to a place where I no longer recognize right from wrong. I pray until my body aches and my mind becomes a series of apologies and pleas for help.

It's some time before I can think clearly again and

longer still before I stop shaking but when there is nothing left in my brain but a dull buzz, I take in my surroundings. Where am I? The sun is sinking, and I'm no closer to Crater City. I slide on the pair of sunglasses I packed, wide banded and dark, then roll my hair under a cap, tucking in the loose strands. With a deep breath to steady my nerves, I step from the building and walk to the closest street.

A car passes through an intersection up ahead. Where there are cars, there are people. I lift my chin and progress toward the intersection with my best impression of confidence. Whatever I do, I can't show fear or give anyone reason to be suspicious of me. I don't want to end up CGEF's next human battery or a Red Dog slave.

Thinking about CGEF brings back a host of memories. My mind darts to the horrors of Dr. Konrad's table and the MRI machine. I try not to think about what Korwin looked like, covered in sores and bruised almost beyond recognition. *Oh Korwin!* The hole in my chest burns. What have I done? I could explode from the hurricane of emotions swirling within me. I am utterly lost, hopeless.

"Miss, you got water in that pack of yours?" a deep voice asks me.

I jump back, tripping off the curb and into the street.

"I'm not gonna hurt you, girlie. Just thirsty and the fountains are done working for the day." The man's voice is raspy, his lips cracked. He's huddled against the dilapidated building between two large bags crammed full of what looks like junk to me.

My instincts tell me to run. The man might be

homeless but he's not harmless. He looks to be in his thirties with longish brown hair and a scruffy face. I should run for the hills, but I don't. With a shaky hand, I reach inside my pack and pull out one of the three water bottles I've stowed there. I hand it to him.

"Thank you," he says. He unscrews the cap and guzzles the contents, then eyes me from hat to shoes suspiciously. "What's an uppercrust like you doing in the deadzone?"

"Do you know how to get to the Oakdale Rehabilitation Center?" I blurt.

"Sure. It's on Mosato Avenue, right before you reach Western."

"Can I walk there from here?"

"Oh no, girlie. It's much too far. You'll need to take a cab."

"Oh," I say, the disappointment evident in my voice. "What street is this?"

"This is Everglade. Tell the cabbie to take you west to Mosato and then take a right. He should charge you for seven miles. Don't let him rip you off and take you the long way."

I force a smile. "Right. Thank you. Again, nice meeting you."

He holds up the water. "I owe you one."

I nod. Seven miles might be too far for an *Englisher* to walk, but where I come from it's a stroll to a friend's house. I head west on Everglade, joining foot traffic on the sidewalk.

An hour or more later, the crowd thickens as I approach Mosato Avenue. This part of the city is developed and has plenty of energy. Electric billboards advertise products above me in the twilight, blinking their full-color pitch over the streets. I decide to rest and take it all in. I sit down on a cement bench, digging in my bag for a nutrition bar and my last bottle of water.

The bench faces a shop window where televisions are for sale. Like the ones at the mansion, they appear static, oil paintings of fruit bowls and a woman smiling. A man pauses in front of the window and the shop owner smiles at him before tapping one of the screens. A woman stops to watch as do several teenagers. All I can see from the bench are flashes of color and light between the bodies of the crowd that's formed to watch.

I return my water to my bag and step toward the group, angling between shoulders so that I can see. It's an advertisement for a show called *Burn*. I glance at the people around me, surprised to find them completely enthralled. The host is a man with a ponytail in a paisley robe. In a melodic voice, he asks, "What are you willing to burn for energy to burn?" People compete for prizes of energy allotments. In order to win the units, the contestants have to prove they want them badly enough to burn their most cherished possessions. In the clip, a woman bawls as her grandmother's rocking chair goes up in flames.

Around me, the spectators cheer and laugh. "I want to see that one!" a girl from the back says.

In the Amish world, the gifts of the past are cherished, and the gift of each other, never sacrificed. How sad to give up your roots, a piece of who you are, for temporary comfort. I must be the only one to think so, though, because the people around me continue to laugh without empathy as another clip from *Burn* plays on.

I'm about to leave when the advertisement ends and Alexandra Brighten's face takes its place. I freeze at the edge of the crowd. *Tonight on Channel 12 News*, Alexandra says. My face is plastered across the screen, as is Korwin's. *Deadly criminals still at large in the capital...*"

I step backward and luckily, the people in the crowd are so centered on themselves and their view of the television that they don't even look at me. Instead, they simply fill in the space I leave in front of the glass, slowly pushing me out. "They've upped the reward to fifteen thousand units!" I hear as I walk away.

With long strides, I break away from the group. I don't run. That could draw attention. Instead, I stroll, as if I'm late for an appointment rather than dodging scrutiny. I tuck a strand of my hair into my cap.

No one seems to notice me. I don't look back and pray my luck holds out.

The CGEF logo is everywhere here, and traffic has accelerated to a frenzied pace. I can't see the drivers because they're moving too fast. I remember this. This is the grid, the innermost roads of Crater City, wired to allow for super speed. I must be close to CGEF headquarters. A chill ripples through me just thinking about it.

It's dark by the time I find the Oakdale Rehabilitation Center. It's inside a skyscraper named the Oakdale Medical Complex that houses a variety of health-related businesses. A map inside leads me to the second floor and the rehabilitation center's front office.

A doughy, curly-headed woman in scrubs gives me a practiced grin from behind the counter. "May I help you?"

"I'm here to see Forrest Woodward," I say, recalling my father's English pseudonym.

"He's in one twenty-two. Sign in, and I'll buzz you back." She points at an electronic tablet bolted to the counter.

I pick up the stylus. I can't use my own pseudonym. Everyone is looking for Lydia Lane. I invent a name— Carly Woodward. The signature fades behind a ticking clock and then the door buzzes. The woman behind the counter doesn't even look up as I enter the rehabilitation floor.

It's hard to believe it's been just over a week since my father's stroke. So much has changed. I've changed. Even if I am able to return to Hemlock Hollow, I'll never be the same. Under the costume of my skin, my blood knows the truth: I am different, down to my cells. For a moment, I am overwhelmed with shame thinking about it. Telling my father isn't going to be easy. Then again, maybe I won't have to. If Jeremiah has already been here, it's possible he told my father everything.

I knock on room one twenty-two, curious if he's been healed or if the stroke has caused permanent damage.

"Come in," my father calls through the door.

At the sound of his voice, a fountain of relief wells up within me. I enter, beaming. He's regained his ability to speak! Once I'm in the room, I can see it's more than that.

228

My father sits at a table, reading an electronic newspaper. He looks strong, almost as good as new.

"Can I help you?" he says to me.

I pull off the glasses and remove my cap.

He stands from his chair on shaky limbs. "Lydia," he whispers.

I cross the room and hug him with everything I have in me. But he pulls away first, glancing toward the door. "You shouldn't be here. Leave now, before they come for you." He spreads the window blinds with his fingers, looking up and down the street.

"Then you know about what happened at CGEF?"

He nods. "It's been all over the news. You've got to get home where you'll be safe."

"It's okay. I signed in as Carly Woodward. No one knows I'm here."

"You don't know what they can do. They could be tracking you right now."

"Dad, has Jeremiah been here?"

He shakes his head and leans toward me. "No. And neither of you *should* be here. It's dangerous."

I frown, wondering what has become of my best friend. My father falls into his chair more by the weight of gravity than his own will. He steadies himself on the table. I sit down across from him.

"You look better," I say.

"I am. I can't say I'm not grateful you sent me here, but some of the therapies…" He shivers and shakes his head. "They're going to release me in a few days." His gaze washes over my hair, my blouse, my jeans. "You cut your hair. You look… different."

"I am different. There's something I have to tell you."

He grabs my wrist and squeezes. "I know."

"I'm not a scamp—"

He squeezes harder. "Don't say it. I know. I know what you can do."

My eyes narrow. "How?"

"Lydia." He wraps his calloused hands around mine. "You have always been my precious daughter."

"But?"

He closes his eyes and shakes his head. "But it's time I told you the truth." His voice is all gravel and his eyes are wet with the threat of tears.

"What are you talking about?"

"You are not my biological daughter. I found you as a baby, when you were only a few weeks old."

His words punch into me and I stop breathing.

"I was an *Englisher* then," he whispers. "A fireman. I worked not far from here. Your biological father left you in my care. He gave me a letter and some money. I hid you."

I shake my head. "No… No…. What about our Bible? We have a complete ancestry in the front of our Bible." I can't figure out why he's saying this. The floor is unsteady under my feet.

"I was raised in Hemlock Hollow," he says, spreading his hands. "Your ancestry is my ancestry. I left Hemlock Hollow for *rumspringa,* just like you did, at seventeen. I met a girl, an *Englisher*, and decided to stay. We married and had a son."

"What—"

"My wife—the woman I told you was your mother—and my son were killed in an automobile accident. That much is true. But when your father left you with me, I ran from this world. At first I tried to hide you in the English world, but everything here is wired. People asked questions. In the end, I returned to Hemlock Hollow and they accepted me as if I'd never left. I was baptized, returned to my roots, and planned to live out the rest of my life there with you."

I cover my mouth with my hand.

"Your biological parents were involved in a research experiment conducted by the government," he whispers. "They had the same abilities you do. Your father died the night he left you with me…saving you from them."

"Why didn't you tell me?" My voice breaks with anger, even though I am careful not to yell.

He scrubs his face with his palms. "We were happy, you and I. You grew up completely normal. I didn't know your biological father's power slept inside of you. If we hadn't left, maybe we'd never know. I planned to tell you someday, if you ever got serious about *rumspringa*. But the timing never seemed right. And then this." He smooths his palms over the small table and leans toward me.

As much as I want to be angry with him, deep inside I understand that he saved me. If he'd kept me in the English world, I'd have ended up like Korwin or worse. Deep grooves around his eyes and mouth testify to the truth. He kept me from this nightmare as long as possible, to protect me. But I can't stop myself from feeling disappointed. I mourn the loss of the heritage I never had. Tears parade down my cheeks.

"Did the man—my biological father—mention others like me? What about my mother?"

"He didn't have time to tell me anything. The note he left with you explained about the study. He believed the Green Republic intended to kill you. I needed to hide you. That's all."

I nod. In my heart though, I still can't accept it. I was so sure of who I was. I thought my power came from God or maybe the radiation from the Outlands. I was wrong. I come from the same place as Korwin. I am manufactured. I am not exactly human.

"I know it's a shock, learning you come from this world, but it doesn't change anything. You are still my little girl. God brought you to me. Maybe not the usual way, but you were a gift just the same. I love you just the same." His voice shakes. The light glints off his wet cheeks.

I stare at my fingers knotted on the table.

"The boy in the video, he's not dangerous like they say, is he?"

"No. Korwin and I... We are the only ones—"

"He's the only one like you?"

"Yes."

"Maybe, when we go back, we can find a way for him to come and visit."

I stare at my hands. Am I going back? Or does knowing that I come from Operation Source Code change everything? There's so much I don't understand.

The sound of shuffling feet in the hallway brings my head around. Without courtesy of a knock, the door slams against the far wall. I leap in front of my father, adrenaline causing my hands to glow. The air around me crackles.

"Hold it right there!" a uniformed officer yells. His familiar face fills me with dread. Officer Reynolds. The same man who arrested me in Willow's Province. The room behind him fills with green uniforms.

He points his metal box toward me, the scrambler. "Think twice before you flame out, Lydia. This device will scramble your neurons. It'll hurt and I'm not afraid to use it. Even if you do get lucky and get out of here, your father won't. Put your hands behind your back."

I lower my hands, extinguishing the blue glow. They move quickly, handcuffing me.

"How did you find me?" I ask.

Officer Reynolds doesn't respond but muscles me toward the door. "Bring the old man," he orders the others.

"No, no!" I beg. I try to fight, to use my power, but the handcuffs they've slapped on me are made of something that absorbs the elastic tickle. The cuffs seem to drain off my power; the more I try to use it, the more exhausted I get.

"Just relax. The cuffs are wired to absorb your energy. I don't want to have to carry you into CGEF." Officer Reynolds forces me through the door and into the hall by the elbow.

My father groans behind me, but I can't see him through the ocean of green uniforms that surrounds us.

They push and pull me through the reception area and out into the street, where a group of black vans wait. One of the uniformed men jogs ahead of me and slides back the side door to the van. Officer Reynolds shoves me inside. With my hands cuffed behind my back, I fall face-first into the cargo area and brace my shoulder on the floor in order to pull my knees in under me. As soon as I do, Officer Reynolds slams the door behind me. The van jerks into motion, and I squirm until I'm able to sit up on my knees. My eyes adjust to the dark interior. I'm not alone.

Handcuffed to the seat at the back of the van, Jeremiah raises his head to look at me.

Chapter 22

The ride from Oakdale isn't long, confirming what I'd suspected. I've come full circle and am in CGEF's backyard. I stare at Jeremiah, wishing I could read his mind. Where's he been? How'd he get caught?

I am afraid to say anything. How much does CGEF know about Jeremiah and me? Anything I say could put us at risk.

When the van door opens, Officer Reynolds pulls me out into a dimly lit garage. Unlike my first visit to CGEF, they aren't bringing me through the front door. They force us inside the building and up the elevator to the clinic. I'm so terrified, my legs give out and Reynolds has to half-carry me into a room with a holding cell. With a shove, he directs me toward the bench at the back. I trip over my feet, landing awkwardly on my hip. He removes Jeremiah's cuffs before backing out of the cell.

"Aren't you going to remove mine too?" I ask, my voice trembling.

"No." Officer Reynolds slides the bars shut and leaves the room, offering no further explanation.

Jeremiah's fingers go to work on my wrists, tugging on the steel bands. "They won't budge. Can you…?"

"No. They know what I am. These will drain me," I

whisper.

He releases the cuffs and settles his elbows on his knees. With my hands bound behind my back, I try in vain to get comfortable on the bench beside him. "I'm sorry I hurt you," I say. It seems like a good way to start.

"Don't." He turns his face away from me.

"I read your letter and I took your advice. I guess Maxwell was right. How did we think we'd ever make it back home this way?" I whisper.

Jeremiah's head snaps around, his sharp look pinning me in place. "What letter?"

"The letter you left on my bed. You said that I'd forgotten who I was and you were going home after checking on my dad."

He leans his face toward mine. "I didn't leave. You did. *You* left *me* a letter."

"What?"

"I found a note from you on my bed." Jeremiah stresses each word. "You said I was in the way. That you wanted to stay with Korwin. That I should go home."

"No. I didn't. I came looking for you when you left."

He slowly shakes his head.

A twisting begins low in my stomach, a compression of razor blades that work their way up my throat and make my eyes burn. "Who?" My voice cracks.

"I don't know." Jeremiah places his hands on my cheeks and lowers his forehead to mine. "But I wouldn't leave you if you didn't want to be left. What's a little thing like you falling in love with someone else to come between lifelong friends?" He gives a weak laugh.

"I never said…" I'm about to finish *I loved Korwin*, but I stop short. I do love him and Jeremiah knows it. His cornflower blues say it all. I've hurt him, deeply. But like me, he isn't willing to give up everything we have. Our relationship is so much bigger than dating, than the physical. I don't want him the way I want Korwin, but I do want him in my life.

"I hoped you'd understand. It just happened. I never intended to hurt you."

He lowers his hands but his gaze drills into me. "Besides, if we ever make it home, who knows?"

I avert my eyes from the sting of his hopeful tone.

"How could I be so stupid?" he says. "You're not sure you're going home."

I can't argue, although staying in this world doesn't make sense either. I am a freak of nature, and the people here want to use me or destroy me. Maybe both. But when I try to picture myself going back, knowing this thing, this power is inside of me, I'm not sure I could put it aside. Would the *Ordnung* accept my abilities as a gift from God or condemn me?

"Right now, I just want to make it out alive," I say.

His eyes dart to mine and the corners of his mouth pull down into a grimace.

The door to the room squeaks open and a parade of green uniforms enters. I gasp as Korwin and Maxwell trip forward from the center of the group, thrust toward the cell doors in handcuffs. The bars slide open and I notice cuts and bruises all over their exposed skin. Maxwell's left eye is swollen to the point of being useless. An officer removes his cuffs and he staggers to the bench. Like with me, they leave Korwin's cuffs on.

Once we are all locked inside the small cell, all of the Greens leave the room.

"I don't understand. How did this happen?" I ask Korwin.

He shakes his head and glances at a round black bubble in the upper corner of the cell. Of course the Greens are watching and listening. Why else would they put us all together? I chide myself for being open with Jeremiah earlier. I've been so stupid. And where is my father? What have they done with him? I have so many questions, but I don't dare say anything now. We wait in excruciating silence.

After maybe an hour, one of the officers returns. "Lydia Lane, come with me."

What should I do? Why are they singling me out? I glance toward Maxwell but he looks away. Korwin meets my eyes and sighs deeply.

"Now!" the officer says.

Reluctantly, I stand and amble to the door. The man locks the cell behind me and then leads me down the hall, and to a neighboring room. I balk when I see Dr. Konrad and another older man I've never met seated at the table. Konrad's expression is as severe as ever with that thin, drawn smile that makes me want to back out of the room. The other man is as warm as Konrad is cold and that scares me even more. He's impeccably dressed in a vintage suit and tie, gray haired and gray eyed, and judging from his fingernails, his hands have never known real work.

"What have you done with my father?" I ask Konrad.

Konrad rakes his eyes over me. "Lydia, I want to introduce you to Senator Pierce. He's the sponsor of Operation Source Code."

I refuse to respond.

"Lydia," Senator Pierce drawls with an accent that isn't familiar to me. His voice is syrupy. "It's a pleasure to make your acquaintance. I'm sorry about the way you and your friends were detained but I promise you, what happens to those folks in that cell and your father is strictly up to you."

"You'll free them if I cooperate?" I ask, meeting Pierce's gray eyes for the first time.

"I'm afraid that won't be possible, but if you cooperate, their lives and yours will vastly improve." He squints and jigs his head when he says "vastly" as if he's selling me a sick horse.

"What do you want? To use me as a human battery like you did Korwin?"

"Oh dear, no." Senator Pierce gives a friendly smile. "Please sit. Konrad, help the lady."

Konrad gets up to pull a chair out for me. I don't sit.

"There's been a huge misunderstanding," Pierce says. "We don't want to drain you, Lydia. We want to work with you. We want to resurrect the program as it was intended and make you part of our security unit."

"That's it? Nothing else? You don't want to experiment on me or Korwin like guinea pigs?"

"That's it." Pierce spreads his hands. "We do want to test your abilities but nothing will happen without your consent. We want to work with you, to be a team."

"And this is the way you invite me to the team," I say through my teeth, turning to show him the cuffs.

"The electrocuffs will come off as soon as we can trust you. There was no other way. The man in that cell, Maxwell Stuart, is the head of the Liberty Party and the cause of one of the worst incidents of terrorism I can remember since the war."

What? I try to stay neutral but I can feel a scowl twist my lips. He's lying! They said the same thing about Korwin and me.

"Ah, you don't know, do you?" Senator Pierce holds up a finger. "The Liberty Party bombed one of our buildings. Killed seven government employees and nine civilians— *children* who were taking a tour of the building." Senator Pierce's chin drops to his chest and he glares at me from under bushy gray eyebrows.

I shake my head. "That's not true."

He rises from his chair. "If I can prove to you that it's true, will you listen to us with an open mind?"

For a moment I'm confused what to do. I'm sure he's lying. "No amount of Green Republic-manufactured proof is going to convince me."

"Oh, that won't be necessary." He looks at the guard behind me and nods.

The officer opens the door and leads me back to the holding cell. Pierce follows.

"Maxwell Stuart," Pierce says, "could you please explain to Lydia who was responsible for the West Hub bombing?"

Everyone in the room stares at Maxwell. He sputters but doesn't answer. His lip is so swollen, I'm not sure he can speak.

"We can get Konrad in here to give you some *motivation* if we need to. Answer me," Pierce demands.

I start to shiver. I can only imagine what type of motivation Konrad could provide.

On cue, the doctor enters with a large leather bag. He opens it, and I see twisted and sharp metal tools inside, horrific tools, some with dried blood in the grooves. Konrad extracts a small box containing a syringe and draws up thick yellow fluid from a vial he pulls from the side pocket.

Maxwell groans at the sight of it. His head lists on his shoulders. "We were after CGEF's West Hub," he mumbles. "We didn't know there was anyone else inside. They were collateral damage."

Korwin jerks at "collateral damage." I've never heard the phrase before, but I can guess what it means. He's saying the sixteen lives were less worthy than his cause. The thought makes me nauseous.

"Korwin, did you know about this?" I ask.

He shakes his head, averting his eyes so that he doesn't have to look at his father.

"Oh no. Korwin was our guest at the time of the bombing," Pierce says.

I stare at Maxwell, my brain digesting that he's a killer, a terrorist.

"All I'm asking, Lydia, is for a chance to give you more of the truth," Pierce says. "Cooperate, and the people you love will be made comfortable, including your father."

I face Pierce. It takes every ounce of resolve I have left to do what I have to do. "Okay," I say. "I'll cooperate."

Senator Pierce claps his hands together and laughs. "Well, hot damn! Guess we won't be needing you after all, Doctor."

Konrad returns the needle to the box, looking slightly disappointed.

"Boys, show our guests to their rooms."

The door is thrown open and a sea of green uniforms floods the cell around me.

* * * * *

"Follow me," an officer says softly. They've separated me from the rest of the group and sent me with a Green who looks about my age. I'm not sure if his politeness is feigned or if he doesn't know why I'm here. He looks too young to wear the uniform. We ride in an elevator to a floor of apartments where he shows me to a door with no number. He presses his palm into the Biolock and the door opens on its own.

"Please," he says, motioning inside. He removes my cuffs and introduces me to a comfortable suite with a bedroom, kitchenette, and plenty of seating. The technology rivals the manor's.

I stare at the Biolock panel, remembering how I'd broken into one to save Korwin. Perhaps I'll be able to break out.

"Just a warning. Don't try the Biolock," the officer says. "It's made to drain off extra energy to evade scampers."

"Oh," is all I can think to say.

"The television is also a control center for music and holographic games," he says. He pokes a painting of a night sky and then points out the different options on the main menu.

I shrug in response. He taps a button and the night sky painting is back.

"There's no cooking equipment. They don't allow it up here, but you can order food." He presses a few buttons on the irradiator, and a square of chicken magically appears inside.

"How does that work?" I ask.

"No idea," he says and laughs to himself. "Something along the lines of teleportation. I never paid much attention in school."

"Me neither," I say absently. Everything I could ever need is available at the touch of a button and I don't want any of it.

I'm relieved when he finally goes, even though I haven't even begun to understand all of the features of this apartment. This place is simply a different kind of cell. The door is still locked and the wall of windows that overlook the city won't open. Even if they did, I'm too high to jump.

Again, I wonder what they've done with Jeremiah, my father, and the Stuarts, but I'm helpless to find out. My brain buzzes but the events of the day are too much. I can't think or feel properly. I just am.

Maybe a drink to clear my head.

The refrigerator contains three different types of soda, stocked in rows to take up an entire shelf. I lift a bottle of root beer from the group and, after reading the instructions, screw off the top. I collapse into the leather chair that faces the window and drink it in the privacy of my cage.

I want to scream. Instead, I let out a subdued moan.

I'm halfway through the bottle when there's a knock at the door. I give the wood panel a deadly stare. It's locked. They've told me not to try to open it. Why do they bother knocking at all?

Reluctantly, I move to the door and yell, "Come in!"

When it opens, I almost drop the bottle in my hand.

Chapter 23

"Jameson!" I stare at the familiar face first in utter surprise and then, as I notice the Green Republic emblem on the folder in his arms, accusation.

"Jameson was my cover. My real name is David, David Snow." He looks at me expectantly. "We have so much to talk about, Lydia."

The pieces of the puzzle snap together. "You're with them. You're working with the Green Republic."

"Yes. Invite me in and I'll explain everything."

"You betrayed the Stuarts."

"Maxwell had it coming. Be thankful I got you and Jeremiah out of there before the Greens raided Stuart Manor. If I hadn't, you'd be in far worse shape. Now, come on. Sit down. Let's talk." He nods his head toward the table.

"And if I don't?"

He says nothing, but with the way he tilts his head, I know I don't really have a choice.

"Come in. Let's talk," I say cynically, turning my back on him.

"You are so like your mother," he says.

I whirl in his direction. "So now you knew my mother?" As the words come out of my mouth, I remember how he said I reminded him of someone. Was that who he meant? My mother?

"I knew your mother quite well." Hastily, he sets the folder on the table and pulls a picture from it.

I snatch it from his fingers. Four women and four men dressed in military uniforms stare back at me. The woman in the middle could be my twin. The man over her right shoulder is a young version of Jameson… I mean, David.

My mouth opens but nothing comes out.

"The man on her left is your father," he says. "He was my best friend."

With the picture pressed between my fingers, I lower myself clumsily into the chair across from him. "You were one of the Alpha Eight."

He pulls the chair out and takes a seat.

My fingers hover over the picture of my mother. She looks strong, determined. The man behind her has a similar countenance. "What were their names?"

"Your father was Michael Fawn. The best and the bravest soldier I've ever known. Your mom, Laura, was a medic. That's how they met. She treated his wounds in the Northern war."

I'm not familiar with the Northern war. The history we learn in Amish school ends with the Great Rebellion when the wall went up. I don't ask though. It's not important to me. "What happened to my parents?"

David's eyes sweep toward the window. "They died."

"Trying to escape." My jaw snaps on the last word.

David shakes his head. "The situation was complex. They weren't in their right minds."

The couple next to my parents is olive-skinned and

familiar. "Korwin's parents?" I ask.

"Yes. Jordan and Sicilia Villanueva."

"Also dead?"

"Yes," he says. "In the same way."

"And these two?" I ask.

"Charles and Rebecca Stone. Assumed dead." David's attention shifts to the folder.

"Assumed?"

"Their bodies were never found."

"Who is this on the other side of you?"

"My wife." His voice cracks, and his expression morphs into hollow misery. She must be dead, too.

I scour every inch of the picture, looking for answers the photograph can't give me. "I want to know the truth."

He folds his hands on the table and I'm struck by how completely different he is. Jameson was stiff and formal. David has shed the black suit for a T-shirt and jeans and casually slumps across from me. Even his mannerisms have changed. "Ask me."

"How long were you undercover at Stuart Manor?" I ask.

With a deep sigh, he leans back in his chair. "Five years. As soon as we discovered Korwin."

"And you've been feeding the Green Republic information on the rebellion ever since."

David doesn't answer. In fact, his face turns to stone, expressionless except for a flick of his pupils toward a light fixture in the ceiling. It's so fast I almost don't notice it. Inside I feel a tug. I don't exactly hear his voice in my head, but my intuition burns. David wants to tell me something but can't.

I thumb the picture in front of me. Korwin has told me about Operation Source Code, but his information was all hearsay. This is physical evidence. A living, breathing member of the study to share exactly how I came to be. I lean forward. "Tell me about Operation Source Code."

"Just over eighteen years ago, Senator Pierce sponsored a project with the goal of revolutionizing biological energy. After the war and the resulting ban on dirty energy sources, there was a huge shortage of power. Pierce thought if people powered their own lives, it would solve the allocation issues. People would naturally use less energy if part of it came from their own personal store."

He stops talking and glances at the refrigerator.

"Would you like a drink?" I ask flatly.

He nods.

I retrieve a root beer and slide it across the table.

After a long drink, he continues. "Konrad was the scientist at the forefront of biotechnical research and was quickly named to oversee the study. The government solicited military personnel to apply to participate. There were four qualifications: the applicant had to be in peak physical condition, between the ages of eighteen and twenty-five, willing to live undercover for an indefinite amount of time, and married, only husband-and-wife teams need apply. The draw? Fame, fortune, glory, and the possibility of unlimited power. Dr. Konrad compared it to being the first man to walk on the moon."

He shakes his head and takes another drink. The face

he makes is tortured, and I recognize the expression as the same one he wore the night he confronted me on the balcony of Stuart Manor. I sense that he wishes he was drinking something stronger than root beer.

"He interviewed hundreds of military personnel and selected the best and the brightest. Four couples. None questioned why Konrad only wanted married couples. It made sense. We were going underground, disappearing off the face of the earth for an indefinite number of years. They wanted us to be stable.

"We were injected with the retrovirus in August, after a series of animal tests. At first, nothing. After a month, I could power my phone. In six months, I could turn the lights on and keep them on with nothing but my mind. After a year—it took a year for us to peak—it was amazing. Not only could we power the test devices, we could shoot lightning from our hands and create heat. But the part that blew everyone's mind was that we could pull electricity from a source."

I clear my throat. "Why was that such a big deal?"

"Because for the first time, Pierce and Konrad viewed us not as test subjects for a retrovirus that would someday be used on the rest of the population, but as weapons. We were able to drain a power supply with nothing but our two hands. Any battery, any power source, our elite force could dismantle in a heartbeat."

"Why would the Greens want you to drain a power source?"

David licks his lips and knots his fingers together on the table. "Our currency is based on units of energy, which means the value of things increases when energy is scarce. It's good for our economy for CGEF to control the amount of energy available to the public." The way David says it sounds like rote memorization. "So that's how they used us. For a while, we were the most celebrated secret agents in history."

"For a while?"

David's face darkens. "Tragedy. Two pregnancies. You and Korwin."

I shake my head. "I don't understand. Why is that a tragedy?"

"When the Fawns and the Villaneuvos found out they were expecting, Konrad was skeptical the babies could be carried to term. But when the pregnancies advanced normally, it posed a problem for the study."

"Why would a pregnancy be a problem?"

"No one knew what you would be. A monster? A cripple? Pierce and Konrad ordered that as soon as you were born you were to be contained for tests, until he knew what we were dealing with. If you were found to be dangerous…" David's face sags.

I tuck my hair behind my ear. "He planned to kill us."

David nods.

"Is that why my parents escaped? To save me?"

"Yes, and it cost them their lives. They couldn't survive outside of the study. Our cells." His hand pats his chest. "My cells are unstable. Around a year into the experiment, we noticed the symptoms. Any energy output would result in electroscurvy." He shakes his head. "We were constantly covered in sores. Luckily, Konrad invented a formula to stabilize our chemistry. With a shot a day, I'm as healthy as you or Korwin, but I need that shot, Lydia, or I will effectively starve to death."

When he says it, the air between us thickens with tension. "Konrad keeps you alive," I say in barely a whisper.

He nods slightly. "When your parents escaped, they knew it was a death sentence. I've heard they lasted only a couple of weeks without Konrad's formula."

I press my fingers into my lips. My parents, two people I never knew, sacrificed themselves for me. I'm overwhelmed. Lowering my hand, I ask the obvious question. "Why are you telling me all of this now?"

David sits up straighter. "Because you're grown, and you're powerful. We need your cooperation. We can resurrect the team. You don't know how amazing you and Korwin are. Your cells are completely stable." David places his hand over my wrist and squeezes, staring into my eyes with brutal intensity. "You are stronger than any of us."

My wrist tingles. I'm not sure why, but a strong feeling tells me to focus on this message: *You are stronger than any of us.* I tilt my head to the side. I don't understand.

"Do you still have your power?" I ask.

David extends his hand and it bursts into blue flame. "As long as I have the formula, I'm a Spark." I blink, and he extinguishes it. "We can be a team again, Lydia. You can follow in your mother's footsteps."

I fold my arms across my chest. "And just like my mother, I don't have a choice, do I?"

He reaches across the table and rests a hand on my

upper arm. "What other choice could there be? You are what you are. Embrace it. Your cooperation will be generously rewarded."

The phrase sounds practiced, and I feel the tug again. I know this. It's similar to when I'm with Korwin. David's cells are enough like mine that we connect too, though not as powerfully and in a different way. Why didn't I notice it before at the mansion? But then, I can't remember David ever touching me. That's when my connection with Korwin is the most noticeable. I had so much anxiety at the mansion anyway, it's possible it was there all along and I didn't see it for what it was. I feel it now though, strong and focused. He's not telling me everything.

"I have to go now. Konrad will come get you in the morning to run some tests. Afterward, Natasha and I will begin lessons in basic hand-to-hand combat." He stands, gathering the folder into his arms, and moves toward the door.

"Who's Natasha?" I ask.

He points at the picture he's left on the table. "My wife."

And then he's gone. The door clicks closed and locks behind him.

I stare at my parents until my eyes burn. I know David left this picture to convince me to cooperate with the Green Republic, as if cooperating will make my parents proud. But all I can think, as I search their faces, is that my parents died to save me from this.

Chapter 24

Head throbbing, I break from my endless cycle of dead-end thoughts and decide to take a bath. I ache to shed my clothes, as if I can shed my uncertainty with them. The only items in the closet are exercise clothes, stretchy pants, and shirts labeled to shed sweat. I snag a gray set and find the bathroom. The controls are similar to the ones at the Stuarts'. I fill the tub with water, as hot as I can stand it, and slip in, one inch at a time, closing my eyes and leaning my neck against the cold porcelain. "Lord, help me," I pray aloud.

"Lydia," comes a muffled voice. "Is that you?"

I sit up, splashing water over the edge of the tub. "Jeremiah?"

"I'm here. We're locked in the apartment next door."

I press my hands against the tiled wall. "Are you okay? Have they hurt you?"

"We're fine. Your father is here with me. He's fine too. And you?"

"I'm well." My voice cracks.

"You don't sound well."

I press my forehead against the tile and begin to weep. Great gulps of air enter my throat in noisy rattles.

"Stay there. I have an idea," he says. Minutes tick by.

Then I hear footsteps.

"Jeremiah?" I say toward the tile.

"There's a door, Lydia. I think our suites are connected. It's locked, but I bet you could open it."

I push myself to my feet and wrap the white robe from the hook around my body. Following Jeremiah's knocks and whispers, I find the door to the left of the kitchen. It isn't hidden in any way but it doesn't even have a knob, just a Biolock. I have a nagging suspicion I'm meant to find it. Why else would they have me next door?

"I'm going to try to open it, but it might not work. They told me the front door is wired to drain off energy if you don't have the bio-key."

"Will it hurt you if it does?" Jeremiah asks.

"I don't know for sure."

"Then wait—"

A tiny pulse of electricity from my hand opens the mechanism. On the other side, Jeremiah smiles at me from an apartment very much like the one I am in. Behind him, my father rests in a recliner. I can't stop the tears.

"I guess it wasn't that kind of lock," I say. I throw my arms around Jeremiah's neck and kiss his cheek hard enough to nearly leave a bruise. Then I hurry to my father's side.

"Dad, are you okay? They didn't hurt you, did they?" I rub his hand between my own.

"Not yet." The corners of his mouth tug down.

Jeremiah takes the seat next to me. "They don't believe us about where we're from."

"You mean Hem—"

My father hugs me, forcing my mouth into his shoulder.

Jeremiah moves closer. "They questioned us for an hour. Of course, we told them the truth—that we came from Willow's Province."

I notice my father's eyes dart up to the light fixture. They're watching us. That's what David was trying to tell me. "Of course. What else would you say?"

"But you see, they're checking with Willow's Province local government because they can't believe you grew up there and they never knew about you," Jeremiah adds.

"They're angry that your abilities weren't reported immediately," my father says. "I explained to them that your talents didn't blossom until this year, but they found that hard to believe."

"Oh. I'm sure the Willow's Province government will clear everything up," I say confidently, but inside I'm a mess. If they dig too deep, we are doomed.

"Of course," Jeremiah says. He rubs his forehead as if he's in pain.

The Green Republic must never know where we're really from. What will become of us if they find out our identities are manufactured? We cannot allow them to point the finger at Hemlock Hollow. Our way of life is dependent on the English underestimating us and believing we stay where we're put. We are like prehistoric creatures, preserved for posterity, kept neatly out of everyday life. Our secret, that we come and go as we please, can never be revealed. It would change everything.

I straighten. "Where are Korwin and Mr. Stuart?"

"They separated us," my father says. "Mr. Stuart has a history. I think it's best we distance ourselves." He rubs his eyes with his thumb and forefinger.

"The Green Republic knows I spent time with Mr. Stuart. Our agreement is that if I cooperate, no one gets hurt. That includes Mr. Stuart. I don't care what he's done—he's part of the agreement." My voice is loud and firm. I want them to hear me. I hope that they're watching.

A strange brew of emotions stirs inside me. I have no love for Maxwell Stuart, not after his forced admission, but he matters for Korwin's sake. Pierce is likely holding them together and I am angry they are unaccounted for. For all I know, both are still in the cell in the clinic.

For the time being, I've earned a comfortable space for my father and Jeremiah. Deep inside though, I know I've made a deal with the devil. Konrad and Pierce will want more and more of me. I'm so deep inside the lie that I am Lydia Lane from Willow's Province, I can hardly remember all of the truth. What will it do to me, living this double life? What will it do to my soul? My soul— already compromised by violence, disloyalty, and deceit. I am filthy with sin.

I pace the small living room between my father who holds his head in his hands and Jeremiah who watches me, looking lost and bitter. We remain silent, fearful of who might be watching.

"Did you say something?" I ask Jeremiah.

"No," he says, brows plunging.

"There's a mumble. Can you hear that?"

"I don't hear anything."

I glance at my father and he shakes his head. My skin begins to tingle, and the hair on the back of my neck stands on end. I check the room, eyes darting to every corner. The windows are closed; we are too high up to hear anything anyway. Again, I hear the mumble and feel the tingle even stronger. This time I *know* what I'm feeling. I cross the apartment and press my ear against the door. Korwin is out there.

I try the door but it's locked. Like a caged animal, I beat against it and then attempt to open the door with a pulse of energy. But this lock must be the same as the one in my apartment because it drains me. It's made of the same stuff as the handcuffs. I double over as it draws my energy until I can break the connection. I pull my hand away, panting.

All of the air exits my lungs at once. My shoulders sag. I wobble to the sofa and flop down onto it.

Jeremiah is at my side in a heartbeat. "What was that all about?"

My father leans toward me in his recliner.

"Korwin," I whisper. "I think they just walked him down the hall. I could feel it."

Jeremiah's face falls, and he pulls his head back as if he's putting distance between us. The way he looks at me, it's like he's seeing me for the first time. Like I'm a freak. Maybe I am.

"There's something you two need to know about me," I say. Better to get this out now. There's no reason to delay. If we ever get out of here, they will have to know why I don't belong in Hemlock Hollow. I trot into my apartment and retrieve the photo from the table. When I return, I hand it to my father. "Jameson visited today. His real name is David. He's the one who turned us in."

Jeremiah's eyes grow wide, and he snatches the picture from my father's hands.

"He was one of the original eight test subjects in Operation Source Code. One of the original Alpha Eight." I explain everything, all I know about Operation Source Code, the Alpha Eight, my real parents, and David. My father and Jeremiah listen in stunned silence.

Finally, my father's left eye wrinkles in that way it does when he's thinking hard about something. "You know what I find interesting about your story? Why would Konrad only use married couples if he didn't want or expect children to be an outcome?"

"David said Dr. Konrad wanted them to be stable since they wouldn't have contact with the outside world."

"Hmm." My father winks at me as if he wants me to make a connection, but I am too exhausted. I can hardly think. He rubs his chin. "You know what I find helpful in these situations? A good night's sleep." He hobbles over to me and places a hand on my shoulder. "Once you can rest and recharge, everything will come together."

A person has to be a problem-solver to make it in Hemlock Hollow. We don't have a store on every corner. If you want something, you have to get it from someone you know or make it yourself. We are dependent on each other and on our heritage, and we trust the wisdom of our past. We have a saying: *Be like the teakettle. When it's up to its neck in hot water, it sings.*

I force myself to smile at my father. "You're right. Let's all get some rest."

I'm in hot water. Tonight I'll sleep. Tomorrow, it will be time to sing.

Chapter 25

"Lydia, I'm not going to call security or cuff you today. You won't disappoint me, will you?"

"No," I tell Dr. Konrad. "I won't."

"Good girl."

To be sure, a Green ushered me from my apartment to this private dining room in cuffs, but I'm free now and have no intention of causing trouble. How can I risk it? Everyone I love is locked in separate rooms in this building. Dr. Konrad could have them all killed with a snap of his fingers. I know he would do it. I have no choice but to cooperate.

David and Konrad sit across the table from me, a heaping plate of ham, eggs, and fried potatoes in front of each of us.

"It's really important you eat it all," David says. "You'll need your strength for the tests."

I cut a slice of ham and force myself to eat it. It tastes like rubber. One of the things I miss most about home is the taste of meat. When Korwin told me chicken was created in a lab, that it was never actually alive, I didn't think much of it. But now, I remember his explanation. This meat is a cell from a pig that was coaxed into being a ham without ever being a pig. On one hand, I can see where it is the compassionate choice. Nothing has to die for me to eat. I've helped slaughter enough pigs to know the task is gruesome for everyone involved.

But the taste isn't the same. Not even close.

I force myself to swallow. "Is that why you practically force-fed Korwin and me at the mansion, David? To fatten us up for testing?"

He smiles. "Using your abilities burns a lot of calories. We want to keep you healthy. We want what's best for you."

I doubt it. Just like Maxwell Stuart, they want me to trust them so that I'll be forthright and show them what I can do.

When I think of Maxwell, it dawns on me that I no longer have any concern for the failure of his planned revolution. I don't care about politics or Maxwell's war. I loathe his methods as much as the Green Republic's. What I do care about is being free. I want my family and friends back. I want my life back. Right now, the doorway to both of those things seems to be through Dr. Konrad. I decide to play his game until I can win my own.

Once my plate is empty, I ask, "What now?"

"Now, if you will follow me to the lab, we'll get started," Konrad says.

David pushes his chair back from the table. "I'll see you after lunch for some additional training based on the results."

Konrad leads me to the elevator. We descend to the clinic and then come to a room that, from the outside, looks eerily similar to Test Room A in the manor. I roll my eyes. Not again. Has my life been reduced to a series of white insulated rooms? I feel more like a guinea pig than ever.

But inside, there is no wood, sand, or metal, just a dark room with padded walls and a mirror at the front disguising the observation booth. I look directly at the square of glass.

"What do you want me to do?"

Dr. Konrad speaks slowly, condescendingly. "We would like a demonstration of your skills, Lydia. By establishing a baseline, we hope to better develop how we can help each other in the future."

"There's nothing in here to demonstrate on," I say.

"Anything in a blue uniform is a target. Avoid the green. Greens are friendlies."

A man appears in front of me, out of thin air. For a moment, I'm confused. Where did he come from? What is he doing in here? Burly and dressed in blue, he looks half-crazed. He draws a gun, points it in my direction.

"What are you doing?" I ask.

Konrad's voice comes over the speaker. "Hit the target, Lydia."

The man pulls the trigger. With a snap of my arm, I spark out to protect myself, but the bullet never hits me. Instead, it passes right through me, shield and all.

It's a hologram, like the game at Korwin's. I blast the man with a bolt of lightning from my hand. He breaks apart on contact. In the resulting flash of light, I notice a thin wire behind his image.

"A weak current," Konrad says. "But effective."

Weak? Does he think that's the best I can do? I didn't know it was a hologram. I certainly didn't give it my best shot. Anger swells within me. If he wants a demonstration, I'll give him one.

"Again." I throw my hands out to the sides, the hot elastic ribbon shooting from my control center into my palms.

A blue soldier rushes me. I blast him to bits. Another jumps at me from the ceiling and earns the same fate. Behind me, a blue soldier reaches for my throat. I see him in the mirror, pivot, and blow him away. More come, ten, twenty. I start to sweat. This is my chance. Maybe I'm tipping my hand by showing him everything I've got, but I want him to know. And it's more than a desire to avoid ever doing this again. I want him to fear me.

Blast after blast I destroy the soldiers, and then something different. A green uniform instead of blue. I'm not supposed to shoot the green. I let him pass me. More blue, both men and women this time, twenty, thirty. I fry an entire legion of them, avoiding the ones in green. I am shaking, dripping with sweat, and glowing brighter than a star.

The room goes dark again and then there is a child, maybe seven years old, in a blue uniform. I narrow my eyes in the direction of the observation booth. I don't want to do this. Even if it is a hologram, it's a line I don't wish to cross.

"Engage the target," Konrad says.

My head is spinning. I'm too hot, too bright. If this was a child, she'd have burnt up in my atmosphere. "No,"

I say. "I won't kill a child, even a pretend child."

Konrad doesn't respond but the next thing I know, the room is filled with children in blue uniforms, knives and guns in their tiny hands. Obviously, Konrad thinks he can push me beyond my limits and force my obedience.

I give my head a shake and then I walk to where one of the children are and grab the wire hanging behind her while the hologram stabs me harmlessly in the stomach. Staring directly at the mirror, I unleash the thing within me, the monster I've kept tethered for as long as I've known how. I throw it into the wire with no intent to call it back or tie it off. I tell it to run, to fly.

My breath comes in ragged pants. My glow fills every corner of the room. The children flicker and fade. The wire in my hand melts and drips soupy silver to the white floor. I wipe my palms free of the remnants. All of the wires have melted, peppering the floor with silver puddles, and the white material on the walls is singed brown. It blisters and melts in my mounting heat, but I do not pull my power back inside.

"Stop!" comes a voice over the speaker.

Stop? How could I stop? It feels so good to let the power out. Only now do I realize how difficult it was to keep it contained. My power glides behind my knees and circles in front of me. The beast has taken form. A twisting blue, dragon-like fire swims around me, pushing at the melting walls. It passes in front of the mirror and the glass cracks, first in one spot at the center and then branching out like a spiderweb to the corners.

The shattering glass and the ever-growing electric

dragon, the corporeal form of my power, bring me to my senses. I have to stop this. If I don't, it will consume me and everything close to me.

Focusing, I begin to draw the power back inside. I tie it off at my elbows, clench my fists so no more can go out. I pull and yank and coil the beast inside like I'm spooling yarn. My head might explode from the effort. I'm not sure the power will fit inside of me anymore. It's too large.

Sprinklers come on above me, water drenching me from head to toe, cooling me. I grab hold of what remains and wrench it back inside. Finally, it obeys and I succeed in containing it.

At the center of the wrecked room, I stare at the cracked mirror, knowing Dr. Konrad is watching. My reflection in the glass is someone I don't recognize. A too-skinny woman, soaking wet, with mascara-darkened eyes and a white T-shirt that clings to her breasts. The muscles in my arms bulge beneath my skin. Blood dribbles from my nose. My chin lowers and my lips peel back from my teeth, not in a smile but an expression more sinister.

I am powerful. I am deadly. Fearfully and wonderfully made. The water drips over my lashes, down my cheeks, and onto my lips. I don't blink. I focus on the crack in the mirror with everything in me, willing him to challenge me with something more.

The mirror shatters, pieces crashing to the floor, revealing the open-mouthed faces of Dr. Konrad and two men in white coats.

"Is that the kind of demonstration you wanted?" My voice sounds husky. I hadn't meant to annihilate the mirror. I'd thought my ribbon was wound back inside. But my power is like a muscle and with all the exercise I've given it, it has grown.

Dr. Konrad finds his voice. "Yes, Lydia. That was perfect." He smiles, breaking into a low chuckle. "You are absolutely perfect. Let's get you some dry clothes and find David."

I walk toward the hole in the wall, stepping through the broken glass and into the room with Dr. Konrad. He swallows hard as I approach but stands his ground. The other white coats scramble away.

All the while I'm watching them scatter, I am drunk with power. Who am I? Not the timid girl from Hemlock Hollow I'm supposed to be, but the owner of a great and terrible power. I'm shocked that a part of me is proud of the way I've made Konrad revere me. And the biggest surprise of all is that I like this feeling. In fact, I love it.

Dr. Konrad motions toward the door. "Shall we go?"

I lead the way into the hall. Eyes twinkling, he bounds after me like it's his birthday and I'm the present he never expected to get.

Chapter 26

By the time David comes to get me, I've changed and had lunch with my father and Jeremiah. They are comfortable but, unlike me, haven't been allowed out of the room. We say little to each other, for fear the Greens are listening.

After Konrad's enthusiasm, I expect David to be in a good mood. Instead his expression is grave.

"Dr. Konrad shared your results with me. He wants to begin combat training."

"Wasn't that what I just did?" I answer. "I fought off an army of blue uniforms. And no electroscurvy." I hold up both arms so he can see. "I did get a bloody nose though."

"You're getting stronger."

I shrug and look away. The confidence and assertiveness I'd shown with Konrad has been replaced by the humility I'm far more familiar with.

"Konrad wants to train you in hand-to-hand combat. You have to be able to defend yourself in the event you are drained or otherwise unable to spark."

I step into the hall and turn right toward the elevators, but David shakes his head. "Let's take the stairs to warm up." He turns left, hugging the south wall.

At first I try to walk beside him, but he keeps stepping

in front of me. The tug is back and I stumble at the odd sensation in my body. I find relief by walking behind him, snug against the south wall. My senses are on high alert. David is trying to tell me something.

We reach the stairwell and he pauses, his hand hovering over the Biolock. An electric breeze courses over me and the hair on my arms stands at attention. I glance toward the second door to my right and then at David.

Korwin is in there. I know it. "When can I see Korwin?"

David lowers his chin slightly, almost imperceptibly, and opens the door. "Not up to me," he says. He begins jogging down the stuffy concrete stairwell, and I join him, matching him step for step.

"There are twenty-one floors between your apartment and the training center," he says. "The training center is on the second floor."

"Konrad and I had an agreement. I cooperate and no one gets hurt."

"Take it up with Konrad."

I nod, then narrow my eyes. "Will Natasha be meeting us there?" He'd mentioned his wife yesterday and said she'd help train me.

He clears his throat. "She isn't feeling well today."

My stomach drops and I'm flooded with panic. I miss a stair and trip. David catches my elbow, and the feeling passes as quickly as it came.

"Are you okay?" he asks, but the concern in his eyes is not for me. I am not imagining our connection. His expression pleads with me, but what is he pleading for?

What is he trying to tell me?

"I'm fine. Just a little drained from this morning's session." I nod my head slowly, deliberately.

"Come on. Almost there." He breaks into a jog again and doesn't stop until we reach the second floor.

The training room has an impressive display of padded mats and racks of weapons. Although the space goes on and on, we are the only ones there. "No one else feel like training?"

"Konrad said you needed your space. You made quite an impression this morning. I'm not sure any of the officers want to be in the same room as you at the moment."

Good. Exactly what I wanted.

My eyes fall on the padded floor. The symbol of the Green Republic is emblazoned on the black rubbery surface. "Sustainable Living Through Government."

"Do they teach you what the symbol means in those Willow's Province schools?"

"I was homeschooled," I say quickly, "and my parents never stressed the subject. What does it represent?"

"I'll make you a deal. If you work hard today, even if the exercises make you uncomfortable, I'll tell you."

I shrug. "I was going to work hard anyway."

"You might not want to once we begin," he says darkly. The gray in his hair seems more pronounced today and the bags under his eyes make him look weary.

"I'll work hard."

"Good. Prove it. Give me an idea of what we are dealing with. Hit me." He stands in front of me, feet slightly spread, arms by his sides.

I pretend to punch, stopping my fist before I make contact with his chest.

"No, Lydia. That's not how we train here. Actually hit me."

David is older than me. Not quite as old as my father but still old enough to be called my elder. "It would be inappropriate."

Without warning, David's fist connects with my jaw. My body slaps the mat and pain radiates through my jaw. "Get up," he growls.

I turn my stinging face in his direction. "I… I don't think I can."

David's foot connects with my ribs, hard enough for me to groan, but I can tell he's holding back. It's more of a push than a true kick. "What's it going to be, Lydia? Are you going to fight or fail? Get. UP."

I scramble to my feet. His fists are raised and I copy his position. "Now, hit me, Lydia."

For a moment, I just stand there, moving my fists in slow circles.

"Stop avoiding. You said you'd work hard. Now do it." He looks me in the eye and lowers his voice. "There is only one way out of this room and it's through me. Now, come on."

I jab at his face. My punch is slow and soft. He could easily move out of the way or block it if he tried, but he doesn't. My fist connects with his cheek. It barely leaves a red mark.

"Good. Now here's how to make it better." David

grabs my wrist and repositions my fist, explaining how to use my hips to throw my weight into the punch. He helps me practice different approaches on a rubber manikin, coaching me on ways to focus the impact. When I've practiced several times with each arm, he grabs me roughly by the elbow. "Now, hit me."

This time, I don't hesitate. What's the point? My fist connects with his chest. A grunt escapes David's lips, and he takes a step back. He smiles fully for the first time. "Not bad. On to blocking skills."

We work for another two hours on blocks and kicks, and then fight each other for practice. David calls this *sparring*, but his punches feel as real as actual fighting. I throw everything I have into protecting myself from his attack, never allowing myself to think too much about what I'm doing.

His fist slides past my arm and connects with my gut. All the air in my lungs comes out and I crumple to the floor, unable to catch my breath.

David's bare feet are near my face, and I cover my head with my arms, expecting him to kick me, but he doesn't. "That's enough for today."

I lower my arms and nod, although I remain curled on my side.

He crosses the training center to his bag and starts putting on his socks and shoes.

"You said you would tell me about the emblem," I say, pointing to the mat.

Hands on his hips, he steps to the symbol. "So I did." He takes a deep breath and lets it out slowly. "The emblem of the Green Republic commemorates its three founding organizations, each powerful in its own way." He squats and points at the greenery that forms the outside of the symbol. "The first was an agricultural company called Next Generation Ag (NGA), represented here by the laurel wreath. NGA invented and patented genetically modified crops and combined forces before the war with a major animal rights group to become the leading proponent of *in vitro* meat production."

"In vitro? You mean, the meat produced in a lab," I whisper, remembering what Korwin has explained to me about their world.

"Yes. NGA believed that the only sustainable food supply was one completely within human control. But they faced a growing public contingent that believed natural, organic food production was better for health. Before the war, NGA understood that the grow-your-own way of life couldn't be sustained. The chemicals people poured on their gardens were ruining our water supply, and farm animals contributed to greenhouse gas emissions."

I have to consciously work to keep my jaw from falling open. I've spent most of my life working on our farm, growing crops and raising animals without any chemicals. It seems like the most basic human right. I can't fathom being dependent on someone else for food, and I find it hard to believe that our way of life is bad for the earth.

"NGA saved the world by banding together with two other groups to form a revolution, the Great Rebellion."

"Who are the other two groups?" I ask, curious.

"I'll tell you when you've earned it."

I groan.

"I know it's hard, Lydia, but you need to know how to defend yourself," David says. "Your enemies are everywhere. Remember that you can't trust anyone. The Stuarts are prime examples. People like Korwin and his father look innocent but have committed heinous crimes. Crimes the Green Republic find unforgivable." He stresses the last word.

The feeling is back, the sense he's trying to tell me more than he actually says, and I know he's warning me about Korwin. My heart sinks into my stomach. What does the Green Republic do to the *unforgivable*?

Chapter 27

The next day, David bangs on my door before the sun is up. He chides me for being late and demands I be ready and waiting every morning by seven. I'm not usually a late sleeper, but my body aches from the paces he's put me through.

"I can hardly move," I complain.

"I thought that might be the case." From a zippered black bag he carries, he pulls out a syringe of clear liquid. Before I can protest, he's grabbed my arm and stabbed my bicep with it.

"Oww. What was that?" I ask, rubbing the injection site.

"Something for the pain. Come on. You'll be fine once we get to the training area."

Warmth spreads from my shoulder outward as I follow David into the hall. The same path as last time, he hugs the wall to the stairwell, making a production about using the Biolock, while glancing at the door where I think they are keeping Korwin, then jogging down the stairs as he counts down from twenty-one. By the time we've reached the training center, the ache in my muscles is completely gone.

He kicks off his shoes and I sink into the fighting stance he taught me. He waves his hand.

"We'll get to that, but first we're going to learn about weapons. Have you used any of these weapons before?" He points at the rack of metal in front of him.

I'm overwhelmed by the sheer number and variety. I attempt to distract him. "Aren't you going to explain the rest of the symbol?"

"Later. When you've earned it." He points at the rack.

Aside from the knives, I can't even name most of them. "No," I say. I don't explain that I grew up in a place where implements of war are forbidden, and he doesn't ask for justification.

"We'll start at the beginning." Methodically, David introduces me to each item on the rack.

There is an entire section of weapons for stabbing—daggers, swords, spears, double-edged knives. He says these tools are used to puncture the enemy. On a diagram of the human body, he shows me where to attack to inflict the most damage. I have to stop myself from vomiting when he discusses with complete detachment how a proper stab to the lung will cause an opponent to drown in his or her own blood.

I'm relieved when he moves on to the next section, but end up just as horrified. These are weapons created to bleed or de-limb your enemy, curved blades and scythes. "Aim for the arteries," he says, demonstrating in the air at the sides of his throat and in front of his inner thigh. "A wrist is easier to sever with this than a shoulder."

I try to block the images that come to mind. Rotating one of the weapons in my hand, I cannot fathom using it.

"With the axes, I recommend you aim for the skull. If

they dodge, chances are you'll hit something on the follow-through."

I nod.

"These here, the blunt objects, they're for breaking bones." He twirls a staff in his hands. "You might not see your enemy bleed with these, but if you use them correctly, the injury will be on the inside."

"Oh." My eyes burn with the desire to cry.

He hands me a dagger and lifts a staff from the rack.

"Attack me," he says.

"You can't be serious." I scoff. "I can't stab you."

He jabs the staff in my direction, and I notice he is glowing. The slight blue aura is barely perceptible in the light. Narrowing my eyes, I stab experimentally at his midsection.

"Ah!" He slaps my hand away with the staff, but not before the tip of the knife bounces off like he's made of stone.

"I suggest you spark out or you are going to get the bruising of your life."

I fold my hands to my heart, then snap them straight. My skin glows to life.

David bows his head slightly, raises his staff, and attacks.

* * * * *

David's electrokinesis is not as strong as mine. We have to stop weapons training, not because either of us is tired, but because a sore has bloomed over the left side of his upper lip. He hobbles over to his zippered black bag against the wall and pulls out another syringe, this one filled with blue fluid. He pulls up the leg of his shorts and plunges the needle into his thigh.

"Do you want me to juice you?" I ask, holding out my hand.

He locks eyes with me as he returns the needle to the bag in silent warning, and I stop talking.

"Hey, you need to tell me more about the symbol," I say to break the awkward silence.

He smiles and takes a seat on the floor by the emblem. "Last time I told you how the laurel wreath represented Next Generation Agriculture. There was another company interested in saving the world." He raises his eyebrows when he says the last, almost like it's tongue-in-cheek, although I do not pick up the same inflection in his voice.

He points to the lightning bolt. "Nucore Energy was a power company with roots in fossil fuels. They'd invested heavily to reinvent themselves to be an alternative energy company. When the global crisis came and fossil fuels were outlawed, Nucore stood to profit from the shift to sustainable energy. Only, nuclear energy was proving to be the more promising short-term solution, despite its risks."

"Like the meltdown."

"Exactly."

"Nucore joined forces with NGA. Their goal was to clean up the planet."

"And to profit from it," I mumble under my breath. David smiles but says nothing.

For a moment, I am mesmerized by the healing of the

sore on David's face. It stitches itself up until the skin is a fresh pink. He catches me staring and I look away, toward the emblem, embarrassed.

"What does the hammer represent?" I ask absently.

David frowns. "That's a lesson for another day."

* * * * *

David retrieves me from my room at sunrise day after day. I'm expected to have eaten breakfast and am made to if I haven't. Almost every day, David has to give me a shot of painkiller to keep me going. My muscles throb without it, and there is not a place on my body that doesn't hurt. I lose track of time. What day is it? How long have I been here? I have no idea.

I learn how to use every weapon in the training room's arsenal and spend hours practicing martial arts techniques. We train until dinner, stopping only when David insists I eat and drink. He never holds back or pulls a punch. Even trying to shield myself, he lands enough thwacks and slams to leave me black and blue. I have a cut under my right eye from losing my concentration and a bandage over my lower abdomen I can't remember putting there. Lapses in memory are becoming my forte. I can't decide if it's the painkillers or the way David gets me in the zone when we fight.

Although I repeatedly ask for him, I never see Korwin. Nor do Maxwell or Natasha make an appearance. I begin to wonder if they are even alive anymore. But I hold to the promise that if I work hard, if I earn the Green Republic's trust, I'll get more privileges, more freedoms, and perhaps the privilege to see Korwin.

"Lydia," my father says that night, staring at me over a roast beef that appeared in our irradiator moments ago. It smells great but it tastes like a kitchen sponge. The potatoes and asparagus aren't any better. "You can't keep doing this. I don't even know how you're still standing. You're a walking bruise."

"Not walking, limping," Jeremiah says. "She hasn't walked straight for over a week."

"A week?" I say. "It hasn't been that long."

Jeremiah scoffs. "It's been almost *three*."

"Three weeks?" I laugh. "Not possible."

Jeremiah glances at my father and then back at me. "You've been distracted." He lifts one brow and leans toward me as he says it. He pulls a square of paper from his pocket. "I've made an x on the back of this every time we've slept."

There are twenty-four X's on the paper. I have vague memories of sitting at this table, eating with them, but it's all a blur. Pressing the heels of my palms into my eyes, I try to see it clearly, behind the kicking, stabbing, and fighting that plays over and over in my head. "What's wrong with me?"

"We don't know," my father says.

"They haven't given you a day off since we got here," Jeremiah continues.

I stare at my hands for a moment, memories flashing in front of me. I've fired a gun. Several different guns, on a firing range deep within this building, but I only remember it as if it were a dream. My body shakes. I look at the place on my shoulder where David has injected me every morning. My arm is covered in needle pricks in various stages of healing. My other shoulder too. I squirm in my chair. There was more than painkiller in that syringe. What has David done to me?

"They don't let us out of here, Lydia. Ever," Jeremiah says. "We don't know what they do to you when you leave. This is the clearest you've been in days."

"Korwin?" I say.

They both shake their heads. My father takes my hand. His eyes flick to the lamp above the table, where we all know the Greens keep a monitor. "A Green stopped up here today to tell us that Willow's Province could not find our records. We told them we have no explanation, but Jeremiah and I thought you should know."

I widen my eyes in alarm. The Green Republic is going to want answers. They will demand to know where Lydia Lane has been these last seventeen years and how I was hidden from detection. The Green Republic's kindness is limited and conditional. If I don't give them answers, who will they hurt to make me?

For some reason, Natasha comes to mind, and I see David's face saying, "She's not well. She can't join us today." He's said that every day. Every day for what I now know is three weeks.

If they're holding Natasha the way I think they're holding Korwin, David and I might have more in common than Operation Source Code. There's no way they're keeping Korwin comfortable in an apartment like my father or Jeremiah. If they were, they would've let me see him. No. Likely, they've been draining him or torturing him. I don't believe Natasha has been sick either. Something has to change. Every day I don't see Korwin is potentially a day the Green Republic draw him closer to death. I'm running out of time, and I can't afford to lose another day.

Chapter 28

"I'm fine," I tell David when he comes to my door the next morning. It's a lie. I can hardly hold my head up. Every part of me aches.

"This will make it easier," he says through thin lips. He moves the syringe toward my shoulder.

I grab his wrist before he can inject me and without thinking, draw his energy in. It's not purposeful, more like my body is thirsty and he's a bottle of water. The blue juice flows up my arm, and I watch my bruised skin heal as it goes. I take more and more until David crumples into the doorframe with a groan.

I release his wrist. I feel renewed. He's covered in sores.

"Come on," I say. I return the syringe to his bag and grab him under the elbow, forcing him into the hall. He goes, hugging the wall just as he always does. Silent. This time, he doesn't hesitate before popping the Biolock. He stops just inside the door.

"Are you crazy?" He props himself against the wall and digs through his bag for another syringe and a vial of blue liquid.

"What have you been giving me every morning?"

He injects himself with the solution. "Painkillers."

I hold out my hand, threatening to touch him again. To drain him. He pulls away. "Also, a supplement to help you retain what you learn."

"Why do I feel like I've lost track of time?"

"That's how it works. You experience things using the part of your brain associated with long-term memory. What I've taught you this week will be second nature to you. You will never forget it."

"Is this some kind of Green Republic torture? Did Konrad put you up to drugging me?"

"Konrad doesn't know. As far as he's concerned, there was nothing but painkiller in that vial."

"Then why?" I step closer to him. He's still recovering, the sore on his arm slowly crusting over. He leans his head against the wall.

"We're running out of time." He meets my eyes. "The things we love most will be used against us."

Korwin. "What do I need to do?" I ask.

"We've got to go. This stairwell is the only place in the complex not monitored, but they'll know something's wrong if we are not in the training center in five minutes." He gathers his things and starts jogging down the steps.

"David, what can I do to help Korwin?" I ask, falling into step beside him.

"First, if you believe in God, start praying that Konrad misses the part where you drew energy from me through touch."

"Why?"

"They don't know you can do that. The participants in Operation Source Code couldn't juice each other. We could draw from things, but not from people and certainly not into people."

Oh, so that was why he'd changed the subject in the training room when I asked if I could juice him.

"Second, I have no idea how you can help Korwin. I don't even know how you can help yourself. But you're strong and you're smart." He pauses on the second floor and points toward the outer wall of the stairwell. "Beyond that wall is freedom."

What?

He opens the door and leads the way into the training center, where he promptly stashes his bag against the wall. I can tell he's still dragging from being drained and the sprint down the stairs has left him breathless.

"Tell me about the last part of the Green Republic's emblem," I say. "I won't practice if you don't."

Relief washes across his features before being hidden away. "Okay. I guess I owe you that much. You've worked hard these last weeks." He sits next to the symbol and motions for me to sit across from him.

"The hammer," I say, reminding him where we left off.

"Right. Frankly, I'm surprised you've waited this long to ask about the hammer. It's the most important part of the origination history of the Green Republic. The hammer represents the Evergreen political party and its army. As the environment became more toxic, the oceans swelled and flooded the coasts and nontoxic fresh water became harder to come by. An international political party rose up from grass roots efforts to combat the environmental damage. They called themselves the Evergreen Party. They won elections to the north and south, across the oceans, and with each win they built a militia focused on the enforcement of sustainable living."

I laugh.

"What's so funny?"

"Don't you find it humorous that it took men and women trained in doling out death to force the populace to think about life?"

A small smile spreads his lips. "Certainly, ironic."

"So, the Evergreen Party militia joined forces with NGA and Nucore to form the Green Republic?"

"Correct. After the tragedy in the Outlands, most people were begging for a savior to clean up the mess, and the Green Republic was ready and willing. With an army supplied by the Evergreen Party, financing supplied by Nucore, and NGA withholding food from the enemy, the Great Rebellion was won, and since then our air is clean, the oceans are healthy, and we have very little waste. It's utopia."

I force myself to smile and nod. Utopia for some maybe. No freedom. No autonomy.

David's face sobers. "Those who refused to accept the Green Republic's way of life were sentenced to die and imprisoned within a concrete wall next to the failed reactor." He shakes his head. "The radiation levels were high enough, most are presumed dead. Those who remain live like wild animals."

I almost laugh at the ridiculousness of his last sentence. But then his words fester like a wound. I clear my throat. "I'd heard that the people behind the wall were a religious group." I swallow hard. Is David warning me about Hemlock Hollow or simply telling me a story? What will the Green Republic do to us if they find out we're not dead or wild animals?

He shakes his head as he gets to his feet. "Most were, but let's just say they had one hell of a bump in membership after the war. Well, until the radiation killed them off."

I chew my lip. If what he says is true, my Amish community is a mixed group of those descended in the faith and rebels escaping the revolution. I'm not sure why this bothers me. After all, everyone worships together now. We dress the same. We uphold the same *Ordnung*. I shake the unexamined feeling off.

"Time to get to work," David says. He's looking better; the solution must have worked. "I think you need more target practice."

I follow him across the room to a door that leads to the shooting range. I've been here before. I've done this before. Without a word, I grab ear protection from the tray and a handgun from the rack. On autopilot, I approach the booth, assume the stance David has taught me, and proceed to unload the ammunition into a man-shaped target. When I'm finished, I've peppered the head and the heart with bullet holes.

Magazine empty, I turn toward David in confusion. He removes his ear protection and motions for me to remove mine. "I told you the supplement would help you remember."

"Remember? I felt like a machine." I blink quickly, still in wonder over what I've done. Before coming here, I'd only seen pictures of guns. I'd never so much as dreamed of holding one, let alone firing one. I certainly did not expect to be good at it. What else has David and his chemical supplement taught me? I stare at my hands, dumbfounded.

"You *are* a machine. Electric power and all." He snorts. "And that brings us to the end of our time together."

"What?"

"Your training is complete." His voice breaks. "What you do with it now is up to you."

* * * * *

"Lydia, I'm very pleased with your performance. Very few initiates pass training in less than a month, even with personal trainers," Dr. Konrad says. "You will be integrated into the Special Ops team and assigned a mission as soon as possible."

I sit in Konrad's office, in the chair across the desk from him. He peruses a stack of papers, my test results, with growing interest.

"Where is Korwin?"

"Safe. Alive. And as long as you face your responsibilities, he will stay that way.

"When can I see him?"

"Soon. First, there's one more thing I need from you."

"What?" I ask. "I've done everything you've asked of me, without question."

"Yes, yes. But you, Lydia, hold the key to our future. We need to take Operation Source Code to the next level.

The next…generation."

"Generation?"

He sighs. "Your trainer David is an Alpha, very unstable. You are a Beta, stable and exponentially stronger, and your baby will be the first Gamma. There's no limit to what we could accomplish with Gamma cells."

Panic rises in my throat with bile. Gamma cells. Like he's not talking about a person but biological fuel.

"Don't worry, honey," Konrad says over his steepled fingers through that thin excuse for a smile. "You won't need to carry it. All we need is your cells. A few of yours and a few of Korwin's. Both second generation. We have technology now that can handle everything else. The procedure is simple."

I don't want to believe what I'm hearing. It's too sinister. What type of monster breeds people like rats? "And what then?" I ask. "Once you have your Gamma, what will happen to the rest of us?"

Konrad shrugs. "As I said before, we're already planning your first mission and once the baby is born, he or she is going to need a mother and father."

So that's it. Two for the price of one. Our forced parenthood will also mean our forced servitude. It is another hook for Konrad to insert into Korwin and me. More leverage to make sure we spend the rest of our lives fighting for the Green Republic. When you make a deal with the devil, he keeps on taking. My father's comfort for my cooperation. Korwin's life for one of my cells. Our baby's life for our ongoing allegiance. When will it stop?

"I think I need to lie down," I say. My eyelids flutter. I

have to grab the desk to steady myself.

"Of course. You've had a very full day, and I'm sure you need some time to process all of this. We can perform the procedure tomorrow."

I swallow repeatedly to keep from vomiting.

Konrad picks up his phone and presses a few buttons. A blond officer who looks too young to wear the uniform enters the small office. "Please escort Lydia to her room."

The blond boy takes my elbow and lifts me out of the chair.

The next thing I know, I'm in my apartment, staring out the window at the sunset. I've lost hours, again. My own mind is hiding from me. I lived those hours, I'm sure. I put one foot in front of the other, followed the officer to my apartment, and sank into this chair, but I'm not here, not really. I am a ghost. Is this a side effect of the drugs David has given me, or my mind's way of shutting out the world, of escaping into an internal oblivion?

My father places his hand on my shoulder and gives it a firm shake. "Are you all right, Lydia?"

I turn my head and look up into his warm brown eyes. "Are you disappointed in me?"

He growls and squeezes my shoulder. "Of course not."

"This life. This isn't what you wanted for yourself or for me."

With a deep sigh, he hobbles to the kitchen to grab a chair from the dinette set and drags it next to the recliner I'm in. When he's settled, he faces me. "You know as well as I do that we don't decide which hand we are dealt, only the way we play it. If my wife and son had lived through the accident, would I have stayed where I was? Most certainly. But the first time I held you, I wanted a very different life than what I had with them. You've been a blessing, an abundant joy. I'm so proud of you, Lydia." A solitary tear etches a trail down his cheek.

"I don't feel joyful, Dad. And I don't think I get to choose how to play my hand. All of my choices have been taken from me."

"You've been dealt a hand a lot like the one I got when the hospital called me about the accident. It's a life changer, sure. But here's what I learned about that. When the other player is cheating, the rules of the game don't apply anymore."

I nod out of habit but he grabs my shoulder harshly and shakes until I meet his eyes again.

"The rules don't apply to you," he says more firmly, emphasizing each word. He rubs my hand. "I've raised you in a certain way in a certain place under a certain set of circumstances. But that doesn't matter now. You're in the devil's playground and here, the devil makes the rules. When you deal with the devil, sometimes you've got to break the rules to save your soul. You've got to know when wrong is right, and the only person who can make that decision is you. I was in your shoes once, when a man who glowed like a star left a baby in my arms."

As serious as his expression is, he looks better, stronger than he has in weeks. "Do you trust me?" I ask. "To play the hand I'm dealt? In any way I have to?"

"Even if it means the end of me," he whispers.

I take a deep breath and slowly let it out. "If it means

your life, there is no choice."

A derisive snort cuts me off. "Lydia, there are always choices. Your problem is, you don't want to have to live with the consequences. You are the strongest young lady I've ever had the privilege of knowing, but I wish you'd known my wife. She'd tell you that the hard part about being a woman is knowing which rivers to row and when to get out of the boat. What consequences are you willing to live with? I'm with you whatever you choose."

"So am I," Jeremiah says from behind me.

I turn to face him. The weeks he's spent in this cage have taken their toll. Dark circles shade his eyes, and he's developed a cynical hunch. It is more than just my life the Green Republic holds in its deadly grip, and I'm beginning to think that death might be better than what lies in store for me.

Chapter 29

"Jeremiah, if anything should ever happen to me, do you promise to take care of my father?"

He grits his teeth. "You know I will."

I gather my hair, refastening my ponytail and pulling it tight. "We've got to do something. We can't remain prisoners here forever."

My father glances at the lamp. We've been so very careful about who's listening or watching.

"I don't care," I say. "I'm sick of all of it. Prepare yourselves." I stand and walk toward the door. It's locked, of course.

"Lydia?" my father asks.

"Prepare," I whisper again.

Jeremiah nods and helps my father from the room.

Instead of trying to unlock the door, I place my hands on the nearby wall. I can sense wires behind the paint, like a regular person might feel a pulse beneath skin. I trace the wires to a square of energy inside the wall to my right. If my theory is correct, this is the source that powers the lock. I use my fingernail to mark the paint over my target.

My father and Jeremiah return with shoes and sweaters on.

Shoulders squared, I face my mark. With a deep breath and a snap of my arm, I draw the power into my hands.

The air around me glows blue and a hum, like an engine roaring to life, comes from the general vicinity of my heart. I hurl my power at my target, into the box behind the wall, a lightning bolt that I cut off from myself, just in case.

Not only does the door open, but a smoking hole appears in the wall. The lights blink on and off. I shouldn't be surprised when the sirens start, but I jump at the noise. Jeremiah and my father stare at me with wide eyes, waiting for my direction. I can't let them down.

"We won't have long," I say. "Go, quickly. Left. To the stairwell. Hug the south wall." The wail of the siren builds to a deafening pitch.

Jeremiah helps my father out the door. I bolt past them to the place where I've felt Korwin's presence. I pray he's still there. I blow another hole in the wall and kick in the door.

The room is nothing like the apartment I've come from. It's a one-room prison. Korwin lies face down on a cot, one arm hanging limply off the side, wearing nothing but thin white pajama bottoms.

"Korwin?" I rush to him and shake his shoulder. He's ashen, like a corpse. I shake him again, harder, and roll him onto his back.

His eyes flutter open. "Drained," he mumbles. The telltale remnants of circular wire attachments are all over his body.

"What have they done to you?"

He doesn't answer but stares at me with dead eyes from under hooded lids.

"I'm going to juice you. We've got to go. It isn't safe."
I cup his face and my blue glow bathes him in light. As I
lower my lips to his, the draw I've felt to Korwin from the
very beginning takes hold. My energy flows into him
freely, in one direction at first, but then just as Maxwell
explained, the flip comes and the power between us
morphs into something else, dividing and multiplying. He
is empty, so it takes some time before the power returns to
me. But when it does, it almost knocks me off the bed.
Our cells feed each other, revolving faster and faster.
Atoms in a perpetual dance of motion heat the air around
us. Energy pours out and in until my muscles twitch and
the paint on the wall behind Korwin begins to peel and
singe.

Korwin breaks the connection and scrambles to his
feet. He paces for a moment, getting his bearings.

"Better?" I ask.

"Oh yeah!" A blue shiver dances under his skin. He
points toward the hall, at the flashing lights and the
blaring sirens. "You?"

"Me." I lace my fingers into his and pull him toward
the hall. "We don't have much time."

"Do you know where my father is?" he yells over the
sirens.

"No. I haven't seen him in weeks, not since the
holding cell."

"There's someone next door. I've heard them...
moaning," he says. "Maybe it's him."

"Let's go."

I bust through the neighboring door, but Maxwell

G. P. CHING

Stuart isn't there. Instead, I find a skeletal woman covered in sores. I have a strong hunch I know who this is.

"Natasha."

She rolls her head toward me on the cot. She's clearly ill. If what David tells me is true, they don't have to drain her. Without Konrad's stabilizer, her body will feed on itself and eventually die. This is why David helped the Greens. Natasha is the hold Konrad has over him.

"We need to take her with us," I say.

"What? We can't." Korwin glances back at the door, then up at the camera in the ceiling.

"She's one of the Alpha Eight."

He shakes his head, his brow furrowing. "She can't be. They all died."

"We don't have time for this, Korwin," I yell. "Trust me. You need to carry her, so I can fight."

For a moment he seems at war with himself but thankfully it doesn't last long. Korwin scoops her into his arms and we rush to meet the others. We make it to the end of the hall, to the locked stairwell door, where Jeremiah and my father wait for us.

"Who is that?" Jeremiah asks.

"A soul who needs our help," I say. Bracing myself, I blast the door. The stairwell is empty. "Twenty-one floors down," I command. "I'll go ahead."

Jeremiah hooks my father's arm around his shoulders, helping him forward, and we begin our descent. The incessant blare of the alarm makes it impossible to listen for footsteps. I jog ahead of them, hands flaming blue. It's a good thing I'm ready. I make it only ten floors before

295

green uniforms fill the stairwell. More than bullets are waiting for me. I dive out of the way and the scramblers barely miss me.

I aim for their knees, electric blue flying from my hands. Screams echo through the stairwell as the men fold to the concrete.

David is a genius. Aside from being the only place in CGEF without security cameras, only so many men can fit on the landing, and they have to come from below, giving me the advantage.

I bound off the far wall, rotating in the air, and kick the door closed. It slams on an entering officer's head, throwing him backward into the man behind him. A scrambler probe hits the wall next to me, one of the fallen men trying to play the hero despite his wrecked legs. With one hand I solder the door closed and with the other I wrestle the weapon from his fingers, thankful that the scramblers take fifteen seconds to recharge—another tip from David.

"Don't even think about it," I say to another who reaches for his dropped scrambler. "I'll fry you like bacon."

He retracts his hand.

Jeremiah and Korwin reach the landing about the time I collect the last weapon.

"Looks like you handled this," Korwin says, almost reverently.

I strap a scrambler to his belt and then to Jeremiah's. Another goes to my father, and I wrap Natasha's limp fingers around one. She's more dead than alive, but it only seems fair.

The officers pound on the welded entryway. "Open the door," Konrad yells. I should have known it was only a matter of time before he joined the party. "There's no way out, Lydia. Think about the consequences."

My thoughts immediately jump to Maxwell, but there's no time to find him. Giving up now won't help anyone.

"We've got to keep moving," I say. I race down the steps, soldering door after door before Green Republic officers can reach us. But I am oddly unchallenged. There's only one way out of this building—and it's on the first floor. I'm willing to bet that's where the officers are waiting. There will be no way out but through them.

"Do you have her?" David's voice cracks from below me. He steps out from the doorway of the training room onto the second-floor landing. By the pounding behind him, I know he's barricaded himself in. There's a bag over his shoulder and his face looks drawn.

"Yes," I say. "She's coming."

He exhales a ragged breath just as Korwin turns the corner with Natasha in his arms.

"Jameson?" Korwin asks, bewildered.

Three stairs at a time, David jogs up the steps to him, lifting Natasha into his arms. "Nat! Nat! I'm here."

"Too late," she rasps.

He jumps to the landing, laying her down on the floor. Removing the bag from his shoulder, he produces a syringe and vial of neon blue liquid. Konrad's serum. With shaking hands he draws up a heavy dose and thrusts it into her thigh.

Her eyes pop open, and she screams like he's ripping her in half.

"David," I yell. "We have to get out of here!"

He stores the needle and cradles Natasha in his arms. Eyes darting between Korwin and me, he scoots back against the door, then nods toward the concrete wall across from him. "You're the strongest of all of us, Lydia. This is only the second floor."

It takes me a second to digest what he's proposing. He wants me to blast through the concrete and leap a full story to freedom. For a moment I turn in a circle, the concrete walls closing in on me. And then I remember. I am powerful. I am dangerous. I am deadly. All my life I've worked to be simple, but now, I can't pretend anymore. Nothing about me is simple. Nothing about me is plain.

I face the concrete wall and power up. "Korwin, you'll need to take my father."

He follows my train of thought and scoops my dad from Jeremiah's side. Resting my palm on the concrete, I close my eyes, weighing the energy in my fingers.

"Get ready. I'm going to make a mess," I say to Korwin. I step back.

He pushes Jeremiah toward David, his body filling the space behind me in blue light.

My father gasps. "Lydia."

I am a star, a supernova of heat and light. An intense spiral of energy courses around me. I concentrate, winding the elastic tighter and tighter at the back of my head. Then I let it go. The stretch reaches the concrete and I know when the wall accepts it because my power flows out of me like fishing line. The atoms in the wall dance for me, pulling my energy, hotter and faster into my target. The entire building shakes. Red blooms and spreads through the white bricks, brighter, hotter. When I think I've weakened the structure, I jump and kick at the center of the red. The wall explodes around my foot.

Concrete blocks and iron cables snap against me but bounce off my shield harmlessly. I land on the edge of a hole I've created in the side of the building, grit and smoke blinding me from what lies beyond. When the dust clears, I turn toward the others. Korwin's shield has worked. The rubble has collected on either side of us but my father and Jeremiah are safe, as are David and Natasha, although the latter looks worse than before.

Fresh night air blows in around us, cold air that stings my cheek. "We have to jump," I say weakly. I'm drained. It will take everything I have left to do this.

Korwin nods. He lifts my father and leaps through the hole I've created. The blue glow strengthens him and he lands on his feet in the lawn on the side of the building.

"I can help you, Jeremiah," I say, motioning for him to come to me.

"Let a man be a man," he says. He pushes me out of the way, then leaps.

"Jeremiah!" I yell, reaching for him. But I'm not fast enough. He lands awkwardly and rolls out of it.

Korwin rushes to his side.

I turn to David. "Come on."

"You first, Lydia. I've got this. Go!" David's eyes blaze.

I nod and jump. The air rushes past my ears, my

ponytail whipping around my head. The ground comes up too fast and I hit hard, rolling sideways across the grass. My energy has kept me from breaking a bone but not from hurting. I twist onto my side and squeeze my knees to my chest, trying to hold myself together. I can't breathe.

Korwin's face appears in front of mine. He rolls me onto my back and cradles my face in his hands. "I have something of yours," he says. He kisses me. Not the kind of kiss you give a friend or a family member. A full-on real kiss that reignites the flame inside of me. He pulls back much too soon. "Come on!"

I leap to my feet, the air crackling with our power and chase after him.

People have gathered in the street. The grid is a parking lot of open windows and gawking strangers. "Don't trust anyone," Korwin says, and this time I agree.

Sprinting for the grid, I find the fastest-looking automobile in the crowd and yank the door open. I drag the screaming driver from the vehicle. His fault for stopping to watch. We pile my father and a limping Jeremiah into the back. Korwin takes the control stick as bullets and scrambler probes barely miss us. The lawn around CGEF is covered in green uniforms. They've only succeeded in frightening the crowd so far, but they're getting closer.

"Korwin, go!" I yell.

"What about Jameson?"

"His real name is David, and he can take care of himself. Go!"

Korwin takes the car off-grid and drives between the traffic, weaving in and out and jumping the sidewalk to get ahead of the others. He veers down a side street and onto the expressway, and then we accelerate to that lightning-fast speed that sinks my stomach. He switches back to the grid and faces us.

"Do you think they're following us?" I ask.

"I'm not sure. To follow us on the grid they need the identification number of this vehicle. They'll be able to get it from the surveillance video or from the driver, but it will take them a few minutes. Then they'll have to contact the tech people, who will find us on the grid. They'll have to enter a code to take control of the vehicle. At our speed, we might have another few minutes for the GPS program to catch up with our location. I'd say ten minutes, tops."

"Not enough time to reach Willow's Province," I say. "Where will we go? Who can we trust?" My voice sounds embarrassingly desperate.

Jeremiah leans forward, poking his head between us into the front seat. "Korwin, who is your father's second in the Liberty Party?"

Internally, I groan. Out of the frying pan, into the fire. I'm not crazy about trusting the Liberty Party after learning about the attack on the West Hub. But what choice do we have?

Korwin's brows knit and then he types an address into the dashboard. "Jonas Kirkland. It's dangerous because his location is close to CGEF."

I vaguely remember Jonas and his daughter from Maxwell's party.

"Jonas," my father says. "I know him."

We all turn to gape at my father. "What are you talking about?"

"I worked with Jonas. At the fire station when I was an *Englisher*. He was a firefighter, like me."

"He's still there. The fire chief now, and acting leader of the Liberty Party while the Greens have my father. I think he's our best bet."

"Will we make it in time?"

"I've set the address for a few miles away, in the deadzone. We'll dump the car and travel by sewer."

Great. I squeeze my eyes shut and take a deep breath. I was beginning to miss the sewer.

Chapter 30

We exit the grid at the cluster of dilapidated buildings near the spot where I'd given the homeless man my bottle of water. Korwin parks the car. This is the deadzone. There's no electricity in this area, so the only light comes from the half-moon. We run three blocks west and duck inside the nearest building. Shuffling toward the back with my father wedged between Jeremiah and me, I notice rows of empty shelves and a few cans of long-expired pet food.

"What was this place?" Jeremiah asks.

"Looks like a grocery store," Korwin says. "We're not even that far out. The deadzone keeps getting bigger. The power goes out and that's all she wrote. People abandon everything and migrate into the city."

We find an office in the back with a door to the alley.

"Give me your sweatshirt," Korwin says to Jeremiah.

He removes the hoody he's wearing and hands it over.

Korwin hangs the sweatshirt off the chair, then dodges back into the store for a moment. When he returns, he pulls the tab back on a can of pet food and buries a plastic fork in it. "Maybe, if they find this, they'll think we've made camp here. It might buy us a few minutes if they search the place."

"Can't we stay here?" Jeremiah asks. "Just for a while.

To rest." He gestures toward my father.

Korwin shakes his head. "They'll track the car, then methodically search everywhere within a five-mile radius. Trust me, we're on borrowed time."

We slip out the back door, travel two blocks down the alley, and enter the sewer. My father is too weak to walk the entire way, so Jeremiah and I take turns carrying him on our backs. We follow Korwin through the maze of pipes for more than an hour before emerging in an alley behind a fire station. There is power here, but the lit streets are quiet because of the time of night.

"There," my father says, pointing at an awning-covered door on the side of the building.

Korwin nods.

The door is unlocked. We enter a garage full of fire trucks and climb a flight of stairs. The second floor is populated with men in blue uniforms—playing cards, smoking cigars, eating from waxed cardboard containers.

"It's exactly how I left it," my father says.

Silence. The firemen stare at us expectantly until a stocky young man in the back rises from his chair and approaches. He brushes his hand over his thinning brown hair.

"I'll be damned. Franklin Stark. You look like hell. What happened to you?"

"It's a long story." My father lists in Jeremiah's arms. "Last time I saw you, Brady, you were hiding behind your father's knee. How is your father?"

"Retired but doing okay." Brady's eyes flick over me, and then Korwin, who is still only wearing a pair of

304

hospital pants. All of us are covered in remnants of the sewer. "What happened to you?"

"We need to see Jonas Kirkland," Korwin says.

A flicker of understanding crosses Brady's face. "Upstairs," he says. He waves a hand at the others in the room. "Go back to what you were doing. I'll take care of this." He motions for us to continue ahead of him and then sees how weak my father is. "There's an elevator. We're required by law to have one but none of us ever use it. No sense burning the energy. It's at the front of the building."

"No, thanks," my father says. He leans on Jeremiah and grabs my elbow.

Together, we slowly ascend. On the third floor, a massive steel door greets us. Brady punches a code into a pad. A tight close-up of the man I met at Stuart Manor appears on screen. Jonas.

"There are people here for you," Brady says.

Korwin and I lean in front of the camera.

"Thank you, Brady," Jonas says. There's a buzzing sound, and the massive door slides into the wall. We walk into a bunker of a room, steel framed with rows of cots, a kitchenette, and a small office space where Jonas sits at a desk.

The door slides back into place behind us and the bolt scrapes into position.

"I never thought I'd lay eyes on you two again. How the hell did you escape from CGEF? We've had no new intel for weeks."

"David helped me," I say.

"David who?"

"You know him as Jameson."

Korwin and Jonas stare at me like I'm speaking a different language. "He's one of the Alpha Eight. He and his wife, Natasha, were recaptured when the other six escaped. Konrad's been using him as a spy, threatening to kill his wife if he didn't help them."

"That filthy mole." Korwin curses. "He's the one who turned us in!"

"He said he had no choice."

Jonas looks flustered. He types furiously on his keyboard. "He could do a lot of damage to our cause, depending on how much he shared. Do you know if he named names?"

"It's been weeks. If he had, I'd think you would know by now."

"Hmm." Jonas runs a hand through his wooly hair. "What makes you think the Greens aren't just waiting for the right time to slaughter us all?"

"He helped me escape. He taught me to fight and showed me the way out. Last we saw him, he was trying to escape himself."

"We can't trust him," Korwin says.

Jonas nods. "I'm putting the resistance on high alert." He finishes typing, then seems to notice my father and Jeremiah for the first time. He squints and stands to get a closer look.

"Franklin Stark? I'll be damned."

"Nice place you got here, Jonas," my father says.

The man's graying eyebrows arch above twinkling

brown eyes. "I convinced the Green Republic that a fire station needs a fireproof room for its firefighters. After what happened the day you left, they couldn't refuse me. We lost a man that day."

"Smart thinking." My father accepts an embrace from Jonas. "This is my boy, Jeremiah."

I start at how he says "my boy," as if Jeremiah is his son.

"What are you doing here?" Jonas shakes Jeremiah's hand but keeps his eyes on my father. "We thought you'd died in the explosions."

"I moved to Willow's Province."

"Ah, Willow's Province. The place people go to get lost and be forgotten." Jonas narrows his eyes and gives a half-smile. He turns toward the window and clasps his hands behind his back, watching the occasional headlight go by on the street below. "I can understand your need to be secretive. This is some deep muck you've gotten yourself into, Frank. Hell, I thought you hated politics. Not to mention, I thought you were dead. And then you show up at my door with Korwin Stuart and Lydia Lane. I think I deserve an explanation."

My father doesn't answer. Funny, learning he isn't my biological father has only made me trust him more. The risks he's taken for me—he is my father in every way, despite the differences in our cells. If he doesn't trust Jonas enough to say I'm his daughter, or to mention Hemlock Hollow, I won't either. While I'm grateful for a place to hide from the Greens, I'm not crazy about returning to the clutches of the Liberty Party, not now that I know they've killed people—children—in their quest to overtake the Green Republic.

My father limps closer to him. "That's interesting, because when I left, you could not have cared less about the Green Republic. Your three girls were your whole world. How are your girls doing, anyway?"

"Fine. Grown. Gainfully employed. Reunion over. I need details."

"All the details you need are standing right there in front of you. These are good kids. You know what the Green Republic will do to them if they catch us again. We need help."

Jonas's eyes fall on Jeremiah. "Who are you, besides Frank's boy?"

"No one. I'm a friend who was in the wrong place at the wrong time." I'm surprised at the daggers Jeremiah shoots at me. Does he blame me for all this?

"Hmph. You, I do feel sorry for," Jonas says. He drifts toward Korwin. "The rebellion needs you, both of you, but I have to know what I'm getting myself into. I need to know every detail. How did they capture you? What does the Green Republic know? How did you escape? The networks are exploding over this."

"We'll tell you," I say. "Everything you need to know. But keep my father and Jeremiah out of this."

Jonas lets out a deep breath and eyes Korwin's state of dress. "Okay. First things first, it's obvious you need a shower, food, and rest. You're no good to the Liberty Party in your current state."

"Thank you," my father says, choosing a chair at the

table. He lowers himself into it with a series of jerky movements. He's exhausted and probably in pain. My heart aches to think that I've ruined him, that he might never be the same because he hasn't completed his rehabilitation.

"It won't be safe for you to stay here for long. I have a feeling we're already on borrowed time." Jonas types on the keyboard at his desk. "I'm sending a message to our supporters. I'll see if I can find you a safe house."

"What about Maxwell?" I ask.

Jonas frowns. "I'm a realist. Maxwell may already be dead, but we'll keep our ear to the ground."

I jump at the word *dead*. As angry as I am at Maxwell, the thought of Korwin losing the only father he has ever known pains me.

"There's something I have to know," Korwin says to Jonas. His face hardens, and he clenches his fists.

The old man looks at Korwin's distressed state in confusion. "What exactly?"

"Did you know about the West Hub bombing?"

The old man goes perfectly still. "Boy, I think you'd better go hit the shower, and while you're in there, think long and hard about the wisdom of dredging up ancient history."

Chapter 31

Thankfully, the fire station has a small bank of showers, useful for the long shifts the firefighters work on a regular basis. Clean and fully dressed, I wait in the tiny vestibule of lockers outside the bathroom for Korwin to emerge, anxious to get him alone.

When he sees me, I don't have to ask what's wrong.

"I've been such a fool." Hands on his hips, Korwin shifts from side to side. "This whole time I thought my father was a hero. You heard what he said when the Greens threatened him. He's a killer. Collateral damage! A murderer... of children."

"It's awful, Korwin, but he said he didn't know."

"And you believe him?"

I spread my hands. "I don't know what to believe, but he's not here to defend himself, and I certainly don't trust the Greens."

He shakes his head. "I've spent enough time making excuses for him, for this whole damn rebellion."

Placing my hands on his shoulders, I turn him so that we are face to face. "I agree with you. Your father's actions are deplorable, but don't you see? This is an evil world. Do you remember what I told you about Hemlock Hollow, about the choice my ancestors made to live behind the

310

wall?"

"Yeah."

"A person can't have it both ways. You either fight or you separate yourself from the evil." My mind spins at the edge of reason. "I... I think, we can't judge what your father or the Liberty Party did any more than we can judge what David did. We're all just trying to survive."

He narrows his eyes. "I'm sick of just surviving. I want a life. A real life, away from all of this."

"What are you saying?"

"I'm saying I don't want to go to a safe house. I want to go with you, to Hemlock Hollow."

* * * * *

As I lie in the dark of Jonas's flat, I ponder how I used to sleep at home in Hemlock Hollow. I miss it. I'd fall asleep when my head hit the pillow and only wake when the rooster crowed. The English world never sleeps. I've been running on stolen moments. My dreams, even my nightmares, used to be hopeful. Now they are filled with explosions and people chasing me. As if our circumstances aren't horrific enough, my brain replays them over and over in my head. It's the middle of the night but I am wide awake while Korwin's chest rises and falls in peaceful slumber on the cot next to me.

I'm not sure how I feel about Korwin's admission that he wants to leave the English world. Part of me is elated. I love him and won't have to live without him. But another part fears this is an escape, a way to not have to face the debunked hero that is his father. Life in Hemlock Hollow isn't easy. It isn't a place to escape personal problems. It's just different.

"Korwin!" Jonas snaps. "Wake up and get over here. You need to see this."

Korwin groggily opens his eyes and runs a hand over his face. I, on other hand, bound from my cot and hasten to Jonas's side. He swipes his finger across the screen, rewinding a television clip to the beginning.

On the monitor is the same blond newscaster I'd seen at Maxwell's house and on the street, Alexandra Brighten, but today there's a man behind the desk as well. SPECIAL REPORT scrolls across the screen. Korwin joins me at the monitor.

Earlier today, rebel terrorists escaped Green authorities before they could be transported to Crater City penitentiary. The fugitives, seen here in their previous escape, are considered armed and dangerous. The clip of Korwin and me bursting through the front window of CGEF flashes across the screen.

The male host turns toward Alexandra. *When you say* armed and dangerous, *should the public consider this a high-alert situation?*

That's right, Marshal. These terrorists are hell-bent on destroying CGEF and our entire nation's way of life. The good news is authorities have captured their leader and a public execution is scheduled for dawn unless the fugitives turn themselves in.

Maxwell's beaten and bloody body flashes across the screen. He is handcuffed and on his knees, his head lists to the side as if he's barely conscious. The barrel of a gun presses against his temple.

A familiar face fills the camera—Officer Reynolds. *The Crater City government does not negotiate with terrorists. Turn yourselves in or he dies.*

The clip fades to Alexandra and Marshal smiling at the camera. *Well, I don't know about you, Marshal, but I feel so much safer knowing the government is serious about capturing these terrorists. Hopefully these criminals will do the right thing and turn themselves in.*

That's for sure. Marshal bobs his head. *In other news—*

Jonas taps the screen and the clip pauses. "I'm sorry it's come to this. I've put the word out that Maxwell's absence appears to be permanent. And I've found a family in Northern Province that's willing to take you in. I recommend we get you out of here on one of the trucks."

"Aren't you even going to attempt to rescue him?" I ask incredulously.

Jonas snorts. "It would be a suicide mission. Trust me when I say there is no way Maxwell Stuart is walking out of CGEF alive. Look at him. He's barely alive as it is."

Korwin scowls. Our eyes meet. No words are said but plenty is communicated. He knows where I stand. We can't leave this undone.

"A suicide mission for you. Possible for us," Korwin says.

Jonas's head snaps around. "Korwin, they'll just kill you, too. Even you can't take on CGEF."

"I have to try."

"I can't let you. You're too important to the rebellion."

"To hell with the rebellion!" Korwin yells. "This is the man who saved me. He took me in and raised me as his own. He could've turned me over to the authorities the day I was left on his doorstep, but he didn't. I'm not leaving him to die on theirs"—Korwin looks at me—"no matter what he's done."

"We can't give ourselves up. They'll just kill him anyway," I say. "After last night, CGEF will be completely locked down. We'll never get back in without being caught."

"You're right. We'll need a distraction," Korwin says. "And we need backup."

"What are you proposing?" Jonas asks.

"You say we are too valuable to the rebellion to risk, but Lydia and I want no part in your politics. I'm proposing that we put my father's plan into action tonight. The rebellion has waited for the right moment to attack. This is it." Korwin's face is tired and desperate. "You attack, and we use the distraction to save my father."

Jonas's eyes widen. "You're talking about organizing a revolution in a couple of hours. It isn't possible."

The brilliance of Korwin's plan dawns on me. This is the only way out. If we allow Jonas to take us to a safe house, this nightmare will never end. We are trapped, pawns in a game of war. To break out, we have to pay the price and make our move, now.

I make my hands glow like stars in the dark room. "Don't tell us what is and is not possible, Jonas." I match his unblinking stare.

In Hemlock Hollow, I would have never disrespected

an elder in such a way. But this world, the world of the *Englishers*, makes promises it can't keep. The rules don't apply here.

I thought coming here would be harmless. Maybe even helpful to make me fully realize who I am. I thought it would make me a better seamstress and wife. Maybe give me something to talk about to my grandchildren when I was old and gray. In a way it has; I am a capable warrior, a leader, and more powerful than I ever thought possible. But by an ironic twist of fate, I am also wise enough to wish I'd never come here or had to use these skills. My hope is that after tonight, I'll never have to again. I want to go home, and if I ever make it back to Hemlock Hollow, I will never return.

"What was Maxwell's plan?" I ask Korwin.

"You and I take down the grid. Once the power's out, the Liberty Party uses the distraction to attack."

I nod. "And in the scuffle, we move in and grab Maxwell. Then we escape to Willow's Province and never come back."

Korwin blinks at me. He knows I mean Hemlock Hollow when I say Willow's Province, and he beams with joy at my invitation.

"Do I get a say in this?" Jeremiah chimes in. "Do I get a vote on whether you risk all of our lives to save a man who is all but dead already? We could escape now, Lydia. We could go back to Willow's Province today, without getting involved in other people's problems."

I turn on Jeremiah, fixing him with a stare that must glow blue because it lights up his face like a spotlight.

"No, you don't get a say." I don't mean to hurt him, but this is not Hemlock Hollow, he is not my husband, and he doesn't make my decisions. I've made up my mind.

Korwin grabs my hand. "It's a good idea. It's the only way."

Jonas's crossed arms and grave expression say exactly what he thinks of our plan.

Korwin pokes a finger toward him. "The grid is going down. I suggest you mobilize the rebellion while you still can. They'll either take the opportunity or they won't, but either way, I can guarantee it won't come again."

Ready for war, I march toward the door, only to see that my father is sitting up on his cot, watching me with concern. I stop, waiting for his challenge, for him to assert his authority over me and try to make me stay. I place my hands on my hips and meet his eyes.

"Go with God's grace, Lydia. You know what it says in the Bible, in the book of Esther? It says, 'Who knows whether you've come to the kingdom for such a time as this?' In other words, we go where we're called. Seems like you're hearing His instructions loud and clear. You trust in that. Don't worry about me."

I run to his bedside and throw my arms around him. "When the lights go out, take Jeremiah and wait for me in the alley. I'll come for you."

He nods and kisses my forehead.

I return to Korwin, taking his hand and leading him to the door. We wait for Jonas to open it.

"Jonas?" I prompt.

"I could keep you locked in. The room is grounded

and fireproof."

I turn my deadliest stare in his direction. "That won't stop me from incinerating what's inside of it."

For a second we play tug-of-war with our eyes. I don't back down. I don't even blink.

He presses a button on his desk and the door slides open. "Give me as much time as you can to notify the others. Please."

I nod. I will give him that.

Chapter 32

"We'll need to break into the power station and override the main transformer," Korwin says. We jog down the alley and take a left at the crossroad. "I'll warn you, it's heavily guarded. This is how I got caught the first time."

I arch an eyebrow in his direction. "I never knew. All this time I've wanted to ask you and never had the chance."

"Jonas has a reason to be nervous. We tried this once before."

"What happened?"

"I was supposed to blow the transformer. I'd practiced for months and thought I was ready. On that night, I joined a team of rebels under Jonas's leadership. Three men. The plan was for the three to get me in and then I would bring it down. When the city went dark, the rebellion would attack."

"What went wrong?"

"I thought I had it. I juiced but there was too much. I couldn't take it all in. So I pulsed. Pushed everything I had into the transformer. Caused a wicked energy surge but it wasn't enough. All I managed to do was call attention to myself. Before I knew what was happening, I was captured and hooked up to the drainer."

I squint my eyes at him. "Didn't the others try to rescue you? The three men? The rebellion?"

"It didn't happen."

"But your father… didn't he even try?"

"I guess the risks were too great. I was collateral damage." His voice sounds strangled.

I shake my head. "The rebellion has a history of cut and run."

"Exactly."

"Which means we're in this alone."

"Yep."

All at once I hate Maxwell Stuart. It's one thing to lose a soldier but another to sacrifice a son. There's no excuse. What reason could there possibly be for abandoning your child? But there is no time for us to wallow in the past. Unlike his father, Korwin has decided to do the right thing. He'll try his best to save Maxwell. That's the man he is. But, truthfully, I'll have no problem leaving Maxwell behind when we go home.

I shrug and pass him a nervous smile. "Just as well," I say. He seems to understand. Our fate is written in our DNA.

Korwin leads me down the back streets and away from the most congested part of the city. The night is cloudy and cool, no moon or stars. It gives the air a stark chill, like we are on the edge of bad weather. I pull my jacket tighter around me.

We walk a few miles, the buildings growing farther apart. Off in the distance I can see the glow of lights and wires, as wide as a city block.

"There it is. This is the hub for the whole city. All the energy created flows through here before it's parceled out to users."

Over the stretch of barren landscape, the building that houses the transformer rises on the horizon. A slight wind picks up the dirt, and it dances in swirls across the air. Aside from a few thin trees and some formidable boulders, there is nothing to mar the view.

"There's almost no place to hide," I say. "What if someone sees us?"

"It could happen, but luckily there's no reason for people to come this way unless they work here. The shift change happens at seven. It's four now, so we have three hours before any new traffic. There's no avoiding the guards. Our only hope is to take them out before they have time to act."

"I'm ready," I say, but the truth is I am far from it. Never in my life did I expect to be here, martyring myself for a cause that has nothing to do with me. I ache for home. I miss my cow and the haymow, even the feel of bread dough between my fingers.

We race across the dirt, swiftly moving between trees and boulders in the darkness. The closer I come to the transformer, the more my confidence wanes. Korwin notices. I'm not sure if it's the sag of my shoulders or the way my steps are growing progressively shorter, but he takes my hand in his and squeezes it.

"I'll take care of you," he says.

I remember the first time he said that to me, after

escaping from CGEF. He'd seemed too weak to help anyone when I found him but he ended up saving us both. There is a good possibility we'll both die tonight. So many things can go wrong. The electricity might overwhelm us. We could get shot or scrambled. Tortured. Drained to the point of death. But as I look at Korwin, all that matters to me is that we try our best to be free.

I've always thought Hemlock Hollow was a type of prison, that living behind the wall with the *Ordnung's* many rules was limiting. Now, in a world that seems bigger, a world without rules, I actually am a prisoner. I'm wanted and jailed for who I am. I long for the freedom of Hemlock Hollow's wall.

"I can see a guard," I say. "And I think he sees us."

Korwin spots the person in the green uniform a hundred yards away. Without pause, he grabs my hand and pushes a focused pulse of energy in the guard's direction. The green uniform collapses. We don't waste any time. We sprint across the field, no turning back.

It turns out the guard is a woman, mercifully close to my size. I remove the electronic device from her ear and place it in my own. Static. I hand it to Korwin, who holds it up to his ear.

"The pulse temporarily knocked out her communicator. It might buy us some time," he says.

He helps me undress the guard and I slip into her uniform. The material is different, more like the type we use in Hemlock Hollow than the stretchy, self-adjusting kind the *Englishers* usually use. I tuck my hair under the gray cap, pulling the bill down low over my eyes. I place the earpiece into my ear; the static cuts in and out ominously. "Larissa? Larissa, are you there?" a voice says. "She's not answering. I'm going to check on her."

I motion toward my ear and pull Korwin against the wall of the building. *Coming*, I mouth because I'm not sure how the communicator works. Korwin understands and turns so that his back is to mine. The man comes from my direction.

"Larissa," he starts when he sees me. He holds up a hand to get my attention, then notices the real Larissa in a heap at my feet. He doesn't have a chance to speak another word. I grab his wrist and twist him into a chokehold until he passes out. The movement is practiced and smooth. Although I am smaller, my victim doesn't even have time to yell for help.

"Where did you learn to do that?" Korwin whispers, a sense of awe in his voice.

"CGEF. David." My voice is flat.

"Why didn't you just pulse him?"

"Saving my energy. More efficient."

Korwin's mouth drops open.

Hurting someone, even a stranger, has consequences. I lower the body of the first person I've ever intentionally injured to the ground while an awful weight settles at the center of my chest. The man's badge says *Quincy*. He has a hooked nose and bushy eyebrows. Is he a father? Brother? Uncle? Have I done permanent damage?

"You can't think about it, Lydia. It's them or us." Korwin tugs at the man's uniform. "Come on. Help me. We don't have much time."

I snap out of my guilt wallowing and go to work on the man's boot. We are not so lucky with Quincy's uniform. The man is smaller than Korwin, as most men are. Korwin can get the pants on but they are three inches too short and the seams of the green jacket strain near the shoulders. As I suspected, the material does not adjust to size.

"Damn cheap Greens," Korwin says, tugging the sleeves toward his wrists. "It'll have to do."

We head for the door. The earpieces cut in and out; panicked voices interrupt clouds of static. Larissa and Quincy do not respond. They can't. We've stowed Larissa's body behind the back of the building and are dragging Quincy behind us. We have a window of opportunity to do what we came to do, and we can't waste a minute.

Korwin uses Quincy's hand to trigger the Biolock, then dumps his body. We enter the building, knowing it's simply a matter of time before we're found out. Korwin leads me to a service elevator at the back of the building. He's done this part before; he knows where to go. I hold my breath as we pass a group of green uniforms. I don't make eye contact and they are too busy talking amongst themselves to notice us. It isn't until we are inside the elevator and the door is closing that one of them stops and calls to me.

"Larissa?" the man asks. "They're calling for you on the cloud."

In response, I give the man a tiny nod and a smile. The doors close and the elevator descends. I blow out my held breath.

"That was close," Korwin says. He removes his earpiece and motions for me to do the same. "These things transmit both ways when they're in your ear but turn themselves off when you take them out. They won't work in here because of the electromagnetic energy field. Can you feel it?"

I close my eyes. The air tastes like honey, and it tingles against my skin. "Yes," I say, opening my eyes again. "I can feel it. We're close."

The elevator doors slide open. Korwin doesn't exit right away. Instead, he pries the button panel off and twists some wires together. "This elevator is officially out of order," he says.

We depart into the outdoors. The building is shaped like a donut and we are inside the hole at the center, in the open air. The transformer rises toward the night sky, to the wires above, and gives off power I can feel.

The alarms blare to life all around us.

Korwin tilts his head up, toward the circle of second-floor windows. "I think they've found the real Larissa and Quincy."

Dozens of nameless faces stare down at us. People point and yell through the glass.

"Ready?" he asks over the hum of the transformer and the buzz of the alarm.

"As ready as I will ever be."

He brushes my cheek. "Then let's do this."

The corners of his mouth lift but not before I notice the lower lid of his left eye twitch. He's afraid. Maybe more afraid than me.

With a shaky hand, I grab one of the exposed cables that run into the pillar of metal in front of me. Korwin does the same.

And at the speed of light, I find out why Korwin is afraid.

Chapter 33

In comparison, the first time I was juiced on the elevator in CGEF was like sipping energy from a cup through a small straw. At the mansion, getting juiced by Korwin's bath was like chugging from a jug. Kissing Korwin could be compared to gulping from a garden hose. But this... Touching the transformer is like being force-fed from a fire hydrant. The power pours into me without limits. It's like I've eaten a bad meal and I need to get sick, only I can't because someone is fisting more down my throat.

"*Breathe!*" Korwin yells. He kicks my leg.

I inhale. It doesn't help. "*I can't take anymore!*"

Our power revolves around the transformer and lights up the night. We are the eye of the hurricane. It's so intense, my hair blows back and my skin sizzles in the mounting energy storm.

Doors across from us open, but none of the officers dare approach our glowing blue forms. They try to shoot at us, but the bullets are absorbed by the aura of power.

"*Pulse it back, Lydia. Send it back where it came from.*"

I tighten my belly and push. Nothing happens. I can see the strain on Korwin's face. It's like trying to deadlift a semitruck. I push harder.

"*You can do it. Pulse!*" Korwin yells.

326

I try again. Somehow, I find the strength to empty the power I've stored back into the transformer. The metal groans ominously.

"Again," he says.

I can tell he's started to juice. I don't want to open myself up to it again, but the pulse can only last so long. Once I'm empty, I'll have to pull my hands away or open myself up to the flow. My eyes start to tear. The tide shifts, and the power plows back into me.

Head shaking, I look at Korwin. "I can't do this anymore."

"You can. Don't give up."

All I can see is his silhouette through the blur of my tears. I want to help but I have to let go. I lift my left hand from the metal, but Korwin won't let me give up. He snatches my hand from the air and smashes it back against the cable. The physical contact ignites the dance that lives between us, and he pulses out the side of our conjoined palms. It helps. The transformer vibrates, creating an eerie shimmer.

Shattering glass fills the night. The lights illuminating the yard extinguish, the blown bulbs raining down all around us.

My skin is on fire. Tiny red dots break out across my arms. Am I bruising from the pressure of the push? I might pass out. I might die. I am too fatigued to scream or pray.

And then a miracle happens. It starts to rain.

I've never appreciated how magical water can be. The gift from the heavens washes over me, cooling my skin.

Steam rises off of us, curling across the dirt at our feet, cloaking us from the officers.

"Juice, Lydia," Korwin orders. "Juice again and send any extra power into the water. Send it into the ground!"

I do as he says. I'm almost empty, and juicing rejuvenates my failing body. The flow isn't overpowering like it once was. We've weakened it. Excited, I smile at Korwin.

"It's working!" he says.

When I can't hold any more, I bleed the excess into the water. It shoots down into the ground, following the moisture that slicks off me. The lights inside the building flicker.

"One more time, Lydia. Pulse on the count of three. One. Two. *Three!*"

I catapult the ribbon out of me and into the transformer. And that's all it takes. The metal explodes in a shower of sparks. The transformer becomes a house-sized hand grenade. The force twists my body, snapping my neck and prying my fingers from the cable. Korwin's arms are around me. He shields me with his body, turning in the air so that his back takes the brunt of the fall. I land on top of him— chest to chest, face to face—in the flickering light.

For a moment, we search each other's eyes. His lips are so close I can feel his breath.

"That hurt," he says. "Let's get out of here."

I want to answer him but there's something wrong. I try to move but I can't. My body twitches uncontrollably. Sweat breaks out across my skin and I heave over his shoulder.

Carefully, he sits up with me in his arms. He brushes back the hair from my forehead. "The surge scrambled you."

I want to know how long I'll be like this, but I can't get my lips to work long enough to ask.

He stands, lifting me into his arms. Although my body won't work, my mind is exceptionally clear. Around us is mass chaos. None of the people here can function without power. Their communication system is down and the doors won't open. I remember the night we escaped from CGEF. Korwin said this was a security measure. Locking everyone inside was supposed to ensure any scampers were locked in too. There's no concern for the workers, only the energy. People are screaming, banging against the glass like wayward birds. Thinking back to my life without electricity, I have to wonder. How could the *Englishers* let themselves get this bad? How could they become so dependent on something so scarce?

Korwin carries me to the nearest door and pulses it open. He climbs the stairwell to the main floor. The staff, the same people who had tried to kill us moments ago, watch us with panicked eyes, backs pressed against the wall.

"We can't help them, Lydia," he whispers. "They'll turn against us. They'll call for help."

He's right. I know he is right. As we leave through the door Korwin pulses open, slamming the heavy metal on the advancing crowd and soldering it shut, what remains of the crystal housing containing the compassion and innocence of my youth cracks open. Those virtues still circulate through my blood, but they are overpowered by my new sense of reality. The world is a bigger place than I've realized. Pain hurts more. Evil is more pervasive. People can't be trusted. This isn't Hemlock Hollow, and to exist in this world, I have to change. A vivid image of David kicking me in the ribs overtakes me. "What's it going to be, Lydia? Are you going to fight or fail?"

Korwin loads me into one of the cars from the parking lot and switches it to off-grid mode. We accelerate toward CGEF. I come alive in the seat next to him, my neurons unscrambling one by one. I can move a finger, then my arm, then my torso. Soon I sit up and reach for his hand. It's time to save Korwin's father. It's time to finish this.

Chapter 34

I am not prepared for the chaos that greets us as we enter Crater City. The streets are congested with parked cars. Drivers hang their heads out their windows, staring at the darkened lampposts and cursing.

"Early morning traffic. It's not the first blackout," Korwin explains. "They're usually short. People are hoping the grid comes back on because nobody wants to spend their own units to get where they're going."

"How do we get around them?"

"We don't. We go through on foot." He stops the car in the middle of the road and exits. I follow, weaving between the people on the street. I can see the mirrored walls and steel frame of CGEF ahead of us. I break into a jog, slamming shoulders with a man who's moving in the opposite direction.

"Hey! Watch it," the man yells. He moves to push me but then sees my green uniform and backs off. I'm still dressed like a government employee.

"Sorry," I call over my shoulder. I veer onto the lawn, following Korwin, who's gaining in speed. "How much time do we have?" I ask him.

Without slowing he glances at his wrist, then at the lightening horizon. "Ten minutes at the most. They'll want to televise the execution. Maybe they'll wait, since the power is out."

At a full-out run, I cross the lawn, leaping over bushes in pursuit of Korwin. A crowd has gathered in front of CGEF. I can't see Maxwell, but I'm guessing he's at the center of the crowd. We slow and shoulder our way through the mass of people. I press myself against Korwin's back, hoping his taller, broader body will make the better plow. Eventually, we can't advance any more. Korwin frowns and touches the nearest shoulder. A tiny zap of blue makes the man jump. The sea of people parts, one shocked individual at a time, and then we reach the action. I see what we came to see.

Maxwell Stuart kneels on the pavement in the circle of light thrown by a battery-operated camera. His hands are cuffed behind his back and a gun presses into his temple. The blond woman from television, Alexandra Brighten, stands holding a microphone between Dr. Konrad and Senator Pierce. A half circle of green-uniformed officers guards their flank.

Several things happen at once. Senator Pierce raises his head and catches my eye. There's a moment of recognition beneath his bushy gray brows and then his hand falls in a sweeping motion. The officer pulls the trigger, and Maxwell Stuart's body jerks.

He collapses to the concrete, twitches, then stills. Blood pools beneath his head.

Korwin shouts, "*No!*" Screams break out in the crowd as he rushes to his father's side, an ominous blue glow radiating from him. The heat alone sends people running.

Oh Korwin! My heart aches. Whatever I felt against Maxwell Stuart flows away like so much blood. How could they do this to him—to us? Anger makes my head throb. The gathering blue swirls, and like a fever, a new truth spreads through me. I believe it as surely as I believe in heaven above and my own being. Pierce and Konrad have to pay for this. I will not go quietly. And I sure as hell won't let them take Korwin.

"He's dead," Korwin whispers to me over the body of his father. "*Dead!*" The word pounds out of him, the air crackling around us as our collective anger makes us grow brighter. People scatter, shrieking, trampling each other to get away from us. Everyone except Konrad, Pierce, and the small entourage of security officers led by Officer Reynolds.

"It's the penalty for your treason," Senator Pierce yells. He looks down his nose at me and runs a finger along the inside of his collar.

One of the officers turns a scrambler on Korwin. I don't give him a chance to pull the trigger. Instinctively, I throw my power. In my anger, the bolt of electricity that flies from my hand is far more than a pulse. It slices through the officer's side, creating a black-fringed hole that pours blood. He crumples to the pavement, gripping the wound and screaming. The faintest shadow of guilt ripples through my soul but it passes quickly, chased away by fury over the scene in front of me.

Dr. Konrad raises a scrambler and points it at me. "Let's all relax and get inside where we can talk."

I step in front of Korwin, blocking his crouched form

with my body. My anger crackles around me in a blaze of light that makes Konrad blink and shield his eyes with his hand as if he's staring into the sun.

"Don't forget, Lydia, you have a father as well. A fleet of officers are already on their way to the fire station. Oh yes, we've known about rebel activity there for months. Our mole didn't know about your little trick with the blackout, but he was quick to inform us of the two who were left behind."

I glare at Dr. Konrad with his silver scrambler and hunch low like an animal protecting her mate. Konrad pulls the trigger. Panic spurs my power into action and, as before, it defends me. I don't even think about it. Heat radiates from my skin, melting the prongs before they can make contact. The weapon drops from his shaking hand and his eyes widen. He turns to run.

I can't stop it. Lightning flies from my hand, and his body hits the pavement, twitching and writhing. I pant from the heat.

Korwin's eyebrows raise. "It was an accident!" I say, but his expression isn't accusing, it's celebratory.

Senator Pierce backs behind the green uniforms. The officers scatter, even Officer Reynolds, weapons clanking on the concrete. Exposed, Pierce bolts for the door to CGEF, but it won't open because the power's still out. Korwin fries him from feet to knees. He slides down the glass, screaming.

What have we done? What am I doing? The power—I desperately try to reel it back in but I can't. It feeds off Korwin's energy and the panic that surrounds us. I can't fight it. Not anymore. I am possessed.

"Lydia, your father," Korwin says calmly. He is next to me, his eyes completely filled with blue. We are so hot the rain evaporates before it reaches our heads. The steam curls around him, like an archangel, an angel of death, something fierce and holy.

The way to the fire station is congested with parked vehicles. We could weave through them or go around them. "It will be faster if we go through them," I say. My voice sounds hollow and tinny, like my throat is lined with silver. Is this real? Or some kind of nightmare?

Korwin's hand skims down my shoulder and his fingers twine into mine. We turn toward the congested grid, toward the people who gawk or run or scream.

"Move out of the way," I whisper flatly.

Korwin chuckles.

I raise my hand and let out the ribbon. Without holding back or tying it off, I let the power flow forward. Cars erupt from the street, exploding into the sides of the buildings as if thrown by an angry toddler. Metal crumples and bends. The resulting fires light our path and the smell of burning, laced with chemicals, fills my nose.

We stride toward the fire station but it's hard to remember what we're going to do there. It's hard to remember anything besides the buzz of power and the chorus of screams. My mind fades in and out, but my body keeps going, animated by this thing inside me. Some part of me insists I have to hold on. I have to fight for the part of me that's still me. Is this what it's like for Korwin too?

GROUNDED

I have to find a way to regain control.

Chapter 35

This isn't right. I grip the thought like a life raft. Deep within me, I find some human strength, some part of me that isn't owned by the power. I'm in church on Sunday, singing hymns with Mary. I hear her voice, as clear and innocent as silver bells. I see my father's work-worn hands, taste freshly baked bread, feel the tops of the wheat as I run to my tree.

"Be in the world but not of the world," Bishop Kauffman says. His voice is solemn and I long for his hands on my shoulders. This is not me. I have a soul. I have a conscience. This violent sport is not who I am. I am a woman of God. A powerful force for hearth and home. I will not allow this world to have me any longer.

I direct my resolve at our coupled hands and somehow find the strength to let go of Korwin.

He turns those radioactive blue eyes toward me like I've committed a grave offense.

"This isn't right," I say, and this time it's not just in my head. I've said it out loud.

"Right?" Korwin repeats. He shakes his head like he doesn't understand.

"We've got to get control," I rasp, but my voice is still not my own.

Korwin continues down the now abandoned street but

his movements are jerky. Mine are too. I think I have it by the tail but it's so big. I wrap and wrap and wrap the power around the spool at the back of my brain but there is just too much. *Oh, the pain!* I want to let it out again but I can't.

We're close to the fire station. It's only when I see my father and Jeremiah huddled beneath the lip of the dumpster that I realize it's still raining. Although it comes down in sheets, none of it touches us. We're still too hot. What is it they're doing? My father has his legs hugged to his chest and is yelling at Jeremiah to do the same.

Ack! My power surges and sweat breaks out across my forehead as I fight it back. Wrap. Wrap! I wind it around the spool and tie it off. Why does my father look afraid? I shake with the effort of concentrating. The puddle! Oh my word, he'll be electrocuted!

"Korwin!" I command. He's twitching next to me. Every few seconds he reaches for me only to pull his hand back. "You have to fight it!"

This time I can tell I'm more me. Without Korwin to recharge my cells, the power has to fizzle out some time. I bite my lip and wind and wind. *Oh!* Will it even fit inside of me?

"It hurts!" Korwin yells.

"Fight it!" I cry.

For what seems like an eternity, I struggle to gain control. Korwin moans next to me. When it gets too much, I scream. It seems to help. I lean forward, catching myself on my knees and yell until my voice goes hoarse. I'm sure I have nothing left to give. Containing this monster will kill me.

A drop of rain is my savior.

It's cool and wet. When it lands on my forearm, it rolls off my skin and drips to the pavement. I jerk my head up. Korwin's glow has faded as well. His skin steams but his hair is wet.

"It's going to be okay, Korwin," I call, but I don't dare comfort him with my touch. Instead, I hobble past him toward my father and Jeremiah. The closer I get to them, the more I can see the fear in their eyes. They huddle together against the metal of the dumpster.

Can't they see how weak I am? But then this thing is a mystery even to me. It must be something out of a nightmare to my father and Jeremiah. I need to show them. If I can prove I'm in control, then maybe they'll trust me again.

I crouch down and gently scoop my father's hands inside my own.

"Lydia?" He gasps.

"Don't worry, Daddy, I'm still me." With the last bit of power I have left, I will energy between his fingers. Exhausted, I release his hands. He opens them and a tiny electric-blue butterfly flutters toward the sky before breaking apart above us. The rain has stopped but something warm and wet drips down my chin. I wipe the back of my hand across my face. Blood.

It's Jeremiah who catches me when I topple toward the concrete.

"No," my father says, but when I search his face he's not looking at me. I follow his line of sight and see a

CGEF Humvee driving in our direction. There's a weapon mounted on top. A huge rocket launcher I only recognize because of David. The officer in control takes aim at Korwin, who is just a few feet in front of us, and triggers the rocket.

I have a second to see Korwin's blue glow blink and fizzle in the rain.

Boom! A barrage of rubble sprays toward us, and then I'm consumed by total darkness.

Chapter 36

I am home. On the wall in front of me is the quilt I made, log cabin style from gray and blue scraps. It is definitely mine; I recognize the sloppy stitching in the right corner where I got lazy. I run my hand down my torso. I'm wearing my white nightgown. Reaching above my head, I smile when my fingers slap the familiar carved wood of my headboard.

"Relax, Lydia. We're home," Jeremiah says. I turn my face toward his voice. He's sitting in the chair next to my bed and by his wrecked hair and the dark circles under his eyes, I'm fairly sure he's been there for quite some time. He stands and approaches the side of the bed. *Oh dear Lord!* A scabbed red gash runs from the outside corner of his left eye to his jawline.

I gasp. I want to ask him what happened but my voice won't work. My throat feels dry and constricted.

"Don't try to speak," Jeremiah says. He lifts a glass of water from the nightstand and brings it to my lips, scooping one arm under my shoulders to prop me up so I can drink. I try but some of the water trickles out the corners of my mouth. "You've been out for four days."

I widen my eyes at him. It hurts. My skin is too tight and I wonder if I've been injured too. I push the sleeve of my nightgown back. My arm is covered in sores.

"Your power protected you and us." He taps the gash on his face lightly. "I was on the edge of your range but this is the worst of it. Your father wasn't hurt at all. You, on the other hand... Electroscurvy, if I remember correctly from Maxwell's briefing, although I would really rather forget."

I swallow hard and try to speak again. A muffled croak is the only sound I can produce. He raises the glass to my lips again.

"We escaped when the Liberty Party attacked. I've heard they failed, but we didn't stick around to find out the details. We used the distraction of the war to come home. No one followed us. In fact, Jacob ventured outside the wall and checked with Bradford Adams. The Green Republic thinks you died in the explosion, or at least that's what they are reporting on Channel 12 News. Your father and I are hoping Operation Source Code is on permanent hiatus. No one else knows about you, by the way. Everyone in Hemlock Hollow thinks your injuries are from the explosion."

I swallow again. My throat is beginning to loosen and I have to ask the question gnawing at me, although I'm afraid of the answer. "Korwin?"

Jeremiah rolls his eyes. He never used to do that and the cynicism in his expression throws me. "Yeah. He's alive. Actually his shield took the direct hit. We just got the fallout when the spilled fuel ignited. The street was running with it from the damaged vehicles."

I grab his wrist and shake. He knows what I want and frowns down at me.

"He's on a cot in the main room. He hasn't woken up yet."

Using his arm for leverage, I pull myself up. My head spins and my muscles ache.

Jeremiah shakes his head. "No, Lydia. You've got to stay in bed. Your father will have my hide if you hurt yourself on my watch."

I fix him with my most determined stare. "Help me."

Groaning, he pulls the quilt back and sweeps my legs over the side. I grin. He's never been able to say no to me, not since we were children. He wraps my arm around his shoulders and heaves me to a standing position. If not for his arm around my waist, I'd be on the floor. My legs are uncooperative, but he carries me into the main room, where I see Korwin.

The only time he's looked worse is when I first rescued him from CGEF. His color is barely darker than the sheet beneath him, and he has more raw, oozing sores than healthy skin. I reach for him but have to wait for Jeremiah to help me. Eventually, he sits me down on the side of the cot.

Placing my hand over Korwin's heart, I feel the familiar tug as my energy flows into him, but I have very little to give. I have to lie down across his chest I'm so weak. But face to face, I see his eyelids flutter. And a tiny spark flows back into me. It's starting. The engine that is us begins a slow churn.

I press my lips onto his and feel the give and take of the energy strengthen. Korwin's eyes open and his hand lifts to my cheek. Our connection is strong. The voltage flip-flops, trickling down my throat through our connection. I'm not sure how long this continues, I lose myself to it. But finally, the faintest blue glow ignites under his skin. Slowly, almost imperceptibly, I notice the sores on his face change. The blue glow strengthens and his flesh knits together. Amazingly my muscles loosen and contract. My skin warms.

His lips part, and in the tangle of sparks that is our connection, I nestle in, absorbing what he gives me as I give it right back. I thread my fingers into his hair. When I smell smoke, I use my newfound strength to pull back. Lip from lip. Hand from chest. Fingers from hair. We've singed the sheets. I perch next to him on the cot, fully healed.

"If we'd known you could do that, we would have put you two together sooner." Jeremiah touches the red gash on his face. "I don't suppose it will work on me?"

I shake my head. "I wish it did, but no."

"Perfect." He runs his hand through his rumpled hair and walks toward the door.

"Jeremiah?"

"I gotta go, Lydia," he says, placing a hand on the doorknob and tipping his head to the side. He glances between Korwin and me. "I'm certain you'll be fine. Clearly, you don't need my help anymore."

I try to respond but he's out the door before I have a chance. I turn back toward Korwin who looks around the room in confusion.

"Welcome to Hemlock Hollow," I say.

In response, he gives me a face-splitting grin. "I feel at

home already."

Epilogue

One month later, when the fields are harvested and the late fall chill has blessed us with an abundance of fat geese, I kneel down in front of my father, Jeremiah, and Korwin, as well as the rest of the *Ordnung*, and remove my *kapp*. The bishop pours water over my head. It runs in cool trails down my face and neck. He says some words about commitment and forgiveness. My soul feels buoyant, a feather in the wind. The light that streams through the Kauffmans' windows is just for me, a sunny celebration of my baptism.

Korwin takes it all in, although I'm not sure he understands the nuances of the ceremony. He's learning our ways and studying our language. If all goes well, he'll become one of us in a few months. The Lapps took him in and we've officially begun courting.

Jeremiah has already been baptized. He says he's happy for Korwin and me, but I see the way he looks at me, how his mouth changes when he thinks I'm not paying attention. Although I still consider him a good friend, he hasn't been the same since we left on *rumspringa*. The boy who was always smiling now carries a permanent darkness. We don't leap off the haymow like we used to.

My father has made a complete recovery, although he's

346

a bit slower at things than he used to be. Lucky for us, Korwin has decided he wants to farm and has taken up helping my father with his work. If everything goes as planned, we will be married, he'll move into the house, and we can care for my father into his old age.

Korwin and I take long walks and talk about how we met. Every once in a while, when we kiss, the power returns and we have to wind it in tightly and tie it off inside our heads so that we don't set anything on fire. We've become very good at controlling it and are sure it's safe for us to be married. I joke sometimes that we should line our marriage bed with stones or bricks, just in case.

But secretly, I'm happy the power hasn't left us, even though we've left the power. The Green Republic could change the rules. They could come knocking and try to transform Hemlock Hollow, try to force us into their world. It's good to know that if that happens, Korwin and I are ready. We don't want to hurt anyone, but, if we have to, we will.

Sometimes I sit in my tree and think about my mother and about the Alpha Eight. She and my father gave up having a normal life for love of their country and then died resisting the corruption of the same. I wonder what they would think of me here in Hemlock Hollow. I'm not ready to give my life for any of the *Englishers*. Let the rebellion die for the rebellion. I am one life, only interested in protecting the ones I love and the freedom I choose.

I think about Natasha and David. What has become of them? Will they find a way to get the serum they require to stay alive? I'm fairly sure they are either free or dead. If not, the Green Republic would have used David against us. He was a prisoner there as much as I was.

All Korwin and I want is to build a life here, far away from wars and politics. He'll be baptized, and then we'll be married and have children. I hope all of them have his hazel eyes. Maybe our kids will have the power we have. Maybe not. Either way, we'll teach them how to be good, God-fearing people.

* * * * *

"You able to chat for a bit?" Mary asks. She takes a seat next to me on my front porch, just finished with her milking. I've finished first, as always, and am having a rest before I make breakfast. Korwin and my father are cleaning the barn.

"Yeah, what's on your mind?"

"There's a rumor going 'round that while you were on *rumspringa*, you had some kind of demon in you. People say that's why you aren't marrying Jeremiah like you should."

"Who would say such a thing? No one knows better whom I should marry than me. Jeremiah and I were never courting."

"I love you, Lydia, but those are not modest words. It was a bold thing to come back here with an *Englisher*. You must've known people would talk."

All I can do is shrug. The sun breaks the horizon, a great ball of fire in the sky. For a moment, I wonder what would have happened if I'd never left Hemlock Hollow. I probably would have lived up to everyone's expectations and been perfectly happy to marry Jeremiah. Maybe I would never know what I really am. But I did go and I changed. I can make myself become modest again, but my life will never be simple. The mere thought of "simple" makes me laugh.

"What's so funny?" Mary asks.

"Nothing." I give her a warm smile. "I'm baptized now, and nothing about *rumspringa* matters. But I love Korwin. You'll see. He'll be baptized too and become one of us. You'll wonder what we ever did without him. And I don't have a demon in me. I'm the same me as always."

"Glad to hear it," she says. "I knew it was just talk anyway."

The sun warms my face. I smooth my apron and tuck a stray hair under my *kapp*.

"Well, time to make breakfast," I say.

Mary hugs me before heading for home.

I move indoors to the kitchen, and pull the dough from its rising spot. On a dusting of flour, I knead it on the counter before rolling it out for biscuits. Here, with dough between my fingers and the log fire I started earlier burning in the hearth, the English world seems a million miles away.

I am plain. I am modest. I am grounded. And, for now, I'm happy to be home.

Flames lick from between my fingers. I yank my hands away. The dough's on fire! I snatch my glass of lemonade from the counter and douse the mounting blaze. The bread is ruined, singed and soaked. I dump the mess into the garbage, then check the window to make sure no one's watching. I'm alone. Mary's already left, and Dad's still in the field.

Hands shaking, I pull the flour from the pantry and start again.

About the Author

G.P. Ching is the bestselling author of The Soulkeepers Series and the Grounded trilogy. She specializes in cross-genre YA novels with paranormal elements and surprising twists. She lives in central Illinois with her husband, two children, and a Brittany spaniel named Riptide Jack. Learn more about G.P. and the Soulkeepers Series at www.gpching.com.

Follow G.P. on:
Twitter: @gpching
Facebook: G.P. Ching

Sign up for her exclusive newsletter at www.gpching.com to be the first to know about new releases!

37696977R00213

Made in the USA
Middletown, DE
01 March 2019